A RAVAGED SKIES CHARACTER NOVEL

QUEEN OF LIKES

DJ COOPER

Find DJ Cooper on the web.

Https://AuthoroftheApocalypse.com

Don't forget to sign up for the spam free newsletter

https://bit.ly/3KmAGjh

"The trouble with the media is that it seems unable to distinguish between the end of the world and a bicycle accident."

—George Bernard Shaw

Contents

ONLY TWO THINGS ARE INFINITE,
THE UNIVERSE AND HUMAN
STUPIDITY, AND I'M NOT SURE
ABOUT THE FORMER.
-ALBERT EINSTEIN

The salt water burned Grace's lungs as consciousness dragged her back to a world that shouldn't exist. Her fingers clawed at wet sand, nails scraping against shells and stones while her body convulsed, expelling brine in violent heaves. The taste of copper filled her mouth—blood from where her teeth cut her tongue during the drowning that wasn't quite drowning.

Sound came in fragments. Waves breaking against rocks. Wind through scrubby pines. Her own gasping, ragged breaths that felt like knives in her chest. Each inhale brought agony, her lungs refusing to believe they could process air again after the water tried to claim them.

"Easy there, girl. You're safe now."

The voice came from somewhere above her, rough with age and cigarettes. Grace's vision swam as she tried to focus, the aurora's green light painting everything in sickly hues that made the world look wrong, alien.

A man knelt beside her, his weathered face creased with concern that registered somewhere in the back of her mind as genuine. Flannel shirt worn soft with age. Work boots crusted with salt. Hands that showed decades of hard labor.

"Where—" The word scraped out of her raw throat. Water came up again, burning through her nose as her body tried to expel every drop of ocean it held.

"Shh, don't try to talk yet. Just breathe." The man's hand rested on her back, steady pressure that somehow helped ground her. "Name's Earl Hutchins. I've got a cabin just up the path. Can you stand? I can carry you if need be."

Carry her. Like she was helpless. Like she was some fragile thing that needed rescuing. Grace's mind rebelled against the idea even as her body betrayed her, trembling violently beneath wet clothes that clung to her skin. Cold. She was so cold that her bones ached with it.

"I can walk," she managed, though when Earl helped her to her feet, her legs buckled. Only his grip under her arm kept her upright.

"That's alright. Take your time. You been through hell tonight." Earl pulled a wool blanket from somewhere—had he brought it with him?—and wrapped it around her shoulders. The scratchy fabric smelled of mothballs and wood smoke, but the warmth felt like salvation.

They moved slowly up a narrow path between granite outcroppings and wind-twisted pines. Grace's bare feet found every sharp stone, every broken shell. When had she lost her shoes? She remembered running from those men at the party, remembered Maddie's voice calling after her, remembered the cold shock of water closing over her head as she jumped from the bridge.

Jumped. She jumped.

The memory hit her like a physical blow, stealing what little breath she'd recovered. She stopped moving, swaying on the path while Earl's grip tightened to keep her steady.

"Almost there," he said, his voice gentle. "Just a bit further and we'll get you warm."

But Grace wasn't listening. She was back in Portsmouth, back at that party where everything went wrong. The men crowding around her, their hands reaching, their breath hot and wrong. Hannah and Maddie pulling her away, their faces tight with concern that looked like judgment. The argument that followed, words tumbling out of Grace's mouth that she couldn't quite remember now but knew had been important, had been true.

They sabotaged her. Her big break with the reality TV scouts and they ruined it.

"Here we are."

Earl's voice pulled her back to the present. A small cabin materialized from the darkness, its old shingles silver in the aurora's strange light. A single window glowed with warm yellow that promised heat and safety. Lobster traps stacked beside the door. A hand-carved sign above the entrance that read "Hutchins".

Grace's teeth chattered so hard she bit her tongue again, fresh copper flooding her mouth. Earl guided her up two wooden steps and pushed open the door, releasing a wave of warmth that made her skin prickle painfully as feeling began to return.

"Sit yourself down by the fire," Earl said, his hands on her shoulders steering her toward a rocking chair positioned near a stone fireplace where flames danced and crackled. "I'll get you some dry clothes and something hot to drink."

The chair received her weight with a familiar creak. Grace sank into it, the blanket falling away as she held her hands toward the fire. Her fingers looked wrong—pale and wrinkled, pruned from too long in the water. How long had she been under? Minutes? Hours? Time felt broken, disconnected, like frames missing from a video.

Her video. Her content.

Grace's hand patted frantically at her soaked jeans, relief flooding through her when her fingers found the familiar rectangle of her phone. She pulled it free, water dripping from the case, and pressed the power button with a trembling thumb.

Nothing.

She pressed it again. Again. Again.

Dead. Completely dead.

"No, no, no," she whispered, turning the phone over in her hands like she might find a hidden reserve of battery life somewhere. Three years of content. Fifty thousand followers. Sponsorship deals and carefully curated posts and the algorithm finally, finally starting to favor her videos. All of it trapped behind a black screen that reflected only her own distorted face.

"Phone's not gonna work out here even if it was charged," Earl said, returning with an armload of fabric. His voice held apology, like he was personally responsible for the lack of cell service. "Tower went down in the first few days after the lights went out. Haven't had a working phone in weeks."

Weeks. The word didn't make sense. Grace stared at him, trying to process the implications. The chaos began yesterday. Maybe the day before? Time felt slippery, but it couldn't have been weeks.

"What day is it?" The question came out wrong, her voice too high and thin.

Earl's brow creased with concern. "Mid-July, near as I can figure. Hard to keep track without calendars working, but I been marking days on a piece of paper. I forget sometimes. I think some days I forgot to mark but some I may have done more than one."

Grace counted the scratch marks on the paper each set of four crossed with a fifth. "five…ten…fifteen…twenty. Twenty four?"

"Near as I can tell," Earl said.

Twenty-four days. Twenty-four days since the lights went out, since civilization fell apart, since she'd been at Harvard preparing for her sophomore year with dreams of going viral with her back-to-school content.

Or, was it twenty-four days since Portsmouth?

The cabin tilted sideways. Grace gripped the arms of the rocking chair, her knuckles white with tension as the room spun. Earl's hand landed on her shoulder again, that same steady pressure.

"Easy. You're in shock. That's normal after what you been through." He pressed the clothes into her lap. "Bathroom's just down the hall. There's towels in there. You get yourself changed into something dry while I heat up some coffee and soup."

Grace's fingers closed on the fabric—soft cotton that smelled faintly of lavender and cedar. A woman's clothes. She looked up at Earl, questions forming, but he'd already turned away toward what she assumed was the kitchen.

The bathroom was small, barely more than a closet with a toilet and sink. A kerosene lamp sat on the counter, its flickering light casting shadows that jumped and writhed across pale blue wallpaper printed with tiny flowers. Grace caught her reflection in the mirror above the sink and froze.

The face staring back at her was barely recognizable. Matted strawberry-blonde hair plastered to a skull that looked too prominent, cheekbones sharp beneath skin that lost its healthy glow. Dark circles under eyes that looked too large, too wild. Scratches across one cheek, a bruise blooming purple along her jaw. Lips cracked and bleeding.

This wasn't her. This couldn't be her. Grace Reynolds was polished, camera-ready, always conscious of lighting and angles and the image she projected to her followers. This hollow-eyed creature looked like something that crawled up from the bottom of the harbor.

Her hands shook as she peeled off wet clothes, the fabric clinging stubbornly to clammy skin. Sports bra. Tank top. Jeans that had been her favorite, now stained with salt and seaweed. Everything smelled of brine and decay.

The dry clothes swallowed her frame—loose sweatpants that she had to roll at the waist, a flannel shirt that hung nearly to her knees. Grace rolled the sleeves back, her movements mechanical, disconnected from conscious thought. In the mirror, she looked like a child playing dress-up in adult clothing.

Fresh water came from the tap when Grace turned it experimentally. Cold, but clean. She cupped her hands beneath the stream, bringing water to her face, trying to wash away the salt and grime. The scratches on her cheek stung. The bruise throbbed. But at least she looked more human now, less like a drowned thing.

When she emerged from the bathroom, Earl set two mugs on a small table near the fireplace alongside a bowl of soup that steamed gently in the warm air. He gestured for her to sit in one of two chairs positioned across from each other.

"It ain't much," he said, settling into the opposite chair with a soft grunt. "Just some canned chicken soup I heated up. But it'll warm your insides."

The first spoonful burned Grace's tongue, but she didn't care. The heat spread through her chest, chasing away some of the cold that settled bone-deep. She ate mechanically, barely tasting the food, while Earl sipped his coffee and watched her with eyes that held too much understanding.

"How long you been on your own?" he asked after she'd finished half the bowl.

Grace's spoon paused halfway to her mouth. "I'm not sure. Days, maybe? It's hard to remember." The admission felt like failure, like she'd lost some crucial part of herself in the water.

"You come from Portsmouth? I seen the aurora acting up strange tonight. Sometimes draws folks down to the water, thinking they might see something worth seeing."

Portsmouth. The word triggered a cascade of fractured memories. The party. The scouts. Hannah's face tight with what Grace interpreted as jealousy. Maddie pulling her away from her big opportunity, her big break, the moment that would have launched her platform into the stratosphere.

"They ruined it," Grace heard herself say, her voice flat. "My friends. They sabotaged me."

Earl's bushy eyebrows drew together. "Friends don't usually sabotage each other, honey. What happened?"

What happened? The question felt loaded, dangerous. Grace set down her spoon, her hands wrapping around the warm mug of coffee instead. The heat anchored her, gave her something to focus on besides the memories that felt increasingly wrong, increasingly distorted.

"There were scouts at a party. Reality TV scouts looking for fresh talent. They approached me specifically, wanted to talk about opportunities. But Hannah and Maddie, they…" Grace's voice trailed off as she tried to remember exactly what happened. "They pulled me away. Said the men were dangerous. But I know what I saw. They had credentials. They were legitimate. And my friends couldn't stand that I was getting attention, that someone finally recognized my potential."

The words sounded right in her head, but saying them out loud made them feel somehow empty, like she was reciting lines from a script she didn't quite believe.

Earl's careful neutrality encouraged her to continue. "And then what happened?"

"We argued. They wouldn't let me go back, wouldn't let me talk to the scouts. So I…" Grace's throat closed around the words. "I left. I ran. And they chased after me, still trying to control everything, still trying to ruin my moment. So I jumped off the bridge. Just to get away from them."

The silence that followed stretched too long. Earl took a slow sip of his coffee, his eyes never leaving her face. When he finally spoke, his voice was gentle but firm.

"Girl, that don't sound like sabotage. That sounds like friends trying to protect you from men who might have bad intentions."

"No." The word came out sharp, defensive. "You don't understand. I know what I saw. I know what they were doing."

"Maybe." Earl set down his mug with deliberate care. "Or maybe you been through trauma that's got your memories all twisted up. Happens sometimes. Brain tries to make sense of things that don't make sense, fills in gaps with stories that feel true even when they ain't."

Grace's hands tightened on her mug until she thought the ceramic might crack. "I'm not making it up. I'm not crazy."

"Didn't say you were crazy. Said you been through trauma. There's a difference." Earl leaned back in his chair, the wood creaking beneath his weight. "My Marianne, she went through something similar after our boy died. Car accident on Route 1. She started telling stories about how it happened that weren't quite true. Not because she was lying, but because her mind was trying to protect her from the real memory, which was too awful to carry."

The comparison felt wrong, insulting. Grace wasn't some fragile old woman who couldn't handle reality. She was an influencer, a content creator who made her living reading people and situations and crafting narratives that resonated with thousands of followers.

"I know what happened to me," Grace said, her voice tight. "I don't need some stranger telling me my memories are wrong."

"Fair enough." Earl raised his hands in a placating gesture. "I'm just saying, maybe give yourself some grace. You almost drowned tonight. You been wandering alone for who knows how long. It's alright to be confused."

But Grace wasn't confused. She was certain. Hannah and Maddie betrayed her, destroyed her big opportunity, drove her to jump into the harbor in desperation. The scouts were real. The opportunity was real. Everything that came after was their fault.

She just needed to get her phone working again so she could tell her story, could expose their treachery to her followers, could reclaim the narrative they'd tried to steal.

"I need to charge my phone," she said, setting down her mug. "Do you have any way to generate power? Solar panels? Generator?"

Earl shook his head slowly. "Even if I did, that EMP fried most electronics. Anything with circuits is basically scrap now. Your phone ain't gonna work no matter how much you charge it."

The words hit like a physical blow. Grace's hand moved instinctively to where her phone sat in the sweatpants pocket, protecting it even though protecting it was pointless.

"But my content," she whispered. "My followers. They're waiting for updates. They need to know I'm okay."

"Honey, I don't think anyone's following anything anymore. Whole world's gone dark. We're all just trying to survive."

No. That couldn't be true. The internet was forever. Her platform was secure. Three years of careful cultivation, of building her brand, of growing her audience—that couldn't just vanish because some lights went out.

"You're wrong," Grace said, standing abruptly. The chair rocked behind her, its movement agitated. "Social media is global. Even if the power's out here, there are servers, backups, redundancies. My content exists. My followers exist. I just need to get somewhere with working infrastructure."

Earl's face showed pity now, which was worse than the concern. "Grace, listen to me. The EMP wasn't just local. From what I heard on the shortwave before it died, it was worldwide. Satellites are down. Power grids are gone. There ain't no infrastructure anymore. Not in any way that matters for your phone or your followers or any of that."

"Stop." Grace pressed her hands to her ears like she could block out the words. "Stop lying to me. You're just like them. You're trying to break me, trying to make me think I'm crazy."

"I'm trying to help you face reality—"

"Reality?" Grace's laugh came out high and brittle. "You want to talk about reality? The reality is that my entire life's work is on this phone. The reality is that I have fifty thousand people who depend on me for content. The reality is that I was about to break through, about to go viral, about to make something of myself before my supposed friends destroyed everything!"

Earl stood slowly, his movements careful like he was approaching a spooked animal. "You need rest. You need time to process what's happened. Why don't you lie down for a bit? There's a spare room down the hall. Marianne's old sewing room. It's got a bed."

The suggestion made Grace's skin crawl. Lie down in a dead woman's room, in a stranger's house, while her phone stayed dead and her followers wondered where she'd gone? While Hannah and Maddie probably celebrated their successful sabotage, probably laughed about how they'd broken her?

"I'm not tired," she said, though exhaustion pulled at her limbs like weights.

"You're dead on your feet. I can see you swaying." Earl's voice held firm kindness that reminded Grace painfully of her father. "Just a few hours. I'll keep watch, make sure you're safe."

Safe. The word felt like a joke. Nothing was safe anymore. The world ended and her friends betrayed her, and her phone was dead and she couldn't even document any of it, couldn't turn her trauma into content that would validate her suffering.

But her body betrayed her again, a wave of dizziness forcing her to grab the back of the chair for support. Earl was there immediately, his hand under her elbow, guiding her down the narrow hallway to a small room that smelled of dust and dried flowers.

The bed was narrow, covered with a faded quilt that showed careful stitching. An old sewing machine sat in one corner, draped with fabric that probably waited for Marianne's hands for years now. Pictures on the wall showed a younger Earl and a smiling woman with kind eyes, their images captured in cheaper frames that spoke of modest living.

"I'll be right outside if you need anything," Earl said, helping Grace sit on the bed. "You just rest now. Everything looks better after some sleep."

Grace lay back against pillows that smelled faintly of lavender, her body sinking into a mattress that cradled her aching muscles. She meant to stay awake, meant to keep her guard up against this stranger who claimed to be a rescuer but might be something more sinister. Her hand found her phone, clutching it against her chest like a talisman.

But exhaustion dragged her down into darkness before she could resist.

Grace woke to afternoon sunlight streaming through thin curtains and the smell of frying fish. For one disoriented moment, she thought she was home, that her mother was making lunch, that everything since that day had been a nightmare.

Then reality crashed back. Earl's cabin. Marianne's clothes. Her dead phone still clutched in her hand.

She sat up slowly, her body protesting every movement. New aches appeared during sleep—her ribs hurt where she must have hit something in the water, her throat felt scraped raw, her head pounded with dehydration.

Voices drifted from the main room. Earl talking to someone, his tone friendly and relaxed. Grace's pulse quickened. Who else was here? Had he called someone? Were Hannah and Maddie already tracking her down?

She crept to the bedroom door, pressing her ear against the wood. Just Earl's voice, she realized. Talking to himself or maybe to a pet she hadn't noticed. The realization should have been reassuring but somehow made things worse.

Grace eased the door open, peering down the hallway toward the main room. Earl stood at a small stove, tending a cast iron skillet where fish sizzled in butter. He was still talking, his words unclear but his tone animated, like he was engaged in active conversation.

With no one.

"So I told her," Earl said to the empty room, "I said 'Marianne, that girl's been through hell. We got to give her time to heal.' And you know what she'd say, don't you? She'd say 'Earl Hutchins, you bring that poor child out here and make sure she eats something proper.'"

He was talking to his dead wife. Grace watched him gesture with a spatula, nodding at responses only he could hear, and something inside her chest twisted painfully. This old man, alone in his cabin, so lonely that he carried on conversations with ghosts.

Just like she carried on conversations with her phone.

The parallel struck her with uncomfortable force. She pushed it away, focusing instead on gathering information. Earl was distracted. This might be her chance to search the cabin, to find out if he really was the kind stranger he appeared to be or something more dangerous.

Grace moved silently down the hallway, her bare feet making no sound on the worn wooden floors. The cabin was small—just the bedroom she'd slept in, a tiny bathroom, and the main room that served as kitchen, living room, and dining area all at once. No hidden spaces. No locked doors. No evidence of anything sinister.

Which made it more suspicious, didn't it? Too clean. Too perfect. Too convenient.

"You're up," Earl said, turning from the stove with a smile that crinkled the corners of his eyes. "Good timing. Fish is almost ready. Caught these this morning off my dock. Nothing fancy, but it'll put some meat on your bones."

He was trying too hard to be nice. The observation crystallized in Grace's mind with sudden clarity. The rescue, the warm cabin, the dead wife's clothes, the home-cooked meals—it was all a performance. Just like her own content, but more dangerous because it pretended to be real.

"Why are you doing this?" The question came out harsher than Grace intended.

Earl's smile faded into something more serious. "Doing what? Feeding you? Because you need feeding. Because it's the right thing to do."

"Nobody does the right thing without wanting something in return. What do you want from me?"

The old man's expression showed hurt, which was probably just more manipulation. "I don't want nothing from you, girl. You were drowning. I pulled you out. That's all there is to it."

"That's what you say." Grace crossed her arms, very aware she was wearing his dead wife's clothes, standing in his cabin, dependent on his charity. The vulnerability scraped against her like sandpaper. "But I know how this works. You 'rescue' me, you play the hero, and then you expect gratitude. Expect me to owe you."

Earl turned off the stove, moving the skillet to a cool burner before facing her fully. "Listen to me. I'm seventy-three years old. My wife died two years ago. My son moved to California before I could convince him to stay. I live alone on this piece of coast because it's all I got left. When I saw you go under tonight, I didn't think about what I might get out of pulling you out. I just thought about how Marianne would never forgive me if I let some girl drown when I could have helped."

The words rang with truth, which made them more dangerous. Grace wanted to believe him, wanted to accept his kindness at face value. But accepting kindness meant letting her guard down, meant being vulnerable, meant giving someone else power over her narrative.

"I need to leave," she said suddenly. "I need to get to somewhere with working communications. My followers—"

"Your followers are gone, Grace." Earl's voice was gentle but firm. "I know that's hard to hear. But you got to understand, the world that existed before ain't coming back. Not the way it was."

"You don't know that." Grace's voice rose, panic clawing at her chest. "You're just some old man living alone in the woods. What do you know about technology and infrastructure and global communications systems?"

"I know that I haven't heard a working radio in three weeks. I know that the shortwave picked up nothing but static before it died. I know that no boats have come past my shore, no planes have flown overhead, no cars have driven the coastal road. I know that when systems that big go down, they don't come back easy."

Grace's hands clenched into fists, her fingernails biting into her palms. "Stop. Stop trying to convince me that everything I worked for is gone. Stop trying to make me believe my life doesn't matter anymore."

"I'm not saying your life don't matter. I'm saying your priorities might need to shift from phones and followers to things like food and shelter and staying alive."

The reasonableness of his words made Grace want to scream. How dare he stand there with his fish and his dead wife's ghost and tell her what should matter? How dare he try to rewrite her story, reshape her priorities, remake her into someone who didn't need her platform?

"You don't get it," she said, her voice shaking. "That phone is all I have left. My content, my followers, my whole identity—it's all there. Without it, I'm nobody."

Earl's expression softened into something that looked like real compassion. "Honey, if a dead phone is all that's keeping you somebody, then maybe it's time to figure out who you are without it."

The words hit like a slap. Grace staggered back a step, her breath coming too fast. Who was she without her platform? Without her followers? Without the constant validation of likes and comments and shares?

She was Grace Reynolds, psychology major at Harvard, daughter of successful parents, friend to Hannah and Maddie—

No. Not friend. Not anymore. They'd betrayed her.

"I know who I am," Grace said, but the words felt hollow. "I'm an influencer. A content creator. Someone who matters to thousands of people."

"You're a girl who almost drowned," Earl said quietly. "A girl who's hurting and scared and trying to make sense of a world that stopped making sense. That's enough. That's all you got to be right now."

But it wasn't enough. It would never be enough. Grace spent three years building her platform, cultivating her image, creating content that resonated with her audience. She'd sacrificed friendships and study time and her own mental health to grow her following. And now this stranger expected her to just let it all go? To accept that it didn't matter?

"The fish is getting cold," Earl said, turning back to the stove. He plated two portions, setting them on the small table where they'd sat the night before. "Come eat something. We can figure out next steps after you get some food in you."

Grace didn't move toward the table. Instead, she watched Earl settle into his chair, watched him bow his head for a moment—a prayer, maybe, or a moment of gratitude. The normalcy of it felt obscene somehow. How could he sit there acting like everything was fine when the world ended?

Unless he was hiding something. Unless his performance of normalcy was calculated, designed to lower her defenses.

"How did you really know I was out there?" The question came out sharp, accusatory.

Earl looked up from his plate, confusion in his eyes. "I told you. I couldn't sleep. I was sitting on my deck—"

"In the middle of the night. In the dark. Just happened to be watching the exact spot where I would surface. That's too convenient."

"Grace—"

"No." She cut him off, her voice rising. "I've been thinking about this. Really thinking. And it doesn't add up. The timing, the location, the fact that you had women's clothes exactly my size. Someone told you I'd be there. Someone set this up."

Earl set down his fork with careful deliberation. "Nobody set nothing up. You want to know the truth? I almost missed you. I was looking the other direction, toward town, when I heard the splash. By the time I got my boat in the water and rowed out there, you'd already gone under. I had to dive for you, had to search in the dark. Nearly lost you to the current."

The detail felt practiced, rehearsed. Grace's mind spun with possibilities. Who would have known she'd jump from that bridge? Hannah and Maddie, obviously—they'd chased her there. Had they called ahead somehow? Arranged for this 'rescue' so they could control the aftermath?

"They sent you," Grace whispered, the realization clicking into place. "Hannah and Maddie. They knew I'd jump. They knew you'd be there. This whole thing is staged."

"Girl, I don't know who Hannah and Maddie are. I never heard those names before you said them last night." Earl's voice held exhaustion now, like he was tired of defending himself. "You're seeing conspiracy where there ain't none."

"That's exactly what someone part of the conspiracy would say."

Earl closed his eyes, took a slow breath, and opened them again. When he spoke, his voice was measured, calm. "Let me ask you something. What would be the point? If your friends really wanted to hurt you, why would they arrange for you to be rescued? Why not just let you drown?"

The logic was sound, which made it more suspicious. "Because they want to control the narrative. If I die, I become a martyr. My followers would elevate me, would share my content forever. But if I'm just... damaged, broken, discredited—then they can say I was always crazy. They can erase everything I built."

"Or," Earl said carefully, "maybe they were trying to save you because they're actually your friends, and they care about you."

"No!" Grace slammed her hand on the table, making the plates jump. "You don't understand! I know what I saw! The scouts were real! The opportunity was real! They sabotaged me!"

Earl stood slowly, his movements telegraphing caution. "Alright. Let's say you're right. Let's say your friends did something wrong. What do you want to do about it? You're here now. You're safe. You got food and shelter. Maybe that's enough for today."

But it wasn't enough. It would never be enough until she could clear her name, until she could expose the truth, until she could get back to her followers and show them what really happened.

Grace's hand moved to her pocket, to her dead phone. Her fingers traced the familiar shape through the sweatpants fabric. All her proof was in there. All her documentation. The photos from that night, the videos she'd taken, the messages from the scouts before the EMP hit.

If she could just power it on. If she could just get to working infrastructure.

"I need to go to Portland," she said abruptly. "They'll have generators there. Emergency power. Someone will be able to charge my phone."

Earl's face showed open concern now. "Portland's probably worse than Portsmouth. Cities go bad fast when the power goes out. Looting, violence, people fighting over resources. You don't want to go there."

"I don't care what I want. I care about what I need." Grace moved toward the door, her bare feet cold on the wooden floor. "Thank you for the rescue and the clothes and the food. But I need to leave now."

"In Marianne's sweatpants and no shoes? You won't make it a mile." Earl moved to block her path, his hands raised in a placating gesture. "At least let me find you proper clothes. Some boots. Some supplies. If you're determined to leave, let me help you do it safely."

The offer was sensible, which meant it was probably a trap. Earl would find her clothes and then what? Lock her in the spare room? Call her friends? Keep her prisoner until she forgot about exposing the truth?

But Grace's feet were already cut from the rocks on the path last night. And Marianne's sweatpants would fall down if she tried to run. And she had no food, no water, no map of the area.

She needed Earl's help even though accepting it felt like surrender.

"Fine," she said, the word bitter in her mouth. "But then I'm leaving."

Earl nodded, relief evident. "Fair enough. Let me see what I can find."

He disappeared into what Grace assumed was his bedroom, leaving her alone in the main room. The fish sat cooling on the table, its smell turning from appetizing to vaguely unpleasant. Through the window, Grace could see the ocean stretching endless and gray beneath clouded skies. No boats. No signs of civilization. Just water and rocks and the ruins of the old world.

Her hand found her phone again, pulling it from her pocket. The screen was black, lifeless, but Grace pressed the power button anyway. Nothing. She pressed it again. Again. Again.

"Come on," she whispered. "Please. Just turn on. Just let me see my content one more time."

But the phone stayed dead, taking her followers with it, taking her identity, taking everything that made her matter.

Grace slid down the wall until she sat on the cold floor, the phone clutched to her chest. Tears burned behind her eyes but she refused to let them fall. Crying was for people who'd given up. Crying was for people who accepted defeat.

She was Grace Reynolds. She had fifty thousand followers. She was an influencer, a content creator, someone who mattered.

Even if the only person who still believed that was herself.

Earl returned carrying a canvas backpack that looked military surplus. "Found some things that might fit. Marianne's hiking boots—might be a size too big but better than bare feet. One of my old work shirts. Some supplies—dried food, water bottles, matches. Even a knife, though I'd prefer you didn't feel like you needed it."

He set the backpack down carefully, like he was approaching a wild animal. "I still think you should stay another day or two. Get your strength back. But if you're set on leaving, at least take this. And here—" He pulled a folded paper from his pocket. "Rough map I drew. Shows the coast road to Portland.

Towns along the way where you might find help. Places to avoid if you can."

Grace took the map with numb fingers. The paper was worn, marked with pencil notes and warnings. "Why are you helping me if you think I'm wrong?"

Earl's smile was sad. "Because Marianne would have wanted me to. And because even if you are wrong about your friends, that don't mean you deserve to die wandering around lost."

The kindness in his voice made something crack in Grace's chest. She wanted to believe him, wanted to trust that someone in this broken world still cared about helping people without expecting anything in return.

But trust was what got you betrayed. Trust was what let people sabotage your dreams. Trust was dangerous.

"Thank you," Grace managed, the words stiff and formal. She took the backpack, feeling its weight settle against her shoulders. "I'll return the clothes when I can."

"Keep them. Marianne would want you to have them." Earl walked to the door, opening it to let in cool morning air that smelled of salt and pine. "You be careful out there. Stick to back roads. Avoid groups of people if you can. And Grace? If you do find working power, if you do get your phone charged—maybe think about whether what you remember is really what happened."

The suggestion felt like betrayal. Grace pushed past him onto the porch, her jaw tight with anger. "I know what happened. I don't need some stranger telling me my memories are wrong."

"Alright." Earl's voice followed her down the steps. "You take care of yourself, Grace Reynolds."

Grace walked down the path without looking back, Marianne's boots loose on her feet, the backpack bouncing against her spine. The morning sun felt too bright after the cabin's dim interior. She pulled out the map, trying to orient herself, but the hand-drawn lines blurred together until she couldn't tell which direction was north.

She made it maybe a hundred yards before the dizziness hit. The trees tilted sideways, the path rising up to meet her face. Grace stumbled, caught herself against a pine tree, its bark rough beneath her palms.

Not now. She couldn't fall apart now. She had to keep moving, had to get to Portland, had to charge her phone and expose the truth.

But her legs refused to obey. Grace slid down the tree trunk until she sat in a pile of dead needles, her vision swimming. The near-drowning took more out of her than she'd realized. Or maybe it was the days before Portsmouth, wandering without enough food or water, her medication long since depleted.

The medication. Grace's hand flew to her pocket, searching for pill bottles that weren't there. When had she last taken her mood stabilizers? Before the EMP? Before the party? Time felt too slippery to grasp, but she knew it had been too long. Weeks, maybe. Without the medication, her mind felt simultaneously too sharp and too scattered, thoughts racing faster than she could process them.

Hannah and Maddie had her emergency supply. She'd given it to them for safekeeping before the party, before everything went wrong. They probably threw it away after she left, probably celebrated that she'd be forced to spiral without it.

Or maybe that was part of the plan. Get her off her meds, wait for her to break, then document her collapse as proof that she'd always been unstable.

Grace's breath came too fast, her chest tight with panic. She needed to calm down. Needed to think clearly. But clear thinking felt impossible when her brain kept generating new conspiracies, new connections, new certainties about betrayal and sabotage.

The sound of footsteps made her look up. Earl stood at the top of the path, his expression shifted and his forehead creased with concern.

"You made it real far," he said, his tone dry but not unkind. "Come on back to the cabin. Rest today, try again tomorrow."

"I'm fine." Grace tried to stand but her legs refused. "I just need a minute."

"You need more than a minute. You need rest and food and time to heal." Earl moved closer, extending his hand. "I ain't gonna force you to stay. But I ain't gonna watch you collapse in my woods either."

Grace stared at his outstretched hand, seeing both genuine concern and potential threat. If she went back to the cabin, would he lock her in? Contact her friends? Keep her prisoner until she forgot about her mission?

But staying here, collapsed against a tree, wasn't an option either.

She took his hand. His grip was firm but gentle as he helped her to her feet, one arm supporting her weight as they walked slowly back toward the cabin. Grace's vision swam with each step, black spots dancing at the edges.

"I hate this," she whispered. "I hate being weak."

"Ain't weakness to need help," Earl replied. "That's just being human."

But Grace didn't want to be human. Humans were vulnerable, fragile, dependent on others. Influencers were brands, carefully curated, always in control of their own narrative. She'd spent three years building herself into something more than just another college girl, and now one near-drowning reduced her back to nothing.

The cabin welcomed them with wood smoke warmth. Earl guided Grace back to Marianne's rocking chair, tucking a blanket around her shoulders despite her protests.

"You got yourself worked up," he said, crouching beside the chair so they were eye level. "That panic attack you were having, that ain't gonna help you get anywhere. You need to calm down. You need to rest."

"Stop telling me what I need." But Grace's voice lacked conviction. The panic still fluttered in her chest like a trapped bird.

Earl stood, moving to the kitchen area. "I'm gonna make you some tea. Marianne swore by chamomile for nerves. You don't have to drink it if you don't want, but I'm making it anyway."

Grace watched him work, his movements economical and practiced. A kettle on the stove, loose tea measured into a strainer, honey from a jar that looked homemade. The domesticity of it felt surreal against the backdrop of civilizational collapse.

"Why do you live alone out here?" The question emerged before Grace could stop it.

Earl glanced over his shoulder. "Got my reasons. After Marianne died, the house in town felt too big, too empty. Too many memories. This cabin was ours—place we'd come on weekends, get away from everything. Made sense to stay here after she passed."

"Don't you get lonely?"

A small smile emerged. "Sometimes. But lonely's better than being around people who make you feel alone. Out here, I got my memories, got the ocean, got enough to keep me busy. That's enough for an old man."

The tea kettle whistled. Earl poured steaming water over the tea leaves, the scent of chamomile filling the small space. He added honey, stirred carefully, and brought the mug to Grace.

"Give it a minute to cool," he said, settling back into his chair with his own mug of coffee. "Then sip it slow. It'll help settle your nerves."

Grace wrapped her hands around the warm ceramic, letting the heat seep into her cold fingers. The chamomile smell reminded her of her mother, of sick days spent home from school, of being cared for before she learned that care always came with conditions.

"Tell me about your followers," Earl said after a long silence. "What made you want to be an influencer?"

The question felt loaded, dangerous. But something about Earl's tone—genuinely curious rather than judgmental—made Grace's defenses lower slightly.

"I wanted to matter," she said quietly. "I wanted people to see me, to value what I had to say. Growing up, I was always just… there. Not the smartest, not the prettiest, not the most talented. Just average. But online, I could be someone different. Someone worth paying attention to."

"And did it work? Did being an influencer make you feel like you mattered?"

Grace took a careful sip of tea, buying time to formulate her answer. "Sometimes. When a post went viral, when brands reached out for sponsorships, when people left comments saying I'd inspired them—yes. In those moments, I felt like I mattered. Like I was more than just another forgettable person."

"And the rest of the time?"

The question cut too close to truths Grace didn't want to examine. "The rest of the time I was terrified that one wrong post would tank my engagement. That the algorithm would stop favoring me. That my followers would get bored and move on to someone more interesting."

"Sounds exhausting," Earl observed.

"It was." The admission surprised Grace. She'd never said that out loud before, never acknowledged that her platform felt like a burden as often as it felt like validation. "But it was also everything. My identity, my purpose, my future. Without it, I'm nothing."

"That ain't true and you know it." Earl's voice was gentle but firm. "You're Grace Reynolds. You're a person with thoughts and feelings and a whole life beyond likes and comments. The fact that you can't see that right now don't make it less true."

Grace wanted to argue, wanted to insist that he was wrong. But the tea and the warmth and the exhaustion were catching up with her, making her defenses crumble.

"I don't know who I am without my platform," she whispered. "I've spent so long being an influencer that I forgot how to be anything else."

"Then maybe this is your chance to remember." Earl leaned forward, his weathered hands clasped between his knees. "I ain't saying what happened to the world is good. It ain't. But sometimes losing everything is the only way to find out what really matters."

The words felt like wisdom Grace wasn't ready to accept. She took another sip of tea, letting the warmth spread through her chest, temporarily quieting the panic.

They sat in silence for a while, the only sounds the crackling fire and the distant call of gulls. Grace felt her eyelids growing heavy, her body demanding rest even as her mind continued racing with plans and conspiracies and half-formed accusations.

"Why don't you lie down for a bit," Earl suggested. "Proper rest this time, in a real bed. I'll wake you for dinner."

Grace wanted to refuse, wanted to insist she was fine, wanted to gather her things and leave immediately. But her body already made the decision, exhaustion pulling her under like another drowning.

"Just for a few hours," she managed.

"Just for a few hours," Earl agreed.

Grace let him guide her back to Marianne's sewing room, let him tuck the quilt around her shoulders, let him close the door softly behind him. The bed cradled her aching body, the pillow smelled of lavender, and despite everything, Grace felt herself relaxing into sleep.

But even in her dreams, her hand stayed wrapped around her phone, protecting the only thing that made her real.

Night returned to find Grace curled in Marianne's rocking chair, the chair creaking gently as she stared into the fire. Earl moved around the kitchen area, preparing dinner from his limited supplies. The domesticity should have been comforting, but instead it made Grace's skin crawl with nameless anxiety.

"You're quiet tonight," Earl observed, stirring something that smelled of canned tomatoes and herbs. "Feeling better after your rest?"

Grace's fingers traced patterns on her phone screen, muscle memory seeking apps that no longer existed. "I dreamed about Portsmouth. About the party."

"Want to talk about it?"

"No. Yes. I don't know." Grace pulled the blanket tighter. "In the dream, the scouts were there again. But this time I could see their faces clearly. They looked wrong. Predatory. And Hannah and Maddie were trying to pull me away, but I kept fighting them because I was so sure they were sabotaging me."

"What happened then?"

"I jumped. Just like in real life. But in the dream, I could see their faces as I went over the rail. They weren't laughing or celebrating. They looked terrified. Like they'd just watched me die." Grace's voice dropped to barely a whisper. "What if I'm remembering it wrong?"

Earl turned from the stove, his expression carefully neutral. "What do you think?"

"I think my medication is supposed to keep me from having thoughts like that. I think without it, my brain lies to me. Makes me see conspiracies that don't exist, makes me paranoid and delusional." The admissions felt like pulling teeth. "I think maybe those scouts weren't scouts at all. Maybe they were just drunk guys at a party. And maybe Hannah and Maddie were trying to protect me, not sabotage me."

The silence stretched too long. Grace couldn't look at Earl, couldn't face whatever his expression might show. Pity, probably. Or worse, validation that she was exactly as broken as she feared.

"That takes a lot of courage," Earl finally said. "Questioning your own memories, especially when they feel so certain."

"I'm not saying I'm wrong about everything." Grace's voice turned defensive. "I'm just saying maybe some details got confused. That doesn't mean they didn't betray me. That doesn't mean they weren't jealous of my platform."

"Maybe not. But maybe it means they were trying to be your friends, and you were too caught up in content and followers to see it."

The words stung precisely because they rang with truth. Grace remembered the arguments before Portsmouth, Hannah expressing concern about Grace's medication compliance, Maddie worried about how much time Grace spent on her phone instead of studying. At the time, Grace interpreted their concern as judgment, as attempts to control her, as jealousy of her growing platform.

What if they'd just been worried friends trying to help someone they cared about?

"I said terrible things to them," Grace whispered. "That last argument before I ran. I accused them of sabotaging me, of being jealous, of trying to destroy everything I'd built. I told them they were toxic and I never wanted to see them again."

"And then you jumped off a bridge."

"And then I jumped off a bridge," Grace echoed. "God, they must think I'm dead. They probably watched me go under and spent the last three weeks thinking they killed me."

Earl brought two bowls to the table, some kind of pasta with tomato sauce. "Or maybe they survived too. Maybe they're out there somewhere, alive and worrying about you."

The possibility felt both hopeful and terrifying. If Hannah and Maddie were alive, if Grace could find them, if she could apologize—but what if they'd already moved on? What if they were better off without her chaos and drama and constant need for validation?

"Eat something," Earl encouraged. "Then we can figure out what you want to do tomorrow."

Grace forced herself to take a bite even though the food tasted like cardboard in her mouth. Her thoughts spun in circles, chasing themselves around possibilities and regrets and the growing certainty that nothing about her situation was what she'd believed.

"What if I really am crazy?" The question emerged small and broken. "What if my brain is so damaged that I can't trust anything I think or remember?"

"Then you learn to live with uncertainty," Earl replied. "You accept that you might not have all the answers, that your memories might be flawed, that you need help to separate truth from delusion. That ain't weakness. That's wisdom."

But Grace didn't want wisdom. She wanted certainty. She wanted to know definitively whether her friends betrayed her or saved her, whether she was a victim or a villain, whether anything about her carefully constructed life had been real.

The pasta grew cold in her bowl as Grace stared into the fire, watching flames dance and twist and consume the wood that fed them. Destruction and creation all at once, just like the content she used to make, just like the person she'd become.

"I should sleep," she said finally. "Tomorrow I'll… I don't know what I'll do tomorrow."

"That's alright. Tomorrow can figure itself out." Earl collected their bowls, scraping most of Grace's uneaten dinner back into the pot. "You get some rest. I'll be out here if you need anything."

Grace retreated to Marianne's sewing room, the space that became a temporary sanctuary. She lay in the narrow bed, staring at the ceiling, her phone clutched against her chest like a security blanket.

In the darkness, Earl's voice drifted from the main room. Talking to Marianne again, his words indistinct but his tone troubled. Grace caught fragments—"…don't know how to help her…" "…too damaged…" "…might be dangerous…"

The words sent ice through Grace's veins. Dangerous. He thought she was dangerous. And maybe he was right. She'd attacked Maddie. She'd run from her friends. She'd jumped off a bridge. What would she do next?

Grace's fingers tightened on her phone until the edges bit into her palms. Earl was a threat. He'd always been a threat. All his kindness, all his patience—it was manipulation. He was trying to break her down, make her doubt herself, turn her into someone helpless and compliant.

Just like Hannah and Maddie tried to do.

Just like everyone always tried to do.

The paranoia rose like bile in Grace's throat. She sat up slowly, listening to Earl's continued monologue in the next room. He was planning something. He had to be. Nobody helped someone without expecting something in return.

Grace slipped from the bed, moving silently across the wooden floor. The backpack Earl gave her sat in the corner, supplies he claimed were for her journey. What if they were poisoned? What if the water bottles contained sedatives? What if the whole thing was a trap?

She eased the bedroom door open, peering down the hallway. Earl sat in his rocking chair by the dying fire, his back to her, still talking to his dead wife.

"…can't keep her here forever…" His voice carried clearly now. "…needs proper help…" "…mental hospital if there were any left…"

Mental hospital. He was going to lock her up. Going to declare her incompetent. Going to steal her story and tell the world she was crazy.

Grace's hand moved to the fireplace poker leaning against the wall beside the bedroom door. The metal was cool beneath her fingers, solid and real. Just like in Portsmouth, when the world felt too confusing and dangerous, violence offered a simple solution.

She moved down the hallway, each step careful and measured. Earl continued rocking, continued talking, completely unaware of the danger behind him. Grace raised the poker, feeling its weight, seeing how the dying firelight caught the metal.

This would be incredible content. The betrayer exposed. The manipulator revealed. Justice for everything he'd tried to do to her.

"…she's just like our boy was…" Earl's voice cracked with emotion. "…before the accident…" "…wish you were here to tell me what to do…"

Grace froze, the poker held high, her breath caught in her chest. Our boy. The son who died. Earl wasn't talking about betrayal or manipulation. He was talking about loss, about seeing his dead child's struggles reflected in a stranger's eyes.

The poker wavered. Grace's arms trembled with the weight of it, with the weight of what she was about to do.

Earl's head turned slightly, just enough to see her standing there with the weapon raised. He showed no surprise, no fear. Just a deep, bone-tired sadness.

"Go ahead if you need to," he said quietly. "But I ain't your enemy, Grace. I never was."

The words should have stopped her. Should have made her lower the poker, made her recognize the kindness he'd shown, made her see that not everyone was part of some grand conspiracy.

But the paranoia had its claws too deep. The certainty that everyone was against her, that trust was weakness, that violence was the only language that made sense anymore.

Grace's arms swung downward.

The poker caught Earl on the side of the head with a sickening crack. He lurched sideways in the rocking chair, his hand flying up too late to protect himself. The chair tipped, sending him sprawling onto the wooden floor.

Grace struck again. And again. Each blow fueled by weeks of fear and confusion and rage at a world that stopped making sense. Earl tried to raise his arms, tried to speak, but the poker found its mark again and again until he stopped moving.

Finally, the rocking chair settled into stillness. Earl lay crumpled on the floor, blood spreading slowly across the worn planks, dark and thick in the firelight.

Grace stood over him, the poker still gripped in trembling hands. Her breath came in ragged gasps. Earl's eyes stared at nothing, his gaze frozen in an expression of sad resignation, as if he'd known this would happen, as if he'd accepted it even before she raised the weapon.

The poker fell from Grace's nerveless fingers, clattering against the floor. The sound echoed through the cabin, impossibly loud in the sudden silence.

What had she done?

Grace stumbled backward, her legs hitting the edge of the rocking chair. It creaked softly, still moving slightly from the violence, marking time in a world that had stopped.

Earl's blood continued spreading across the floor, reaching toward the braided rug near the fire. In the kitchen, his abandoned mug of coffee sat on the counter where he'd left it. In the corner, the backpack he'd prepared for her journey rested against the wall, filled with supplies he'd gathered to keep her safe.

To keep her safe.

"No," Grace whispered. "No, no, no."

She sank to her knees beside Earl's body, her hands hovering over him but afraid to touch. His chest didn't rise. His eyes didn't blink. The kindness that had creased his aged face was gone, replaced by the empty stillness of death.

"I didn't mean—" Grace's voice broke. "You were trying to—they sent you—I had to—"

But the excuses were weak, even as she spoke them. Earl hadn't been part of a conspiracy. He'd been a lonely old man who saw his dead son's struggles reflected in a stranger's eyes.

He'd pulled her from the harbor. Fed her. Given her clothes and supplies and kindness.

And she'd killed him for it.

Grace's hands found her phone, pulling it from her pocket with shaking fingers. She pressed the power button frantically, desperately, as if seeing her content might somehow undo what she'd just done, might make the last few minutes disappear like a deleted post.

The screen stayed black. Dead. Useless.

Just like Earl.

The reality crashed down on Grace with suffocating weight. She'd murdered someone. Taken a life. Ended a person who'd done nothing but try to save her.

Her hands were sticky with blood. Earl's blood. The poker lay beside his body, its metal now stained red.

"Mommy," she heard herself whisper, her voice small and broken like a child's. "Mommy, I'm scared."

She curled up on the cold floor beside Earl's body, her arms wrapped around her knees, rocking back and forth. The phone clutched against her chest. The fire burned down to embers, casting the cabin into deeper darkness.

"Mommy, I want to come home." Tears streamed down Grace's face, hot against her cold skin. "Please, Mommy, make it stop. I want to go home. I don't want to be here anymore."

But there was no home to return to. No mother to comfort her. No way to undo the violence that stained her hands.

Grace Reynolds, influencer with fifty thousand followers, psychology major at Harvard, friend to Hannah and Maddie— that person was gone. Drowned in Portsmouth harbor along with whatever sanity she'd been clinging to.

What remained was something else. Something broken and dangerous and alone.

"I'm sorry," Grace sobbed into the darkness. "I'm sorry, I'm sorry, I'm sorry."

But sorry couldn't bring Earl back. Sorry couldn't undo the crack of the poker against his skull. Sorry was just another empty word in a world that had run out of meaning.

The fire died to nothing. The cabin grew cold. Outside, the aurora painted the night sky in shades of green and purple, nature's indifferent witness to one more death in a world already drowning in them.

And Grace stayed curled on the floor beside Earl's cooling body, whispering for her mother into the darkness, the dead phone clutched against her chest like a talisman that had lost all its power.

Hours passed. The night stretched on, endless and unforgiving.

Grace's sobs eventually quieted to hiccups, then to silence. She lay on the floor, staring at nothing, feeling nothing except a vast emptiness where her sense of self used to be.

She was a murderer now. That was her identity. Not an influencer. Not a content creator. Not even Grace Reynolds anymore.

Just a girl who killed a kind old man because her broken brain couldn't tell truth from paranoid delusion.

The first light of dawn began to creep through the cabin windows, painting everything in shades of gray. Grace finally sat up, her body stiff and aching. Earl's body lay where it had fallen, the blood dried now, dark against the wooden floor.

She should leave. Should run. Should put as much distance as possible between herself and what she'd done.

But where would she go? Portland? To charge a phone that would never work again? To find followers who no longer existed?

Grace stood slowly, her legs shaking. She looked around the cabin—at the rocking chair now stained with blood, at the fireplace poker lying in a pool of red, at Earl's coffee mug still sitting on the counter.

Evidence of kindness. Evidence of murder.

She couldn't stay here. But she couldn't seem to make herself leave either.

Grace sank back down into Marianne's rocking chair, the one Earl hadn't been sitting in. She pulled the blanket around her shoulders and stared at the dead fire.

"Mommy," she whispered to the darkness, her voice small and broken. "Mommy, I'm scared. I want to come home. Please, Mommy, make it stop."

The dead phone lay beside her, its black screen reflecting nothing at all.

Three days. That's how long she sat there, barely moving, barely thinking. The cabin grew cold around her. Earl's body began to smell. Grace's phone battery stayed dead.

But, she'd learned the most important lesson of the apocalypse and that is…

In a world without rules, violence was the only currency that mattered.

Grace's eyes opened to afternoon light filtering through cabin windows crusted with salt spray. Her body ached in ways she couldn't name, muscles stiff from days curled on the wooden floor. The air tasted thick and wrong, sweet decay mixing with wood smoke and something copper that her brain refused to identify.

She sat up slowly, her hand finding the familiar weight of her phone beside her. Three days. Had it been three days? Time felt slippery, disconnected, like frames missing from a video. Her thumb moved automatically to the power button, muscle memory from thousands of check-ins.

Press.

Nothing.

Press again.

The screen flickered. No, not flickered. Glowed. Came alive with notifications scrolling past faster than she could read. Comments. Likes. Shares. Her followers finally, *finally* responding after the longest content drought of her career.

"Oh my god," Grace whispered, her voice raw from disuse. She blinked at the screen, watching engagement metrics climb. "You're all still here. You waited for me."

We missed you, Grace!

Where have you been???

QUEEN is back!

The comments flooded her screen, warm and validating and real. Grace's chest loosened, breath coming easier. She wasn't alone. She'd never been alone. Her platform survived. Her followers survived. Everything she built still existed, still mattered.

She struggled to her feet, legs shaking beneath Marianne's oversized sweatpants. The cabin spun slightly, hunger and dehydration making her vision swim. When had she last eaten? The pan of cold pasta sat on the stove. Had that been yesterday? Three days ago?

Grace positioned her phone carefully against the sugar bowl, angling it to catch the best light through the window. Her fingers smoothed down her hair, adjusted the flannel shirt, checked her reflection in the phone's black surface before the camera activated.

"Hey everyone!" Her voice came out bright and practiced despite the rasp. "I am so, so sorry for going dark on you. I know you've been worried, but I'm okay! Actually, I have the most incredible survival story to share."

She moved through the cabin with renewed energy, her audience's presence filling the empty space. The main room looked different somehow. Darker. Something about the floor near the rocking chair caught the light wrong, but Grace's eyes slid past it, focusing instead on the rustic charm Earl maintained.

"So as you can see, I've been staying in this amazing off-grid cabin. Very authentic apocalypse aesthetic." Grace panned her phone across the room, narrating like she used to do for tours of places she visited. "Notice the authentic wood stove, the hand-braided rugs, the vintage furniture. You literally cannot buy this level of rustic charm."

Her stomach cramped with hunger. Grace moved toward the kitchen area, keeping her phone steady. "Let me show you guys some survival lifestyle content. It's so important to maintain proper nutrition even when infrastructure collapses."

The kitchen held canned goods, dried beans. A half-empty coffee tin sat on the counter. Grace pulled items from shelves with her free hand, displaying each for the camera.

"The owner of this cabin, poor Earl, he passed away recently. Heart attack, I think. Very sudden." The words came easily, naturally, like she'd rehearsed them. "But he would absolutely want his supplies to go to good use. No sense letting things go to waste in a crisis, right?"

She found crackers, peanut butter, a jar of honey that caught the light beautifully. Perfect content. Grace arranged them on the small table, avoiding the section near the rocking chair where a dark stain dried into the wood grain.

"Okay. So, survival tip number one," Grace addressed her phone propped against the sugar bowl. "Always inventory your resources. Take stock of what you have available. The cabin basically has everything needed for off-grid living."

Her hands shook slightly as she unscrewed the peanut butter jar. When did she last eat? The question felt important but distant, like it belonged to someone else. Grace spread peanut butter on crackers with a butter knife while her mouth began to water.

"And you want to be mindful about portion control. Resources are finite now." She bit into the cracker, the salt and protein hitting her system like a drug. "Though honestly, Earl was super prepared. He has enough supplies here for weeks."

Are you okay Grace?

You look really thin

Where exactly are you?

The comments scrolled past. Grace's smile widened as she read them between bites.

"I'm totally fine, you guys! Better than fine, actually. This whole apocalypse thing is really helping me reconnect with authentic living. No more worrying about algorithm changes or engagement metrics." She laughed, the sound high and bright. "Well, I mean, I'm still tracking metrics obviously. But it's different now. More organic."

She ate three more crackers, washing them down with water from one of Earl's jugs. The liquid soothed her raw throat. How long since she'd had any water? The cabin felt warmer now, less oppressive. Her followers' presence made everything better.

"Let me give you the full cabin tour." Grace grabbed her phone, moving through the small space with renewed confidence. "So, this is obviously the main living area. Very open concept, which I love. The wood stove provides heat and cooking capability. Totally sustainable."

She panned past the rocking chair, her eyes sliding across the floor without registering the dark stains. "Authentic vintage furniture throughout. That rocking chair is probably an antique. And check out this braided rug. Hand-made, super rustic."

The bedroom door stood open. Grace moved down the narrow hallway, narrating continuously.

"Down here we have the sleeping quarters. I've been staying in the guest room, very cozy." She showed Marianne's sewing room, with its narrow bed and faded quilt. "Notice the authentic quilting work. This is real craftsmanship, not some mass-produced thing from Target."

This place looks creepy

Grace seriously where are you

Are you sure you're safe?

"Safe? Oh my God, totally safe. This is literally the safest I've felt since the day." Grace's voice carried absolute conviction. "Earl was so kind to let me stay here. Poor guy. His heart just gave out, but at least he didn't suffer. Very peaceful."

She moved back to the main room, positioning herself by the window where afternoon light painted everything gold. Perfect for her complexion. Grace checked her reflection in the phone screen, adjusting angles.

"Okay so, real talk with you guys." Her voice dropped into the intimate tone she used for serious content. "The last few weeks have been absolutely wild. Like, civilization-ending level wild. But I really feel like I'm finding my authentic self through all this chaos."

You're scaring me Grace

Please tell someone where you are

This doesn't seem right

Grace scrolled past the concerned comments, focusing on the positive engagement. Someone sent hearts. Another comment praised her resilience. These were her real followers, the ones who understood her vision.

"I know some of you are worried, but trust me, I'm exactly where I need to be." She smiled at the camera, the expression practiced and perfect despite her sunken cheeks. "This is all part of my journey. My authentic apocalypse survival story."

Something outside made a sound. Engine noise, growing closer. Grace's head snapped toward the window, her livestream forgotten for a moment. Vehicles on the coastal road. Multiple vehicles.

Her heart rate spiked, paranoia flooding through her system. Who would be driving out here? Had Hannah and Maddie tracked her down? Were they coming to finish what they started in Portsmouth?

"Guys, someone's here." Grace whispered to her phone, suddenly moving to the wall beside the window. "I need to see who it is before they see me."

Three trucks pulled into view, grinding to a stop in Earl's gravel drive. Men emerged, seven of them, moving with casual confidence as though they were out for an afternoon stroll. Not military. Not police. Something else.

Grace pressed herself against the wall, her phone clutched to her chest. The men moved toward the cabin, their voices carrying through the thin walls.

"Smoke was coming from this chimney a couple of days ago. Someone was here."

"Probably that old fisherman. Easy pickings."

"Check the dock first. Might have a boat we can use."

Raiders. The word crystallized in Grace's mind with perfect clarity. These were the people everyone warned about. Looters. Criminals. Taking advantage of collapsed civilization.

Or were they?

Grace's racing thoughts reorganized themselves around a different possibility. The trucks. The coordinated movement. The way they operated as a team. These weren't random looters.

These were scouts. Professional scouts looking for talent.

Just like Portsmouth. Just like the men at that party who recognized her potential before Hannah and Maddie sabotaged everything.

Grace's fear transformed into something else. Opportunity. Vindication. A chance to prove that her platform, her brand, her vision had value even in the apocalypse.

She straightened, smoothing down her hair and adjusting Marianne's oversized flannel. The phone stayed in her hand, ready to document everything. Her followers needed to see this. Needed to witness her comeback story.

"Okay, guys," she whispered to the camera, her voice steady now. "This is huge. I think talent scouts just arrived. Real professionals who can help me rebuild my platform for the post-apocalyptic market."

Grace no

Those are dangerous men

Please hide

The comments scrolled past but Grace dismissed them. Haters. Jealous followers who couldn't handle her success. Her real audience understood. Her real audience wanted to see her thrive.

The cabin door rattled. Someone testing the knob from outside.

Grace positioned herself in the center of the main room, phone held at the perfect angle to capture both her and whoever entered. Her influencer smile locked into place, the one she'd practiced for thousands of selfies. Approachable but aspirational. Friendly but professional.

The door opened.

A man filled the doorway, broad-shouldered and dangerous in a way that should have terrified her. Behind him, two more men crowded the threshold. They all covered their faces, one even gagging. They took in the cabin carefully, their eyes cataloging resources and threats.

Then they saw Grace, standing in the middle of the room with her phone held high, smiling like she was greeting fans at a meet-and-greet.

"Hi!" Grace's voice came out bright and confident. "Welcome! I'm Grace Reynolds. You might know me from my lifestyle and wellness platform. Fifty thousand followers across all channels before the chaos. I'm currently working on pivoting my brand for the post-apocalyptic market, and I would absolutely love to discuss collaboration opportunities."

The men stared at her. One of them, a wiry guy with a tactical vest, started to laugh. But the one in front, the leader, his eyes traveled past Grace to the floor near the rocking chair.

To the blood that Grace couldn't see.

"Well, well." The leader's voice carried dark amusement as he stepped fully into the cabin. His boots tracked across the wooden floor, moving deliberately toward the rocking chair. "Looks like someone's already here."

"That must be the smell," one of the men in the doorway said.

Grace followed his gaze, confused. What was he looking at? The antique furniture? The authentic rustic decor?

The leader crouched beside the chair, his hand touching something on the floor. When he straightened, his fingers came away dark red. He studied Grace with new interest, something calculating entering his expression.

"You kill the old man?" The question came casually, conversationally.

"What? No!" Grace's influencer smile faltered. "Earl had a heart attack. Very tragic. But I've been taking care of his cabin, making sure nothing goes to waste."

The leader moved past the rocking chair, disappearing down the hallway. Grace heard him checking the bedroom, the bathroom. When he returned, his expression shifted into something that made her skin prickle despite her delusions.

"Heart attack." He repeated the words like he was tasting them. "With a cracked skull and defensive wounds on his hands."

"I don't know what you mean." Grace's voice stayed bright, her phone still recording. "This is all just a tragic accident. But since you're here, I really think we should talk about my platform. I have incredible engagement metrics and—"

"Kyle." One of the other men spoke up, the wiry one in the tactical vest. "She's completely insane."

Kyle. The leader. Grace filed the name away, already thinking about how to frame this for content. First meeting with new management. Behind the scenes of her comeback story.

"Maybe." Kyle moved closer, studying Grace like she was a curiosity. "Or maybe she's exactly what we need."

Grace's smile brightened. "I knew you'd see the potential! My authentic apocalypse content is going to revolutionize survival lifestyle branding. I've been developing concepts for months and—"

"Shut up for a second." Kyle's voice cut through her pitch. He turned to his men. "Nate, Pete, check the rest of the property. See what supplies the old man had stocked."

The two men moved past Grace toward the kitchen and storage areas. She started to object about them touching Earl's things, but Kyle's hand on her shoulder stopped her.

"Let me explain how this works." His voice stayed conversational but something underneath made Grace's survival instincts finally wake up. "You killed someone. Maybe on purpose, maybe not. Either way, that makes you interesting."

"I have a platform," Grace insisted, her phone still held between them. "Fifty thousand followers. Brand partnerships. I'm a professional content creator."

"You're a crazy girl with a dead phone, talking to nobody." Kyle's thumb pressed against her collarbone, not quite threatening but close. "But crazy can be useful. Especially crazy that doesn't mind violence."

Grace run

Please get out of there

Those men are going to hurt you

The comments scrolled past her vision but Grace dismissed them. Haters. They didn't understand her vision. Didn't understand that this was networking, brand development, strategic partnership building.

"So here's what's going to happen." Kyle released her shoulder, moving to the table where she'd left the peanut butter and crackers. He picked up a cracker, examined it, ate it thoughtfully. "You're going to come with us. You're going to keep being your authentic crazy self. And when we need someone to distract people while we do our work, you're going to perform."

"Perform?" Grace's influencer instincts activated. "Like, create content? Because I have so many ideas for apocalypse lifestyle series. Survival fashion, authentic living tutorials, community building strategies—"

"Sure, kid. Whatever you want to call it." Kyle's smile didn't reach his eyes. "But you do exactly what we say, when we say it. And if you get any ideas about running off or causing problems, remember we know what you did to the old man."

The words should have felt like a threat. Should have triggered fear or resistance. Instead, Grace processed them as validation. These professionals recognized her value. Saw her potential. Wanted her talent enough to bring her into their operation.

"This is going to be such incredible content," she breathed, already planning the announcement for her followers. "Exclusive behind-the-scenes access to survival operations. My audience is going to love this."

Kyle exchanged a glance with the wiry man—Nate— who'd returned from checking the storage room. Something passed between them, some unspoken communication that Grace's fractured mind couldn't interpret.

"Boss, she's got Earl's hiking gear in the bedroom." Nate jerked his thumb toward the hallway. "Good boots, couple of packs, camping supplies. And there's a root cellar out back full of preserves."

"Load it up." Kyle turned back to Grace. "Get changed into something that fits. You've got five minutes."

Grace looked down at Marianne's oversized clothes, suddenly conscious of how ridiculous she looked. "Right. Yes. Professional appearance is crucial for brand consistency."

She hurried to the bedroom, her phone clutched in one hand while she grabbed Earl's hiking gear with the other. The boots fit better than Marianne's. The cargo pants and work shirt transformed her from drowning victim into something else entirely.

Grace caught her reflection in the small mirror above Earl's dresser. Hollow-eyed. Sharp featured. Dangerous in a way that excited rather than frightened her. This was her authentic self emerging. Raw. Powerful. Unfiltered by society's expectations.

"Perfect aesthetic," she whispered to her phone's camera. "Apocalypse warrior princess meets survival influencer. This is exactly the rebrand I needed."

Please Grace

This is wrong

You're in danger

The concerned comments kept scrolling but Grace's attention fixed on the positive engagement. Someone had sent fire emojis. Another comment praised her resilience. These were her real followers. The ones who understood her vision.

When she returned to the main room, Kyle and his men worked efficiently through Earl's supplies. They'd found his emergency cash, his ammunition, his tools. Everything useful disappeared into their packs and trucks.

"Ready for your first collaboration?" Kyle asked, shouldering a pack that looked like it might burst, it was so full.

"Absolutely." Grace positioned herself for optimal camera angles, her phone held steady despite her racing heart. "Where are we heading?"

"North. Into Portland. We're setting up the… uh… production center in the hotel. It'll be our base of operations while we… uh… gather our audience."

Nate snorted a chuckle, but Kyle flashed him a threatening look.

"You see, Grace. We need you to really dial in on this… uh… apocalypse branding so that we can—" He glanced at his men. "Help them rebuild." Kyle moved toward the door, his men falling in behind him. "You're going to help us convince them to share and join with the… uh… relief efforts."

The thinly veiled violence in his words registered somewhere in Grace's consciousness but couldn't penetrate her delusions. This was content. This was her platform expanding into new markets. This was survival lifestyle branding at its most authentic, and they wanted her to be the spokesperson.

She followed Kyle outside, where afternoon sun shimmered on the quietly rolling waves of the ocean that she felt was the perfect backdrop for an impromptu cameo. She posed with her two fingers held up in a peace sign and wide grin to snap the new profile image for the new image of this movement. The trucks waited in the gravel drive, engines rumbling. Grace climbed into the passenger seat of Kyle's truck without being told, already planning how to frame this for maximum engagement.

"This is going to be such an amazing series," she told Kyle as he started the engine. "Behind the scenes with my new team. Building community through authentic resource sharing. My followers are going to love this direction."

Kyle glanced at her, something dark and amused in his expression. "Yeah, kid. They're gonna love it."

The trucks pulled away from Earl's cabin, leaving it empty except for the blood Grace's mind refused to see and the body she'd forgotten about completely. In her lap, the dead phone's black screen reflected only her own face, hollow and bright with manufactured enthusiasm.

But Grace saw engagement metrics climbing. Saw comments flooding in with validation. Saw her platform growing stronger with every mile toward whatever new content Kyle had planned.

For a flash, her mind returned to the small cabin and Earl, the truth of this death blipped in and then out of her mind in an instant. But truth didn't matter anymore. Only performance mattered. Only content. Only the story Grace told herself and her imaginary followers about who she was and what she could become.

And in the confined space of Kyle's truck, surrounded by men who recognized her capacity for violence and wanted to weaponize it, Grace Reynolds smiled at her dead phone and whispered:

"Don't forget to like and subscribe."

The truck's vinyl seat stuck to Grace's thighs through Earl's cargo pants. Sweat pooled in the creases behind her knees despite the cool morning air rushing through the open window. Her stomach cramped again, the fourth time since they'd left the cabin, and Grace pressed her phone harder against her abdomen like it might somehow ease the hollow ache.

"You look like shit," Kyle said without taking his eyes off the coastal road.

Grace checked her reflection in the phone's black screen. Gaunt. Her cheekbones cast shadows across her face that the morning light emphasized rather than softened. The hiking boots Earl owned felt too large even with two pairs of socks, and the work shirt hung loose across shoulders that used to fill out her college sweatshirts.

"Just need better lighting," she managed, her voice thinner than intended. "The aesthetic is very authentic survival, very raw. My followers appreciate genuine content."

Kyle's jaw tightened but he said nothing. In the truck bed behind them, Nate and Pete's voices carried through the rear window, discussing something about a strip mall off Route 1. Grace's ears rang too loudly to make out details.

The truck hit a pothole. Grace's stomach lurched, threatening to expel the crackers and peanut butter she'd forced down hours ago. She swallowed hard, tasting bile, and repositioned her phone to capture the ocean view through her window.

"Okay, so, road trip content," she narrated to the phone's blank screen. "Day one with my new production team. We're heading to Portland to establish our base of operations and really build out the infrastructure for my platform expansion."

"Put that down for a second." Kyle's voice carried an edge that cut through Grace's performance. He reached behind his seat, producing a protein bar and a bottle of blue electrolyte drink. "Eat this. Drink that. You're no good to us if you pass out."

Grace stared at the offerings. The protein bar's wrapper showed a mountain climber reaching a summit, all determination and triumph. The drink was the electric blue that tasted like chemicals and sugar.

"This is so thoughtful," Grace said, her influencer voice automatic even as saliva flooded her mouth at the sight of food. "You really understand how to take care of your talent. That's what separates good management from great management."

Kyle's expression flickered with something Grace's fractured mind interpreted as validation. She missed the calculation in his eyes, the way he assessed her like a tool that needed maintenance to remain functional.

The protein bar dissolved into sawdust on Grace's tongue but she forced herself to chew, to swallow, to take small sips of the blue drink that burned down her raw throat. Her stomach accepted the food grudgingly, cramping around each bite.

"We're making a stop first," Kyle said as Grace worked through half the protein bar. "Need to pick up some supplies. You can grab whatever you need too."

"Oh my God, really?" Grace's energy spiked at the possibility. "Because honestly, Earl's clothes are very authentic rustic but not exactly on-brand for my platform. I need to think about visual consistency."

Something like amusement crossed Kyle's face. "Yeah. Sure. Visual consistency."

The strip mall materialized from the morning haze like a ruin from another world. Parking lot cracked and overgrown with weeds. Shopping carts scattered and overturned. Windows broken but not recently. This place died weeks ago, looted in the first desperate days after the EMP when people still believed help would come.

But signs of life emerged as they drove closer. Smoke from a barrel fire near the old CVS entrance. Laundry hanging between light posts. Figures moving between storefronts. People who'd claimed this space, turned it into something resembling a community.

Kyle parked the truck three rows back from the main cluster of activity. Grace's eyes scanned the storefronts, cataloging possibilities. CVS. Dollar General. And there, at the end, a boutique with mannequins still visible in the window.

"That one," Grace said, pointing. "That's perfect. I need a complete wardrobe refresh for the Portland operation. You can't build a brand without proper visual identity."

Kyle looked at the boutique, then at Nate climbing out of the truck bed. "Take her. Make sure she doesn't wander off."

"Babysitting duty." Nate's voice dripped sarcasm but he jerked his head toward the boutique. "Come on, princess. Let's get you dressed up."

Grace clutched her phone and followed Nate across the parking lot. The electrolyte drink and protein bar worked through her system, chasing away the worst of the weakness. Her steps grew steadier with each passing moment.

The boutique's door hung open, one hinge torn away. Inside, racks of clothes stood untouched. Most looters prioritized food and weapons over fashion. Grace's heart raced as she stepped through the doorway, her phone already framing shots of the interior.

"Oh, wow! This is incredible," she breathed. "Look at this selection. This is exactly what I need for the rebrand."

Gunshots cracked outside, sharp and close. Shouting followed, a man's voice pleading, then the crash of breaking glass. Grace paused mid-reach for a hanger, tilted her head like she was considering distant music, then continued scanning the racks.

"Probably just negotiation tactics," she said to the empty store. "Very assertive management style."

A sound from the back of the store made both Grace and Nate freeze. A woman emerged from behind a rack of evening wear, hands raised, eyes wide with terror. Forties maybe. Thin from hunger. Dirt smudged across her face.

"Please," the woman whispered. "I was just looking for something warm. I'm not stealing. I'll leave."

Grace's smile brightened. "No, no! This is perfect! You work here, right? Fashion retail?"

The woman's confusion showed clearly but Grace's manic energy steamrolled over it.

"I need a complete wardrobe consultation. Something that says 'apocalypse chic' but also 'aspirational survivor.' Do you understand the aesthetic I'm going for?"

Nate leaned against the doorframe, rifle across his chest, watching with dark amusement. The woman's eyes darted between Grace's eager face and Nate's weapon, calculation happening behind the terror.

"Yeah, sure," the woman said slowly. "I can help you with that."

"Excellent! See, this is what I'm talking about. Professional service even in crisis conditions. This is the kind of content my followers love." Grace handed her phone to Nate. "Can you film this? Behind the scenes wardrobe selection. Very exclusive content."

Nate took the phone with a smirk that Grace interpreted as professional collaboration. The woman moved between racks with trembling hands, pulling pieces that somehow balanced Grace's delusional requirements with actual functionality.

A silver sequined top that caught light like water. Black cargo pants that actually fit Grace's frame. A leather jacket that probably cost more than most people's rent before the collapse. Combat boots with silver buckles. Everything shimmered and gleamed, turning survival gear into performance costume.

"Yes," Grace breathed, running her hands over the sequined fabric. "This is exactly right. This says 'I'm thriving, not just surviving.' This says 'content creator with vision'."

"The dressing room is back here," the woman said, her voice steady despite her shaking hands. She understood her role now. Play along or face the man with the rifle.

Grace took the phone from Nate and followed her to a dressing room with mirrors still intact. She stripped off Earl's cargo pants and work shirt without hesitation, her body reflected from three angles in the mirror arrangement. Ribs too prominent. Hip bones sharp. But the new clothes transformed her.

The sequined top caught the dim light filtering through the boutique's front windows, making Grace shimmer like something supernatural. The cargo pants sat low on her hips, held up by a studded belt the woman produced from somewhere.

The leather jacket added structure to her thin frame. The combat boots made her taller, more imposing.

Grace turned in front of the mirrors, her phone held high for selfies with angles she'd perfected over three years of content creation.

A man's voice screamed through the broken boutique window. "Please, that's all we have!" A sickening thud followed. Then silence.

Grace adjusted her pose, turning to capture her profile. "The leather jacket adds such great structure. Very editorial."

The woman behind her flinched, her eyes darting toward the window. Grace noticed nothing beyond her reflection.

"This is everything," she said. "This is the rebrand I needed. Very post-apocalyptic fashion forward. My followers are going to love this evolution."

The woman stood behind her, visible in the mirror's reflection. For just a moment, their eyes met in the glass. The woman's expression held something Grace's psychosis couldn't quite interpret. Pity maybe. Or horror at what she was witnessing.

"You look beautiful," the woman said, the words hollowed out by fear.

"I know, right?" Grace grabbed another sequined top, this one in gold. "I'll take multiples. You never know when you'll need wardrobe changes for different content themes."

She emerged from the dressing room in her new outfit, Earl's old clothes left in a pile on the floor.

A child's high-pitched wail cut through the air outside, raw and terrified. The sound of someone being dragged across pavement, heels scraping against concrete. Something heavy hit metal with a hollow clang.

The boutique woman's hands shook so badly she dropped the gold sequined top she'd been folding. Grace picked it up cheerfully, brushing off imaginary dust.

"Don't worry about it! Customer service in crisis conditions is always challenging. You're doing amazing."

Nate pushed off from the doorframe, looking her up and down with an expression that might have been appreciation or mockery or both.

"Kyle's gonna love this," he said, but the sarcasm was thick enough to choke on.

Grace gathered armfuls of clothes, the woman helping pack them into shopping bags that still had the boutique's logo printed across them. Sequins and leather and shimmer, everything catching light, everything performance.

Through the window, Kyle moved across the parking lot like a predator. He grabbed the older man from the barrel fire by his collar, said something Grace couldn't hear, then drove his pistol into the man's face. Once. Twice. The man crumpled. Kyle stood over him for a moment, waiting. The man didn't move.

Grace held up two tops, one silver, one gold. "Which one says 'approachable but aspirational'? I'm thinking the silver for daytime content and gold for evening segments."

"Thank you so much for your help. You can see my production team for payment," Grace said as they prepared to leave. "This is exactly the kind of professional service that builds customer loyalty. I'll definitely mention your store in my content."

The woman said nothing. Her hands clutched the edge of a clothing rack, knuckles white with pressure.

Outside, Kyle and Pete had finished their work at the CVS. Three children stood in the truck bed now, silent with shock. Supplies filled every available space. The older man from the barrel fire sat on the pavement, blood running from a cut above his eye. The woman who'd hung laundry had disappeared.

Kyle's eyes traveled over Grace's new outfit, taking in the sequins and leather and silver buckles. His expression revealed nothing.

"You look ready for television," he said flatly.

"Exactly!" Grace climbed into the passenger seat, her shopping bags crowding the footwell. "Visual branding is so important. You can't build a platform without consistent aesthetic identity."

The truck pulled out of the strip mall parking lot. Grace checked her reflection in the side mirror, adjusted the leather jacket, positioned her phone for the perfect angle. Behind them, the woman from the boutique stood in the doorway, watching them leave with an expression Grace would never see.

"So that was incredibly productive," Grace said as they merged onto Route 1. "Supply procurement and wardrobe refresh. Very efficient use of time."

In the truck bed, the children huddled together, their eyes empty. Grace glanced back at them through the rear window.

"Are they coming to Portland for the audience development initiatives?" she asked.

"Something like that," Kyle said, his attention on the road ahead.

The blue drink and protein bar worked through Grace's system, bringing energy and clarity that only fed her delusions. She felt powerful now. Professional. Ready for whatever content opportunities the afternoon would bring.

The sequins caught afternoon light as they drove north, making Grace shimmer like something not quite real. The leather jacket creaked with each movement. The combat boots pressed against the truck's floorboard, solid and grounding.

She was ready for her close-up.

She was ready for her close-up.

The farmhouse sat back from the road, connected by a long gravel drive lined with overgrown lilacs. White clapboard siding. Red barn. Fields gone wild with summer growth. Chickens pecked in the yard. A dog barked from somewhere behind the house.

Normal. Untouched. Like the world never ended.

Kyle parked the truck at the end of the drive, far enough back that they'd have warning if anyone tried to run. The afternoon sun beat down on the metal roof, but Grace barely noticed the heat. The sequined top felt like armor, the leather jacket like a second skin.

"We walk up together," Kyle said, checking his rifle. "Grace, you're out front. All smiles. Tell them we're looking to trade, build community connections, whatever influencer garbage comes natural to you. Keep them distracted while we assess the situation."

"I can absolutely do that." Grace's hands smoothed down the sequined top, adjusted the leather jacket. "Friendly approach, establish rapport, create authentic connection. This is literally what I trained for."

Nate laughed from the truck bed, the sound sharp and ugly. "Yeah. Harvard prepared you great for home invasion."

Grace's smile never wavered. "Marketing and psychology double undergrad major. Understanding human behavior and motivation is crucial for effective audience engagement."

They walked up the drive in formation. Kyle and Pete flanking Grace, Nate hanging back near the truck with those they'd brought from the strip mall. Grace's sequined top caught the afternoon light with each step, sending flashes of silver across the farmhouse's white siding. The dog's barking grew more frantic. A screen door creaked open and a man stepped onto the porch, rifle in hand but pointed down.

Fifties maybe. Lean from farm work. Suspicion carved into the lines around his eyes.

His gaze fixed on Grace first. The sequins. The leather. The silver-buckled boots. Confusion crossed his face, like his brain couldn't process what he was seeing.

"That's close enough," the man called when they reached the bottom of the porch steps.

Grace stepped forward, her influencer smile bright and disarming. Phone held up like a peace offering. The sequins shimmered with the movement.

"Hi! I'm Grace Reynolds. These are my associates. We're traveling through the area, documenting survival communities and building connections between isolated groups. We'd love to talk with you about collaboration opportunities."

The man's eyes moved from Grace's glittering outfit to Kyle to Pete, calculating odds and finding them poor. "We're not interested in collaborating."

"I totally understand the hesitation." Grace climbed two steps before Kyle's hand touched her back, stopping her. The leather jacket creaked. "Trust is hard to build in times like these. But we're all in this together, right? The more we can share resources and information, the better chance we all have of making it through."

A woman appeared in the doorway behind the man. Younger, thirties maybe. Flour dusted her hands and apron. Behind her, Grace caught movement. Children. At least two.

The woman stared at Grace's outfit with naked incomprehension. Sequins and leather in a world of dirt and survival. The cognitive dissonance showed plainly on her face.

"We don't have much," the woman said, her voice tight. "Barely enough for ourselves."

"We're not asking you to give up anything you need." Grace's tone stayed warm, persuasive. The sequins caught sunlight and threw it back in dazzling fragments. "We're just hoping to establish dialogue. Maybe sit down, share a meal, talk about what's working for you. This is incredible content actually. Mind if I film? My followers would love to see how rural communities are adapting."

"Your phone doesn't work," the man said flatly. "And what the hell are you wearing?"

Grace looked down at her outfit, genuine confusion crossing her face. "This? This is my professional wardrobe. You have to maintain brand consistency even in crisis situations. Visual identity is crucial for audience engagement."

"It's not getting restored," the man said, but his voice had lost some conviction. Grace's outfit, her manic energy, her complete disconnect from reality unsettled him more than Kyle's obvious threat.

"Okay, but that's actually a really pessimistic mindset." Grace climbed another step, the sequins sending light dancing across the porch. "We need to maintain hope. We need to believe we can rebuild. That's what my platform is all about. Authentic optimism in the face of adversity."

Kyle moved past Grace, up the steps with confident aggression that made the man raise his rifle. Pete circled left toward the barn. Nate drifted right toward the chicken coop.

"I said that's close enough." The man's knuckles whitened on his rifle. "Turn around and leave. We don't want trouble."

"See, that's the thing about trouble." Kyle's voice dropped the false friendliness. "It's already here."

Everything happened fast. The man tried to swing his rifle toward Kyle. Kyle was faster, closing the distance and ripping the weapon away from him. The woman screamed. Children's voices rose in panic from inside the house.

"No, wait." Grace rushed up the steps, sequins flashing in the sunlight, phone held high. "This is going wrong. We need to de-escalate. We need authentic dialogue, not conflict."

Kyle shoved the man against the house siding. Nate appeared with a chicken in each hand, their wings beating frantically. Pete kicked in the barn door, the wood splintering with a crack that echoed across the fields.

"Please," the woman begged, moving to shield the doorway behind her. "Please, we have children. We'll give you whatever you want. Just don't hurt anyone."

"This is terrible optics," Grace said, positioning herself to film the woman's face. The sequined top caught light with each movement of her arms. "Can you try to stay calm? The fear response is very authentic but it's not the narrative we want to portray. Think about the message we're sending to other communities."

The woman stared at Grace like she was speaking another language. The sequins. The leather. The complete insanity of the performance. It was too much to process alongside the terror.

Kyle dragged the man into the house. Grace followed, her combat boots loud on the wooden floor, sequins throwing light across family photos on the walls. The interior smelled of baking bread and wood smoke. Children's drawings held to the refrigerator with magnets. Two kids huddled in the corner of the living room. Boy and girl, maybe eight and ten.

Normal. This was a normal family trying to survive.

"Okay, so, family dynamics segment," Grace narrated, the sequins on her top shimmering as she moved around the room. "This is really important content. Shows how traditional social structures adapt in post-collapse scenarios."

The man tried to pull away from Kyle. Kyle's fist caught him in the kidney, doubling him over. The woman screamed again. The children cried. The girl stared at Grace's glittering outfit with incomprehension that bordered on madness.

"See, this is the problem with violence," Grace said, moving closer to film the man's face as he gasped for breath. In a grotesque display of light, reflections off her sequins danced across his features. "It creates this adversarial dynamic when what we really need is collaboration. Can everyone just take a breath? Maybe we start over with proper introductions?"

"Shut her up," the woman sobbed, pulling her children closer. "Please, just make her stop talking."

Grace's smile faltered. The leather jacket creaked as she shifted position. "You're ruining the shot. I'm trying to help. I'm trying to make this a positive experience for everyone."

Pete returned from the barn carrying a hunting rifle and a box of ammunition. Nate entered with a chicken under each arm, their necks already wrung. The kitchen yielded flour, sugar, home-canned vegetables lining shelves in the pantry. The bedrooms held blankets, clothes, everything a family needed.

Kyle's crew worked with efficient brutality, stripping the farmhouse of anything useful while Grace circled the living room, her sequined outfit catching every stray beam of light, filming the family's terror through her lens of delusion.

"The emotional authenticity here is incredible," she narrated, the sequins shimmering with each gesture. "You can't fake this level of genuine reaction. This is the kind of content that really resonates with audiences. Raw. Unfiltered. Real."

The man made one more attempt to fight back when Nate started loading supplies into his arms. Kyle hit him hard enough that blood sprayed across the family photos on the wall. The woman's screams reached a pitch that made Grace wince.

"The audio is a bit much," Grace said thoughtfully, adjusting her leather jacket. "We might need to add a content warning for sensitive viewers."

The girl in the corner, the ten-year-old, stared at Grace with naked hatred that finally penetrated the layers of psychosis. For just a moment, Grace saw herself reflected in that child's eyes. Saw the monster she'd become. Saw the obscenity of her glittering costume against the backdrop of violence.

The clarity lasted three seconds.

Then Kyle grabbed the woman by her hair, asking where they kept their medications, and Grace's phone swung to capture it, the sequins throwing fractured light across the scene, the moment of horror forgotten in the need to document everything for her imaginary followers.

"Medical supply inventory is so important," Grace said, the leather jacket creaking as she moved. "You never know when you'll need antibiotics or pain management resources."

They stripped the farmhouse bare. Food, supplies, weapons, medicine, blankets. The family watched helplessly as their survival margin disappeared into the crew's packs. Kyle debated taking the man with them, decided he was more trouble than value. But the woman and children…

"Bring them," Kyle ordered. "They'll be useful."

"Audience development," Grace said brightly as Nate pulled the woman to her feet. The sequins still shimmering in the afternoon light streaming through the windows. "Building our community in Portland. This is actually perfect. We can do a whole segment on integration and mutual support."

The woman fought until Kyle pressed his rifle against her son's head. Then she went limp, defeated, allowing herself to be led outside. The children followed in silence, their eyes empty with shock. The girl's gaze stayed fixed on Grace's shimmering outfit, her young mind trying to reconcile the nightmare with the costume.

Grace walked behind them, sequins flashing with each step, filming everything, narrating their journey to the truck in the language of lifestyle content and community building. The woman climbed into the truck bed without resistance. The children huddled against their mother. The man crawled out onto his porch, blood running down his face, watching his family disappear down the drive.

"We should do a follow-up," Grace said as Kyle started the engine. Her leather jacket creaked against the vinyl seat. "Check in on how they're settling into the Portland community. Show the progression from initial resistance to full integration. That's the kind of character arc that really builds audience investment."

No one responded. Grace settled into her seat, the sequins still catching light, scrolling through photos on her dead phone, selecting the best shots for her imaginary feed.

They pulled out of the driveway, and with the last vehicle in their caravan, a gunshot rang out, followed by a scream. Grace took it as a celebratory firing when the reality of what it meant for this family completely escaped her.

The afternoon bled into evening as they drove north. Grace's energy, sustained by adrenaline and the protein bar, began to crash. The sequined top felt heavier now. The leather jacket pressed against her like a weight. Her hands trembled as she held her phone. Her vision blurred at the edges.

"Almost there," Kyle said, but his voice sounded distant, echoing from somewhere far away.

Portland emerged from the twilight. Empty streets. Dark buildings. Smoke rising from fires scattered throughout the downtown core. They navigated around abandoned cars and debris until Kyle pulled up in front of a hotel. Eight stories. Glass doors. A banner hanging crooked across the entrance advertising rates that no longer mattered.

"Home base," Kyle announced. "Pete, get those supplies inside. Nate, take the new arrivals to the holding area. Grace…"

But Grace didn't hear the rest. The day's events crashed over her all at once. The strip mall. The boutique. The woman's trembling hands. The farmhouse. The children's faces. The girl staring at her sequins with incomprehension. All of it compressed into a single moment of overwhelming exhaustion.

She opened the truck door, intending to step out, to continue documenting, to keep performing. The sequined top caught the last rays of dying sunlight, throwing fractured light across the hotel's facade. Instead, her legs buckled. The pavement rushed up to meet her. Her phone clattered from her hands, skittering across the asphalt. The silver buckles on her boots scraped against concrete.

"Grace!" Kyle's voice, far away.

Darkness pulled her down, offering the same oblivion as the harbor water. Grace surrendered to it, her last conscious thought already reframing the collapse into content. The sequins pressed against the dirty pavement, still catching light, still shimmering.

Her followers would understand. They always understood.

The darkness took her, and Grace Reynolds disappeared into it, still smiling, still glittering, still completely insane.

Grace woke to the smell of cigarette smoke and mildew. Her cheek pressed against rough carpet that reeked of old beer and cleaning chemicals. The sequined top bit into her ribs where she'd twisted during sleep. Every muscle in her body screamed protest as she pushed herself upright.

The hotel room swam into focus. Beige walls water-stained near the ceiling. Heavy curtains drawn against morning light that leaked through gaps in the fabric. A queen bed with sheets that looked gray even in the dimness. Kyle sat in a chair by the window, rifle across his lap, watching her with an expression she couldn't quite read.

"About time," he said, flicking ash into an empty soda can. "You've been out for twelve hours."

Grace's hand flew to her pocket. Her phone. Still there. Relief flooded through her even though the screen stayed black when she pressed the power button. She clutched it against her chest, feeling her heartbeat slow to something approaching normal.

"Where are we?" Her voice came out hoarse, throat raw from dehydration.

"Portland Hotel. Fifth floor. Your room." Kyle stood, stretching muscles with joints that cracked audibly. "We've been setting up while you slept. Got about thirty people here now. Some came willingly. Most not. They're all downstairs waiting to meet the talent."

The word sent electricity through Grace's exhausted body. Talent. He said talent. Recognition of her value, her platform, her brand. This was what she'd been working toward since that first viral post three years ago.

She struggled to her feet, the leather jacket skritching in protest to the movement. The sequined top caught weak light filtering through the curtains, throwing tiny stars across the water-stained walls. Her combat boots found purchase on the disgusting carpet.

"I need to freshen up first. Can't meet my audience looking like this." Grace caught her reflection in the mirror above the dresser. Hair matted on one side and mascara smeared on one cheek. Her hands drew her skin taught, her face too thin. "Do we have makeup? Professional lighting? I need to think about production aesthetics."

Kyle's jaw tightened, a muscle jumping beneath the stubble. "Grace. Listen to me. These aren't followers. They're prisoners. You understand that, right? We took them. Some of them watched us kill their families. They're not here because they want to be."

"Obviously there's going to be resistance at first." Grace moved to the window, pulling back the curtain to look down at the street below. Empty. Trash scattered across the pavement. A few of Kyle's men patrolled the perimeter. She spun back toward him with her hands out palms up. "That's normal with any major platform shift. But once they see the vision, once they understand what we're building here, they'll get on board. It's all about authentic engagement." She trailed off, looking back out the window and pulling her matted hair back. "I could really use a shower. Can you have someone bring me my wardrobe?"

"Dammit." Kyle ground his cigarette into the soda can with more force than necessary. "You really are completely insane."

"I prefer 'visionary.'" Grace turned from the window, her influencer smile locked into place despite the exhaustion pulling at her features. "And I need a production team. Makeup artist, wardrobe assistant, maybe someone to handle lighting and camera work. We can't build a platform without proper production infrastructure."

Kyle stared at her for a long moment, a darkness moving behind his eyes. Then he laughed, the sound ugly and sharp. "You want a production team. Fine. I'll get you a production team." He moved toward the door, paused with his hand on the knob. "But Grace? When they don't perform up to your standards, when they mess up your lighting or forget your coffee or whatever the hell influencers get mad about, you remember something. I'm the one who decides who lives and who dies here. Not you. Me."

The threat should have registered. Should have triggered fear or at least caution. Instead, Grace heard only the promise of support, of resources, of her platform finally getting the infrastructure it deserved.

"That's perfect," she said. "Clear hierarchy is so important for team dynamics. I'll handle creative direction and audience engagement. You handle operations and personnel management. This is exactly the kind of partnership that builds successful brands."

Kyle shook his head and left without responding, the door clicking shut behind him with a finality that Grace's fractured mind interpreted as professional boundary-setting rather than barely controlled fury.

Alone in the room, Grace moved to the bathroom. The fixtures were old but functional. Water still ran from the taps, cold and metallic-tasting but clean enough. She stripped off the sequined top and leather jacket, washing herself with hotel soap that smelled of fake lavender.

Her reflection in the bathroom mirror showed every rib, every sharp angle of bone beneath skin that stretched too tight. When had she gotten this thin? The question felt important but distant, like it belonged to someone else's story.

She pulled the sequined top back on, the fabric clinging to damp skin. The leather jacket settled across her shoulders like armor. Her fingers combed through tangled hair, working out the worst knots. She had no makeup, but the natural look was very authentic survival chic. Her followers would appreciate the raw aesthetic.

A knock on the door made her turn. "Come in!"

A woman entered, thirties maybe, with dark hair pulled back in a ponytail. Her eyes stayed fixed on the floor, shoulders hunched like she was trying to make herself smaller. Behind her, two more women followed. One older, graying hair and hands that trembled. One younger, barely twenty, with bruises blooming purple across her cheekbone.

"Kyle sent us," the first woman said, her voice carefully neutral. "He said you needed a… a production team."

Grace's smile brightened, genuine excitement flooding through her. "Oh, yes! This is perfect! Okay, so first, introductions. I'm Grace Reynolds. You might know me from my lifestyle and wellness platform. Fifty thousand followers before the collapse. And you are?"

The women exchanged glances loaded with meaning Grace couldn't decipher. The first woman spoke again, each word precisely placed. "I'm Jennifer. This is Carol and this is Amy."

"Excellent! Welcome to the team!" Grace moved to the bed, sitting on the edge and gesturing for them to come closer. The sequins caught light with each movement. "So, here's my vision. We're building something revolutionary here. Authentic, you know? Post-apocalyptic content that shows real survival, real community building, real human connection. No filters, no fake aesthetics. Just raw, honest storytelling."

Carol, the older woman, made a sound that might have been a laugh or a sob. Amy's hands clenched into fists at her sides. Jennifer's expression stayed carefully blank.

Grace put her hands up as though stopping their thoughts. "I know you're probably wondering about roles and responsibilities," Grace continued, oblivious to their reactions. "Jennifer, I'm thinking that you can handle wardrobe coordination. Make sure I have outfit options for different content themes. Carol, you'll be in charge of makeup and hair. Keep me camera-ready at all times. Amy, you're on lighting and general production assistance. Does that work for everyone?"

"We don't have a choice, do we?" Amy's voice came out small and broken.

Grace's smile faltered slightly. "Well, I mean, obviously there's going to be a learning curve. None of us trained for content creation in apocalyptic conditions. But that's what makes this so exciting! We're pioneering a whole new genre of lifestyle media."

"My daughter is downstairs," Carol said suddenly, her voice shaking. "She's eight years old. They took her from our house yesterday. I haven't seen her since we got here. I don't know if she's alive."

The words should have meant something. Should have triggered empathy or at least recognition of the horror being described. Instead, Grace's mind reorganized the information into content opportunities.

"Family separation anxiety is such an important topic," she said, pulling out her phone to make notes that would never save. "We could do a whole segment on maintaining emotional resilience during a crisis. Very relatable content. Your daughter could even participate if she's comfortable on camera."

Carol's face crumpled. Jennifer grabbed her arm, steadying her before she collapsed. Amy backed toward the door, her eyes wide with something that looked like terror mixed with disbelief.

"We should get started," Jennifer said, her voice tight with control. "What do you need from us first?"

Grace stood, the sequins throwing light across the women's faces. "I need to address my audience. Everyone downstairs. This is my debut as the face of the Portland operation. First impressions are everything, so we need to make this perfect."

She moved to the small desk in the corner where someone, probably Kyle's crew, piled supplies from the raids. Grace rifled through clothing until she found a gold sequined top that matched yesterday's silver. She held it up, examining the way light caught the fabric.

"This one," she decided. "More aspirational than the silver. Shows growth, evolution. Carol, can you do something with my hair? Nothing too polished. We want authentic but intentional. Like I just naturally look this good even in the apocalypse."

Carol's hands shook as she approached. Grace sat on the desk chair, presenting her matted hair for styling. The older woman's fingers moved through the tangles, her face carefully blank.

"My daughter's name is Sophie," Carol whispered, so quiet Grace barely heard. "She's terrified of the dark. They put her in a room without windows."

"Sensory deprivation creates such interesting psychological responses," Grace said thoughtfully while scrolling through her dead phone. "Very authentic fear reaction. That's the kind of raw emotion that really resonates with audiences."

Carol's hands paused in Grace's hair. For a moment, they pressed against Grace's skull with enough pressure to hurt. Then they released, continuing to work through the tangles with trembling efficiency.

Jennifer pulled clothing from the pile, organizing options across the bed. Grace was mostly oblivious but glanced up in the mirror to see her working on coordinating each outfit, like she was trying to disappear into the task. Amy stood by the door, one hand on the knob, looking like she might bolt at any moment.

"Amy, I'm going to need you focused," Grace said, catching the young woman's eye in the mirror. "This is a huge opportunity for all of us. If you're not committed to the vision, if you're going to be negative and drag down team morale, then maybe you're not the right fit for this production."

The threat was clear even wrapped in influencer-speak. Amy's hand dropped from the doorknob. She moved into the room, her body language screaming trapped animal, but she moved.

"Good," Grace said, her smile returning. "Now, makeup. Carol, what do we have to work with?"

The older woman produced a small bag from her pocket. Inside, cheap drugstore makeup, probably looted from the strip mall or one of the farmhouses. Foundation two shades too dark. Mascara dried almost solid. Lipstick in a color that would look garish under normal circumstances but might work for the aesthetic Grace was building.

"Perfect," Grace breathed. "Very grassroots. Very authentic survivor chic."

Carol's hands applied makeup despite her trembling hands. Foundation covered the worst of Grace's hollow cheeks. Mascara made her eyes look larger, more dramatic. The lipstick, bright red and slightly smeared, gave her mouth a quality that was both glamorous and slightly unhinged.

Grace examined the result in the mirror. She looked like a fever dream, like something that crawled out of civilization's collapse wearing its skin. The sequins, the makeup, the sharp angles of starvation dressed up as high fashion.

"It's perfect," she whispered. "This is exactly the vibe we need."

A commotion from downstairs made them all freeze. Shouting. A woman screaming. The crack of something hard against flesh. Then silence that felt worse than the noise.

"That's probably my cue," Grace said, standing. The gold sequins caught every bit of available light, making her shimmer like something not quite real. "Time to meet my audience."

She moved toward the door, but Jennifer stepped into her path. The woman's carefully blank expression cracked, showing something raw and desperate underneath.

"Please," Jennifer said, her voice barely above a whisper. "Please just stop. Stop pretending this is normal. Stop acting like we're here voluntarily. Stop talking about content and platforms and audiences. These people are terrified. Children are crying. Families are separated. People are dying. And you're worried about lighting."

The words hung in the air between them. Grace stared at Jennifer, her mind struggling to process the accusation. Somewhere deep in her psychosis, a small voice tried to surface, tried to make her see what she was doing, what she'd become.

Then Kyle's voice echoed up the stairwell. "Grace! Get down here! Your audience is waiting!"

The moment of clarity vanished. Grace pushed past Jennifer, the sequins brushing against the other woman's arm with a sound like breaking glass.

"Showtime," Grace said, her voice bright with enthusiasm. "This is what we've all been working toward."

She descended the stairs with Jennifer, Carol, and Amy trailing behind like prisoners in a procession. The lobby opened below, transformed from abandoned hotel into something that looked like a twisted parody of a production set.

Kyle's crew worked throughout the previous night. They cleared furniture to create an open space. Positioned people along the walls, sitting on the floor with their backs pressed against peeling wallpaper. Thirty faces, maybe more. Some from the strip mall. Some from the farmhouse. Others Grace didn't recognize, collected from raids she'd been unconscious for.

Kyle stood in the center of the space, rifle across his chest, waiting. Nate and Pete flanked the exits. Two more of Kyle's men, whose names Grace didn't know, patrolled the perimeter.

Every eye turned to Grace as she reached the bottom of the stairs. The gold sequins caught morning light streaming through the lobby's tall windows, throwing fractured brilliance across faces marked by fear and exhaustion and hopelessness.

Grace's influencer smile locked into place. She moved to the center of the lobby, positioning herself where the light hit best, phone held high even though its screen stayed black.

"Good morning, everyone!" Her voice echoed through the space, bright and enthusiastic and completely disconnected from the horror surrounding her. "I'm Grace Reynolds, and I am so excited to be here with all of you today. I know the circumstances that brought us together weren't ideal, but I really believe we can build something amazing here."

Silence. Not the respectful silence of an engaged audience, but the stunned quiet of people watching something so divorced from reality that their minds couldn't process it.

Grace continued, undeterred. "So, here's my vision. We're going to create the most authentic post-apocalyptic content platform the world has ever seen. Real stories. Real survival. Real community building. And all of you get to be part of it! How exciting is that?"

A man near the back, older with gray stubble and dried blood on his shirt, made a sound between a laugh and a sob. "You're insane. You're completely fucking insane."

Grace's smile never wavered. "I prefer 'visionary'. But I understand skepticism. Change is always scary. But trust me, once you see what we're building, once you understand the impact we can have, you're going to be so glad you're part of this journey."

"My wife is dead," the man said, his voice rising. "Your people shot her when we tried to run. My wife is dead, and you're talking about content and platforms like any of this matters!"

The lobby held its breath. Kyle moved toward the man, but Grace raised her hand, stopping him. She needed to handle this. Leadership meant addressing negativity directly, turning critics into supporters.

"I'm so sorry for your loss," Grace said, her tone shifting into the practiced empathy she'd used for sponsored mental health content. "Grief is such a valid response to trauma. And I want you to know that your story, your pain, your journey through this loss, that's exactly the kind of authentic emotional content that resonates with audiences. If you're comfortable, I'd love to do an interview about your experience."

The man stared at her, his mouth opening and closing without sound. His expression showed naked incomprehension, like his brain was trying and failing to process what he just heard.

Then he lunged. Crossed the space between them with surprising speed for someone his age. His hands reached for Grace's throat, fingers curled into claws, his face twisted with rage and grief and the desperate need to destroy the thing in front of him that wore a human shape but spoke in algorithms.

Kyle moved faster. His rifle butt caught the man in the temple with a crack that echoed through the lobby. The man dropped, blood spreading across the cheap carpet. He twitched once, twice, then went still.

Grace stepped back, the gold sequins catching light, phone still held high like she was filming. "Wow. That's, um. That's very aggressive. Kyle, can you handle that? I need my audience calm and engaged, not violent."

Kyle dragged the body toward the door, leaving a smear of red across the floor. Nate grabbed the man's feet and together they hauled him outside. The sound of the door closing felt obscenely loud in the silence that followed.

"Okay, so," Grace said, her voice slightly higher than before but still maintaining that bright influencer tone. "Let's move past that negative energy. Who's excited about the content opportunities here? Show of hands?"

No one moved. Thirty faces stared at her with expressions ranging from terror to disgust to the blank dissociation of trauma. A child whimpered somewhere in the back. A woman rocked slowly, her arms wrapped around her knees.

Grace's smile faltered. This wasn't working. They weren't engaging. Weren't responding to her energy or her vision or her carefully crafted performance. They were just… sitting there, staring at her like she was a monster.

The thought tried to surface again. That small voice deep in her psychosis asking if maybe, possibly, they were right.

Then Kyle moved to her side, his hand finding the small of her back, warm and solid through the leather jacket. His voice dropped low, meant only for her.

"They need time. They'll come around. But Grace? You need to give me something to work with here. I'm selling this to my crew as using you for distraction, for breaking people down psychologically. But some of them think you're more trouble than you're worth. You need to prove your value."

The words sent ice through her veins despite the warmth of his hand. Value. Proving worth. These were concepts Grace understood intimately. Her entire platform was built on proving she deserved attention, deserved followers, deserved to matter.

She turned to Kyle, pressing closer, feeling his breath on her face. The sequins caught light between their bodies, throwing stars across his chest.

"I can prove my value," she said, her voice dropping into a register that had nothing to do with content creation. "I'm very good at giving people what they need."

Kyle's expression shifted, something predatory entering his eyes. His hand moved from her back to her hip, fingers pressing against her side.

"Later," he said quietly. "Right now, perform. Make them afraid of you. Make them understand that compliance is their only option. Can you do that?"

Grace's mind reorganized his words into opportunity. Make them afraid. Create emotional investment. Build tension that would resolve into engagement. This was just advanced audience psychology.

She turned back to the assembled prisoners, her smile returning but colder now, sharper. The gold sequins threw harsh light across faces that flinched away from the glare.

"Let me be very clear about something," Grace said, her voice dropping the forced enthusiasm. "This is my production.

My platform. My vision. All of you are here to support that vision. Some of you will be on camera. Some will work behind the scenes. But everyone has a role to play."

She moved through the space, the combat boots scuffing loudly against the carpet, sequins flashing with each step. People pressed back against the walls as she passed, trying to make themselves smaller.

"And if you don't want to play your role?" Grace stopped in front of a woman holding a young girl against her chest. The woman's arms tightened protectively. "Well, Kyle just demonstrated what happens to people who disrupt my production schedule."

The woman's eyes filled with tears but she said nothing. The child buried her face against her mother's shoulder.

Grace crouched down, bringing herself to eye level with them. The sequins threw light across the child's dark hair.

"But I'm not a monster," Grace continued, her voice soft now, almost gentle. "I understand you're out of your element. I understand this is a big change. So here's what I'm offering. Cooperate. Do your jobs. Support my platform. And I'll make sure you and your daughter stay together. I'll make sure you're fed. I'll make sure Kyle and his men leave you alone. That's a good deal, right?"

The woman nodded, tears tracking down her cheeks.

"I need to hear you say it," Grace pressed with a tone more threatening than comforting.

"Yes," the woman whispered. "Yes, it's a good deal."

"Excellent!" Grace stood, the sequins catching light as she moved back toward the center of the lobby. "See? This is exactly what I'm talking about. Authentic dialogue. Mutual understanding. Building community through honest communication."

She addressed the entire room now, her voice projecting the confidence of someone who'd given hundreds of presentations to imaginary audiences.

"Here's how this works. Every morning, you report to this lobby. I'll assign daily tasks. Some of you will help with supply organization. Some will work on set preparation. Some will participate in content creation. At the end of each day, we'll do performance reviews. Top performers get extra rations, better sleeping arrangements, family visitation for those who've been separated."

Grace paused, letting that sink in. Then her voice hardened.

"And poor performers? Well. I'm a fair manager, but I have very high standards. If you're not contributing to the vision, if you're creating negative energy or disrupting production, then you're essentially firing yourself. And we all saw what happens to people who quit this operation."

The threat landed. It was not in any way veiled or even presented with the bubbly disassociation she offered earlier. They were threatening her very platform and she was not going to let that stand. Grace saw it in the way shoulders slumped, in the way eyes dropped to the floor, in the way the last traces of resistance drained from faces marked by violence and terror.

"Now, I know some of you are thinking about leaving," Grace continued, moving through the space with the confidence of someone completely secure in their power. "But let me save you the trouble. Kyle's production crew controls every exit. They have the means to maintain order. You don't. They're organized. You're not. And even if you somehow got past them, got outside, where would you go? The city's full of dangers. At least here, you have food, shelter, and the protection of my platform."

She stopped in front of Jennifer, who stood against the wall with Carol and Amy. The three women who'd helped her prepare now looked like they'd been present at an execution.

"Jennifer, you're my wardrobe coordinator, right?"

Jennifer nodded, swallowing hard.

"So coordinate. I need outfit options for tonight. Something that says 'powerful but approachable.' Can you handle that?"

"Yes," Jennifer whispered.

"Carol, I need you to start training others on hair and makeup. We're going to need multiple people camera-ready at all times for content purposes. Put together a team."

Carol's mouth opened but no sound came out. Finally, she managed, "My daughter. Sophie. You said if I cooperated…"

"Right! Of course!" Grace's smile returned, bright and terrible. "Kyle, can we reunite Carol with her daughter? She's been very cooperative. Positive reinforcement is so important for team morale."

Kyle nodded to one of his men, who disappeared up the stairs. Minutes later, he returned with a small girl, maybe eight, her face streaked with tears. Carol made a sound between a sob and a prayer, reaching for her daughter. The girl ran to her mother, burying her face against Carol's chest.

"See?" Grace addressed the room. "Cooperation gets rewarded. This is how we build trust. How we build community. How we build something that matters."

She moved back to the center of the lobby, positioning herself where the light hit best, the gold sequins throwing brilliance across the assembled prisoners.

"I know this is hard. I know you're unsure. But I promise you, if you commit to the vision, if you trust the process, we're going to create something revolutionary here. Something that will matter long after the world rebuilds. You're all part of history now. Part of my platform's evolution. And isn't that exciting?"

No response. Just the sound of Sophie crying against her mother's chest and the distant crack of gunfire from somewhere outside.

Grace's performance deflated slightly. They still weren't engaging. Weren't responding to her energy or her promises or her threats. They were just existing in survival mode, waiting for whatever horror came next.

A moment of anger rose and her voice took on a menacing edge when she repeated, "Isn't that exciting?"

The people along the walls yelled back. Some through sobs, others barely audible. "Yes!"

Grace's eyebrows rose and she smiled in satisfaction. Kyle was right, this was working even better than she hoped. They just needed some motivation.

Kyle moved to her side again, his presence solid and grounding. His hand found her hip, fingers pressing through the leather jacket with possessive pressure.

"Good work," he said quietly. "They're compliant. That's useful. But Grace? We need to talk. Upstairs. Now."

He guided her toward the stairs, his hand firm against her back. Grace followed, confusion made her pulse quicken despite the exhaustion pulling at her limbs.

They climbed to the fifth floor in silence. Kyle opened the door to her room, pushing her inside before following and closing the door behind them. The lock clicked with finality.

"What the hell was that?" Kyle's voice came out low and dangerous. "You threatened to kill a child. A mother and her daughter. You talked about performance reviews and firing people when we both know 'firing' means execution."

"I was establishing boundaries," Grace said, confused by his anger. "Setting expectations. Creating a framework for—"

"You're completely insane." Kyle moved closer, crowding her against the desk. "You know that, right? You're so deep in your delusions that you can't see how fucked up this is."

The words should have hurt. Should have triggered defensive anger or at least confusion. Instead, Grace felt a dangerous excitement building in her chest.

"But you need me," she said, her voice dropping. "You said it yourself. I break people down. I create the psychological pressure that makes them compliant." She gained some purchase and stood closer to him in sure conviction. "Without me, you're just another raider crew. With me, you have something unique. Something valuable."

Kyle's jaw clenched, the muscle jumping beneath his skin. His eyes moved over her face, the heavy makeup, the sharp angles of starvation, the gold sequins that caught lamplight and threw it back in fractured brilliance.

"You're a liability," he said, but his voice lacked conviction. His hand moved from her hip to her waist, fingers pressing against the sequined fabric.

"I'm an asset." Grace leaned into him, feeling his breath on her face, reading the conflict in his expression. "And you know it. You see how they respond to me. The gripping attention. The way I make them question reality. That's power, Kyle. That's exactly what you need to control them."

His other hand came up to her throat, not squeezing, just resting there, thumb against her pulse point. A threat or a promise or both.

"You're going to get us all killed," he said, but his body pressed closer.

Somewhere deep inside she knew what she was becoming but didn't care. She only cared about that rush. The attention.

"Or I'm going to make us legendary." Grace's hands found his chest, feeling the solid muscle beneath his shirt. "Your crew takes resources. I take minds. Together we're unstoppable."

The tension between them pulled taut, dangerous, electric. Kyle's thumb pressed harder against her throat, cutting off air for just a moment before releasing. His eyes searched her face, looking for something, maybe sanity, maybe confirmation of his own descent into whatever this was becoming.

Then his mouth crashed against hers, brutal and claiming. Grace responded with equal ferocity, her hands fisting in his shirt, pulling him closer. The desk bit into her back as he pressed her against it. The gold sequins scraped between their bodies with a sound like tearing metal.

When they broke apart, both breathing hard, Kyle's expression reflected something between disgust and fascination.

"This doesn't change anything," he said, his voice rough. "You're still a tool. Still something we're using. Don't forget that."

Her smile widened with satisfaction.

"Of course," Grace said, her influencer smile returning despite her racing pulse. "Clear professional boundaries. That's very important."

Kyle stepped back, adjusting his rifle, his face settling back into the cold calculation she'd first seen at Earl's cabin. But something shifted between them. Some unspoken understanding that they were both descending into darkness and might as well enjoy the fall.

"Get some rest. I'll send up some food," he said, moving toward the door. "Tonight we're hitting another settlement. A bigger one. I need you performing at full capacity."

"I'll be ready." Grace touched her lips where they felt bruised. "This is going to be incredible content."

Kyle paused at the door, looking back at her. The gold sequins caught light, making Grace shimmer like something not quite real. "You really are insane."

"I prefer 'visionary,'" Grace said, but her smile held sharp edges now. "And Kyle? Tonight's performance is going to make you glad you kept me around."

He left without responding, the door closing with a soft click. Grace stood in the empty room, her reflection visible in the dark window.

She looked like a monster playing at being human. Or maybe a human who'd finally stopped pretending to be anything else.

Her phone sat on the desk where she'd left it. Grace picked it up, pressing the power button, watching the screen stay dark. But in her mind, the notifications scrolled. Likes. Comments. Shares. Her followers responding to her evolution, her transformation, her rise to power.

"Don't forget to like and subscribe," she whispered to her reflection.

8

Grace perched on the hood of Kyle's truck, legs crossed, scrolling through her dead phone while dawn painted the Portland skyline. Pink camouflage cargo pants caught the early light, paired with a silver sequined tank top that threw fractured brilliance across the parking lot. Her combat boots swung rhythmically against the truck's grill.

"Okay, so looking at last week's metrics," she announced to the assembled crew, her voice carrying across the hotel's front lot where Kyle, Nate, and Pete gathered for what Grace insisted on calling 'morning content strategy meetings'.

"Our farmhouse raid content performed really well. Authentic emotional reactions, good production values, strong narrative arc. But the strip mall footage?" She made a disapproving sound. "Honestly, guys, we can do better."

Kyle leaned against the truck's side panel, arms crossed, watching Grace with an expression that mixed calculation and concern. Two weeks of this. Two weeks of her treating every raid like a production meeting, every victim like an audience member, every act of violence like content creation.

"Grace," he started, but she held up one hand.

"Let me finish the analytics breakdown first. Nate, your performance last week was solid. Very authentic tough-guy energy. But Pete?" She turned to face him, her sequined top catching light. "We need to work on your camera presence. You keep standing with your back to me during key moments. Remember, if the camera can't see it, the audience can't engage with it."

Pete's jaw clenched. "We're not performing for a camera, Grace. We're stealing supplies."

"We're creating content while acquiring resources," Grace corrected, her tone patient, like she was explaining something obvious to a child. "There's a difference. It's all about mindset and brand consistency."

Nate shifted his weight, the gravel crunching under his boots. Two weeks since this insane girl joined them, and he still couldn't decide if Kyle was a genius for using her or an idiot for keeping her around. "What's today's target?"

"Excellent question!" Grace hopped off the hood, her phone clutched in one hand. "Today we're hitting a settlement about fifteen miles north. Intel says maybe twenty people, some families, trying to establish a farming collective or something. Very community-focused, which is perfect for our brand expansion narrative."

"It's a supply raid," Kyle said flatly. "We go in, take what we need, get out. Simple."

"Simple is boring." Grace moved through the crew, her pink camo pants swishing with each step. "Simple doesn't build audience investment. We need drama, conflict, emotional stakes. We need to think about production values."

Nate caught Kyle's eye, his expression asking the same question they'd all been asking for two weeks: how long are we going to let this continue?

Kyle's slight head shake reiterated what they all knew. It was working, and they'd keep it up as long as she was useful.

"Okay, so character development notes before we head out." Grace stopped in front of Nate, studying him like a director reviewing an actor. "Nate, I'm thinking we lean into your tactical expertise angle. Very professional operator vibes. Pete, you're comic relief but with an edge. And Kyle?" She turned to face him, her smile bright. "You're obviously the mysterious leader with a dark past. Very brooding protagonist energy."

"I'm not brooding," Kyle said.

"You're totally brooding. It's part of your appeal." Grace pulled out her phone, framing an imaginary shot. "The strong, silent type who commands respect through presence rather than words. My followers eat that archetype up."

"Your phone is dead," Nate pointed out.

Grace's smile faltered for just a moment, something dark flickering behind her eyes. Then it returned, brighter than before. "The phone is just a tool. The content lives in here." She tapped her temple. "I'm documenting everything for when infrastructure returns. Building my archive. My followers are patient."

The crew loaded into two trucks, Grace claiming her usual spot in Kyle's passenger seat. She spent the drive north narrating into her dead phone, describing the landscape like she was hosting a travel show.

"And here we see authentic post-apocalyptic Maine wilderness," she said, phone held up to film abandoned cars and overgrown fields. "Notice the way nature is already reclaiming human spaces. Very powerful visual metaphor for the impermanence of civilization. My audience is definitely going to appreciate the artistic composition here."

Kyle's hands tightened on the steering wheel. "Grace, when we get there, I need you to stay back. Let us handle the actual negotiation."

"Negotiation?" Grace lowered her phone, confusion crossing her features. "Why would we negotiate? That's so passive. We need to establish dominance immediately. Set the tone for authentic community integration."

"We negotiate because it's faster and safer," Kyle said, his voice tight with forced patience. "We tell them we're taking supplies. They give us supplies. Everyone lives. Simple."

"But that's terrible content!" Grace's voice rose with genuine distress. "Where's the conflict? Where's the drama? How are my followers supposed to stay engaged with that kind of boring narrative structure?"

"Your followers don't exist," Pete said from the back seat.

The temperature in the truck dropped. Grace turned in her seat, her expression shifting into something cold and dangerous that sat wrong on her skeletal features.

"My followers absolutely exist," she said quietly. "Fifty thousand people who believe in my vision, who trust my content, who wait for my posts. Just because *you* can't see them doesn't mean they're not real. That's very narrow-minded thinking, Pete. Very algorithm-unfriendly energy."

Pete opened his mouth to respond, but Kyle cut him off. "Everyone shut up. We're here."

The settlement materialized ahead, a cluster of houses surrounded by newly planted fields and makeshift fencing. Smoke rose from chimneys. Laundry hung between buildings. Children's toys scattered across a yard. Normal. People trying to build something normal in the ruins.

Grace leaned forward, her phone already raised. "Oh, this is perfect. Look at that authentic community aesthetic. Very heartwarming before the disruption. Great narrative contrast."

Kyle parked both trucks at the settlement's entrance, far enough back to avoid seeming immediately threatening. A woman emerged from the largest house, maybe forty, with graying hair pulled back and dirt under her fingernails. Behind her, two men appeared carrying hunting rifles pointed down but ready.

"That's close enough," the woman called. "We don't want trouble."

Kyle stepped out of the truck, his hands visible and empty. "We're not here for trouble. Just looking to trade. We have medical supplies, ammunition. Willing to negotiate for food and water."

Grace climbed out of the passenger side, her pink camo and sequins immediately drawing confused stares. She held her phone high, framing shots of the woman's face.

"Don't mind me," Grace said brightly. "Just documenting authentic survivor interactions. This is incredible content. The whole 'wary but hopeful' vibe you're giving? Very genuine. My followers are going to love you."

The woman's eyes moved from Grace's outfit to her dead phone to Kyle's carefully neutral expression. "What is she talking about?"

"Ignore her," Kyle said. "She's harmless. Just a little confused. Let's talk about supplies."

"Confused?" Grace lowered her phone, her smile tightening. "Kyle, that's really undermining my credibility with the audience. We talked about this. Supportive team dynamics are crucial for brand consistency."

The woman took a step back. "I think you should leave."

"See, this is exactly what I was talking about," Grace said, moving forward despite Kyle's warning hand on her arm. "You're approaching this all wrong. You're being defensive when you should be receptive. We're here to help integrate your community into our larger network. It's a partnership opportunity!"

"We're not interested in partnerships." The woman gestured to the men with rifles. "Please leave. Now."

Grace's expression shifted, something dangerous moving behind her eyes. "You're not understanding the value proposition here. We have resources. We have organization. We have a platform. All you have to do is cooperate, and we can build something amazing together."

"Grace." Kyle's voice carried a warning. "Back to the truck."

But Grace wasn't listening. She moved closer to the woman, her phone still raised, her pink camo bright against the drab settlement colors. "Let me explain this in terms you might understand better. We're not asking permission. We're offering you the opportunity to participate voluntarily in content creation and resource sharing. But if you're going to be difficult, if you're going to create negative engagement energy, then we'll have to adjust our approach."

One of the men raised his rifle. "Lady, I don't know what drugs you're on, but you need to get back in your truck and leave. Right now."

The world shifted. Grace's face went blank, then twisted with fury that seemed to come from nowhere and everywhere at once. "Drugs? You think I'm on drugs? I'm a professional content creator! I have fifty thousand followers! I built my platform through authentic engagement and consistent posting schedules! How dare you suggest I'm not in complete control of my faculties!"

"Grace, enough." Kyle grabbed her arm, trying to pull her back. But Grace wrenched free with surprising strength, her voice rising to a shriek.

"This is exactly what they did in Portsmouth! Questioning my judgment, undermining my authority, trying to sabotage my opportunities! Well, I'm not letting that happen again! You don't get to bring down my algorithm! You don't get to ruin my content!"

She lunged forward, phone raised like a weapon. The man with the rifle stepped between Grace and the woman, his barrel swinging up. Kyle moved fast, his pistol appearing in his hand, the shot cracking across the morning air. The man dropped, blood blooming across his chest.

The settlement erupted. The other man fired, his shot going wide. Pete and Nate returned fire from behind the trucks. The woman screamed, running toward the houses. Children's voices rose in panic.

Grace stood in the center of the chaos, her phone still raised, her face twisted with rage and something that looked almost like joy. "Yes! This is perfect! This is exactly the kind of authentic conflict that drives engagement! Keep filming, keep filming!"

Kyle grabbed her again, this time harder, dragging her back toward the truck as bullets snapped through the air around them. "Get down, you insane—"

"We need to secure the settlement!" Grace fought against his grip, her voice cutting through the gunfire. "This is crucial footage! We can't let them ruin the narrative arc!"

The men poured from the second truck, their weapons blazing. The settlement's defenses crumbled under coordinated assault. Three minutes. That's all it took to turn attempted negotiation into massacre because Grace needed drama for her imaginary audience.

Kyle shoved Grace behind the truck, his face inches from hers. "Stay here. Don't move. Don't do anything. We're cleaning up your mess."

But Grace smiled, her eyes bright with manic energy. "This is so much better than negotiation. The emotional stakes, the visceral action, the authentic fear responses. My followers are going to be so invested in this story arc."

The gunfire died down. Kyle's crew moved through the settlement with efficient brutality, clearing houses, securing survivors. Grace peeked around the truck, filming everything, narrating in breathless excitement.

"And here we see authentic community integration in action. Notice the tactical precision of my crew, the way they move with purpose and coordination. This is professional-level content creation, folks. This is what separates amateurs from true influencers."

Kyle returned, blood spattered across his shirt, his expression carved from stone. "Eight dead. Twelve survivors, mostly women and children. All because you couldn't keep your mouth shut."

"Eight? That's a solid engagement number." Grace checked her phone like she was reading metrics. "And the survivors will be perfect for follow-up content. We can document their integration journey, show the transformation from resistance to acceptance. Very compelling character development."

Kyle stared at her, something between horror and fascination in his eyes. "You're proud of this."

"I'm proud of my team's performance," Grace corrected. "This could have been a boring supply run. Instead, we created meaningful content with authentic emotional stakes. That's what separates good creators from great ones. The willingness to embrace dramatic escalation when the narrative demands it."

Nate approached, carrying a bag of supplies. "Found their stash. Medical supplies, canned goods, ammunition. And this." He pulled out a pistol with a bright pink handle, probably spray-painted by someone's daughter before the collapse. "Thought you might want it. Matches your outfit."

Grace's face lit up. She reached for the gun like a child receiving a birthday present, turning it over in her hands, testing the weight. The pink handle caught morning light, garish and wrong against the backdrop of blood and smoke.

"Oh, my God, this is perfect," she breathed. "This is exactly the kind of signature accessory my brand needs. Very on-theme. Very consistent with my aesthetic vision." She checked the magazine, found it loaded, and tucked the weapon into her waistband with the pink handle visible above her pink camo pants.

"Grace." Kyle's voice carried a warning she didn't hear.

"Let's get the survivors organized," Grace said, moving toward the settlement's center where Kyle's crew herded prisoners into a group. "I want to do individual interviews. Get their stories on record. Build audience connection with their transformation arcs."

She walked past bodies cooling in the morning sun, past blood soaking into dirt, past a child's stuffed animal lying abandoned in a doorway. Her phone stayed raised, filming everything, her narration bright and enthusiastic.

"And here we see the reality of post-apocalyptic resource sharing. It's not always pretty, folks, but it's authentic. That's what my platform is all about. No filters, no fake aesthetics. Just real survival, real community building, real human experience."

The survivors huddled together, their faces marked with terror and grief. A woman clutched two children against her chest. An older man bled from a shoulder wound. A twenty something girl stared at nothing, shock stealing her expression.

Grace positioned herself in front of them, her phone held high, her smile bright and terrible. "Good morning, everyone! I'm Grace Reynolds, and I'm so excited to welcome you to our extended community network. I know the circumstances of our meeting weren't ideal, but I really believe we can build something amazing together."

The woman with the children made a sound between a sob and a laugh. "You're insane. You're completely fucking insane."

Grace's smile tightened. Her hand moved to the pink-handled pistol, fingers tracing the grip. "That's really negative language. Very unconstructive. We're going to need to work on your attitude if you want to participate successfully in our community integration program."

"Grace." Nate moved beside her, his voice low. "Maybe ease up. They just watched their people die."

"Which is exactly why we need to establish positive energy now," Grace said, her voice taking on that patient, explaining-to-children tone. "Trauma bonding is a crucial part of community development. If we let them wallow in negativity, it'll poison the whole group dynamic."

She turned back to the survivors, her phone still recording their faces. "So here's how this works. You're all joining our operation. Some of you will help with supply management. Some will participate in content creation. Everyone has a role to play. And if you cooperate, if you commit to the vision, we'll make sure you're fed, sheltered, and protected. That's a fair deal, right?"

The girl, the one staring at nothing, suddenly focused on Grace. Her voice came out flat, emotionless. "You killed my father. He was the one who tried to stop you. You got him killed for your phone that doesn't even work."

Grace's expression flickered. For just a moment, something almost like recognition crossed her features. Then it vanished, replaced by that bright influencer smile. "Loss is part of the survivor experience. It's tragic, yes, but it's also an opportunity for growth. For transformation. Your father's story will live on through my content. That's a kind of immortality, when you think about it."

The girl's empty stare never wavered. "I hope someone kills you."

The settlement went quiet. Kyle's hand moved toward his weapon, but Grace raised her free hand, stopping him. She crouched down to the girl's eye level, her pink camo and sequins catching light, the pink-handled pistol visible at her waist.

"That's a very authentic emotional response," Grace said softly. "I appreciate the honesty. But here's what you need to understand. I'm not your enemy. I'm not the villain of this story. I'm the protagonist. The hero. The one building something meaningful from the ashes of the old world. And you can either be part of that story, or you can be a *cautionary tale* about resistance. Your choice."

The girl spat in Grace's face.

Everything happened fast. Grace's expression went from patient to furious in a heartbeat. Her hand closed on the pink-handled pistol, pulling it free. The girl's mother screamed, throwing herself forward. Kyle shouted something Grace didn't hear.

Grace pressed the pink barrel against the girl's forehead. "You don't get to disrespect my platform. You don't get to bring down my algorithm with your negative energy. You don't get to sabotage my content!"

"Grace, no!" Kyle grabbed for her arm but Grace twisted away, her finger on the trigger, her face twisted with rage that seemed to come from all the memories flooding back. From Portsmouth, from Earl's cabin, from every perceived slight and sabotage she'd imagined over the past weeks.

"This is what happens," Grace hissed, her voice venomous. "This is what happens when you try to ruin everything I've built. When you question my vision. When you bring down my engagement metrics with your toxic attitude!"

The mother grabbed Grace's leg, sobbing. "Please, please, she's just overwhelmed. She didn't mean it. Please don't—"

Grace looked down at the woman clinging to her pink camo pants, at the girl frozen with the pistol pressed to her head, at Kyle and his crew watching with expressions between horror and fascination. In her mind, her followers watched too. Fifty thousand people waiting to see what she'd do. Waiting for content. Waiting for drama. Waiting for her to prove she was strong enough, ruthless enough, authentic enough to deserve their attention.

She pulled the trigger.

The shot cracked across the morning air. The girl's head snapped back, her body crumpling to the dirt. The mother's scream tore through the settlement, raw and animal. The other survivors pressed back, some crying, some too shocked for tears.

Grace stood, the pink-handled pistol still raised, smoke curling from the barrel. Her phone in her other hand, capturing everything. Her face showed no remorse, no horror, just satisfaction with a scene well executed.

"And that's what happens when you disrupt production," she said to her imaginary audience. "Negative energy has no place in authentic community building. Everyone needs to understand that cooperation isn't optional. It's the price of participation."

She turned to the remaining survivors, her voice brightening back into that enthusiastic influencer tone. "Now, who's ready to start their integration journey? Show of hands? Remember, positive attitudes get positive outcomes!"

No one moved except the mother, still crouched over her daughter's body, her sobs the only sound in the terrible silence.

Kyle grabbed Grace's arm, spinning her to face him. His voice came out low and dangerous. "What the fuck was that?"

"That... was content," Grace said simply. "Dramatic escalation. Clear consequences for resistance. Very effective messaging. My followers needed to see that I'm serious about my platform. That I won't tolerate sabotage."

"She was just a young woman!"

"She was a disruption." Grace pulled free of Kyle's grip, tucking the pink pistol back into her waistband. "And she was bringing down the algorithm with her negative energy. I gave her a chance to cooperate. She chose poorly."

Pete moved closer, his face pale. "Boss, we need to talk about this."

"Later." Kyle's jaw clenched so hard Grace could see the muscle jumping. "Pete, Nate, get the survivors loaded. Take anything useful. We're leaving in five minutes."

Grace watched his crew work, her phone still raised, still filming. The mother had to be dragged away from her daughter's body, her screams echoing across the settlement. The other survivors moved like automatons, too shocked for resistance.

"This is such powerful footage," Grace narrated. "The raw emotion, the authentic grief, the reality of loss in post-apocalyptic conditions. This is exactly the kind of content that builds deep audience investment. People don't just want to see survival. They want to feel it."

Nate loaded the last of the survivors into the truck bed, his eyes avoiding Grace. Pete gathered supplies without a word, his face carefully blank. One of the guards stood by his vehicle, watching Grace with an expression that might have been fear.

Kyle returned to Grace's side as smoke began rising from the settlement. Someone set fire to the buildings. Can't leave resources for anyone else. Grace filmed it all, narrating the visual storytelling elements, the symbolism of transformation, the authentic destruction that marked their passage.

"Okay, so that was an incredibly productive morning," Grace said as they climbed back into the truck. "Nine eliminations, eleven new community members, solid supply acquisition, and some really powerful dramatic footage. My engagement metrics are going to be through the roof with this content."

Kyle started the engine without responding. His hands gripped the steering wheel hard enough to make his knuckles white.

"You're mad," Grace observed. "But you shouldn't be. I handled that perfectly. Established dominance, set clear expectations, eliminated resistance. That's professional-level community management."

"You murdered her."

"I eliminated a threat to platform cohesion," Grace corrected. "There's a difference. She was poisoning group dynamics with her negativity. Sometimes you have to remove one person to protect the integrity of the whole operation. It's basic community management."

Kyle drove in silence, his jaw clenched. In the back seat, Pete and Nate exchanged glances but said nothing. Behind them, the other truck followed, carrying survivors and supplies and the weight of what Grace just did.

Grace scrolled through her dead phone, reviewing imaginary footage, selecting the best shots. The pink-handled pistol pressed against her hip, comfortable and right. Her first real kill since Earl. Her first time choosing violence, not from paranoia, but from genuine fury at someone disrupting her content.

It felt powerful. It felt right. It felt like exactly what her platform needed.

"This is going to be such an amazing episode," she said to Kyle's silence. "The escalation, the consequences, the clear messaging about cooperation. My followers are going to be so invested in where this story goes next."

The settlement burned behind them, smoke rising into the morning sky. Grace filmed it through the rear window, her narration bright with enthusiasm.

"And here we see the transformation complete. Old structures destroyed to make way for new community development. Very symbolic. Very powerful. This is exactly the kind of authentic content that separates real influencers from wannabes."

She turned back around, settling into her seat, the pink pistol's handle visible above her pink camo waistband. Her phone rested on her lap, screen dark, waiting for followers who would never come.

She smiled at her reflection in the truck's side mirror and whispered to her phone: "Don't forget to like and subscribe."

Grace positioned herself at the center of the hotel lobby, morning sunlight streaming through tall windows and catching the silver sequins on her tank top. She wore pink camouflage cargo pants again today, the ones that matched her new pistol perfectly. Visual consistency mattered. Brand identity mattered. Her followers expected polish even in crisis conditions.

The settlement survivors sat arranged along the walls where Kyle's crew positioned them during the night. Eleven faces stared back at her, some marked with bruises, all hollowed by shock. Grace held her phone high, framing the shot, scrolling through imaginary notifications with her thumb.

"Good morning, everyone!" Her sing-song tone echoed through the space, bright and enthusiastic despite the stale air that reeked of sweat and fear. "I'm Grace Reynolds, your community integration host. I know yesterday was intense, but today we're going to focus on positive momentum and authentic relationship building."

The woman from the settlement sat in the front row. The mother. Grace's mind skittered away from specifics about why the woman's eyes looked so empty, why dried tear tracks marked her face. Irrelevant details. What mattered was content. What mattered was the platform.

Grace moved between the survivors, her combat boots loud against the lobby's tile floor. The sequins threw light across faces that didn't react, didn't respond. They just watched her with expressions that made something cold crawl up her spine.

For a moment, just a flash, their faces rippled. Skin pulled tight over skulls. Eyes sank into shadowed sockets. Mouths stretched too wide, showing too many teeth. Ghoulish. Hungry. Reaching for her with skeletal fingers that wanted to drag her down into whatever darkness they inhabited.

Grace blinked hard. The faces returned to normal. Tired. Traumatized. Human.

She pressed her thumb against her phone's dead screen, feeling the solid delusion of it anchor her. Her followers were watching. Fifty thousand people waited for her content. She couldn't let them down. Couldn't let these people sabotage her platform like Hannah and Maddie tried to do.

With that thought, anger rose like bile and she spun on her heel away from the prisoners, taking a moment to swallow it down before speaking.

She twirled like the whole thing was one massive Broadway show, and with her newly recovered high pitched tone, said, "So, here's how our integration program works." Grace stopped in the center of the space, positioning herself where the light hit best. "Everyone gets assigned a role based on their skills and aptitudes. Some of you will work on resource management. Some will handle logistics. And some of you get to participate directly in content creation, which is obviously the most prestigious position."

A man near the back, older with gray stubble, shifted his weight. The movement drew Grace's attention. His face flickered for just a moment. Skin peeling away from bone. Eyes rotting in their sockets. Then normal again. Just an exhausted man trying not to collapse.

"Questions?" Grace's smile stayed locked in place despite the sweat forming on her palms. "Comments? This is a collaborative process. I value authentic input."

Silence. The kind that pressed against her ears and made her thoughts race faster, spinning through possibilities and threats and the constant need to maintain control of her narrative.

The mother finally spoke, her voice flat and dead, "You killed my daughter."

Grace's sequined top caught the light as she turned to face the woman fully. "I understand you're processing grief. That's totally valid. But what happened yesterday was necessary for maintaining positive community dynamics. Your daughter was creating toxic energy that threatened group cohesion."

"She was twenty-three years old." The mother's hands clenched in her lap. "She spat at you for murdering her father. And you shot her in the head."

The other survivors shifted, their attention sharpening. Grace felt their focus like weight pressing against her chest. Their faces flickered again. Ghoulish. Hungry. Threatening.

She blinked it away and raised her phone higher, framing the mother in the shot. "This is exactly the kind of authentic emotional content my followers connect with. Raw grief. Unfiltered loss. Would you be willing to do a testimonial? Share your journey through trauma with our audience?"

The mother stared at her. Something moved behind those dead eyes. Something that looked almost like comprehension of just how insane Grace truly was.

"A testimonial?" The mother repeated slowly.

"Yes! Just a few minutes on camera. Talk about your feelings. Your process. How you're finding strength through adversity." Grace's voice brightened with genuine enthusiasm. "This is an incredible opportunity for you. Most people never get platform exposure like this. And the algorithm really favors authentic emotional content."

The mother's face did something Grace's fractured mind couldn't quite interpret. A twist. A collapse. Then she laughed. The sound came out broken and wrong, like glass grinding against metal.

"You want me to talk about finding strength?" The mother stood slowly, her movements careful and measured. "You want me to share my grief journey. For your dead phone. For your imaginary followers?"

"They're not imaginary." Grace's fingers tightened on her phone. "I have fifty thousand verified followers. My platform is built on authentic engagement and consistent content delivery."

"Your phone doesn't work." The mother took a step forward. Around her, the other survivors pressed back against the walls, their faces showing the first signs of hope. Maybe this woman would do what they couldn't. Maybe she would make the glittering monster stop talking.

Grace's vision wavered. The mother's face rippled, became something ghoulish and threatening. Skin stretched too tight. Eyes sinking into darkness. Mouth opening to reveal rotting teeth that wanted to tear Grace apart, wanted to destroy everything she built.

"Stop." Grace raised her free hand, the one not holding her phone. "You're disrupting production. You're creating negative energy that poisons the algorithm."

"My daughter is dead." The mother's voice rose, gaining strength. "You murdered her. And now you want me to smile for your broken phone and pretend any of this is normal?"

The lobby held its breath. Kyle stood near the entrance, his rifle across his chest, watching with an expression that showed both wariness and calculation. Nate and Pete flanked the exits, their hands on their weapons. They'd seen Grace snap before. They knew what came next.

Grace's thumb moved across her dead phone screen, checking metrics that existed only in her fractured mind. Engagement dropping. Negativity spreading. The mother was poisoning her entire platform with toxic energy.

"I'm offering you an opportunity." Grace's voice dropped lower, losing the forced brightness. "A chance to participate voluntarily in content creation. To share your story in a way that helps others process their own trauma. That's valuable. That matters."

"No." The mother's word cut through the lobby like a blade. "I won't participate in your insanity. I won't pretend this is anything other than what it is. You're a sick girl playing with a broken phone while people die around you. Nobody's watching Grace! No one cares!"

The faces rippled again. All of them this time. The survivors transformed into ghoulish things with hungry eyes and reaching hands. They wanted to drag her down. Wanted to sabotage her platform. Wanted to destroy everything she worked three years to build.

Grace's hand moved to the pink pistol at her waist. The handle felt warm against her palm, comfortable and right. Her voice low and menacing she asked, "You're refusing to cooperate?"

"Yes." The mother lifted her chin. "I'm refusing. Kill me if you want. I don't care anymore. But I won't play along with your sick fantasy."

"This isn't a fantasy." Grace pulled the pistol free, the pink handle catching morning light. "This is my platform. My content. My vision. And you don't get to ruin it with your negative energy."

She raised the phone higher, framing the shot, making sure the angle captured everything. The mother standing defiant. The other survivors pressed against the walls. The pink pistol steady in Grace's hand.

"This is what happens when you disrupt production," Grace announced to her imaginary audience, her voice shifting into that bright narration tone. "When you refuse to participate in authentic community building. When you let toxic attitudes poison group dynamics."

The mother closed her eyes. Waiting. Ready.

Grace squeezed the trigger.

The shot cracked through the lobby, impossibly loud in the enclosed space. The mother's body jerked backward, blood spraying across the tile floor. She collapsed, her head hitting the ground with a sound that made several survivors cry out.

But Grace kept filming. Kept narrating. "Notice the authentic emotional response from our community members. This is real grief. Real shock. Real human experience. You can't fake this level of genuine reaction."

She moved closer to the body, the sequins on her top throwing fractured light across blood spreading in a dark pool. The mother's eyes stared at nothing, her face finally peaceful after all the pain.

Grace crouched down, still filming, her voice maintaining that enthusiastic pitch. "And this is what accountability looks like in post-apocalyptic community management. Clear consequences for disruption. Clear messaging about cooperation. Very effective leadership technique."

The phone slipped in her grip, her fingers suddenly slick with something warm. She'd stepped in the blood without noticing. The screen stayed black but in her mind, notifications exploded. Comments. Likes. Shares. Her followers responding to the dramatic content with overwhelming enthusiasm.

"Oh, my God!" Grace's voice rose with genuine excitement. She held the bloody phone up, watching imaginary metrics climb. "Look at this engagement! The likes are flooding in! This is going absolutely viral!"

She stood, turning in a circle, the sequins catching light and throwing it across survivors who pressed themselves against the walls like they could disappear into the peeling wallpaper. Their faces flickered between human and ghoulish, between real and threatening, but Grace barely noticed. Her attention fixed on her phone, on the numbers climbing in her fractured mind.

"Fifteen hundred likes in thirty seconds! Twenty-five hundred! This is incredible! This is exactly the kind of authentic content that breaks through the algorithm!"

The lobby door opened. Grace registered the sound distantly, peripherally, but her focus stayed on her phone. On the engagement. On the validation pouring in from followers who understood her vision, who appreciated her willingness to create dramatic content that other influencers wouldn't touch.

"Three thousand likes!" She squealed, spinning again, the pink pistol still in her other hand, blood on her boots and sequins. "My best performing post ever! This is revolutionary! This is platform-changing content!"

A voice cut through her celebration. Male. Unfamiliar. Carrying an edge of disbelief that bordered on horror.

"What the hell?"

Grace finally looked up from her phone. A man stood in the doorway, broad-shouldered and dangerous in the way all of Kyle's crew seemed to be. But this one was different. Older. More weathered. His eyes moved from Grace to the body on the floor to Kyle standing near the entrance with an expression that showed both pride and growing concern.

The stranger's arm extended toward Grace, his gesture encompassing the blood, the phone, the sequins, the pink pistol, the complete insanity of the tableau before him.

"You got this…" He paused, searching for words adequate to describe what he witnessed. "This Queen of Likes, just executing people?"

The title hit Grace like validation from the universe itself. Queen of Likes. Not just an influencer. Not just a content creator. A queen. Royalty. Recognition of her platform's power and reach and cultural significance.

Her face lit up with genuine delight. "Oh, my God, yes! That's perfect! That's exactly the kind of aspirational branding my platform needs!" She moved toward the stranger, phone still raised, blood still on her boots. "I'm Grace Reynolds. You must be here for collaboration opportunities. I'm so excited to discuss cross-platform synergies and audience development strategies."

The man stared at her, his expression cycling between shock and calculation and something that looked almost like fascination. "You're completely insane."

"I prefer visionary." Grace stopped a few feet away, holding her phone up to film him. "But Queen of Likes is absolutely genius. Very memorable. Very shareable. My followers are going to love this rebrand."

Kyle moved closer to the stranger, his voice low and tense. "Sherman. We need to talk."

Sherman. Grace filed the name away, already planning how to introduce him to her audience. Strategic partner. Military advisor. Supporting character in her platform's expansion arc.

"Talk?" Sherman's voice carried dark amusement. "Kyle, what the fuck is this? You called me down here because you needed help managing territory, and I show up to find some skeletal girl in sequins shooting people while talking to a broken phone?"

"She's useful." Kyle's jaw clenched. "She breaks people psychologically. Makes them compliant faster than threats or violence ever could."

"She's insane," Sherman repeated, but his eyes stayed on Grace, studying her like a problem that needed solving or a weapon that needed understanding.

Grace tucked the pink pistol back into her waistband, the handle visible above her pink camo pants. She smoothed down her sequined top, adjusted her hair, checked her reflection in her phone's black screen. Camera ready. Professional. The Queen of Likes addressing her court.

"Insanity is just misunderstood genius." She moved past Sherman toward Kyle, her voice shifting into the tone she used when directing her crew. "Kyle, can you handle our new arrival? Get him settled, brief him on our operations, coordinate security protocols. I need to finish processing the morning's content and prepare for afternoon production meetings."

She'd treated Kyle as her handler, her partner, even her protector over the past two weeks. But something shifted in that moment. The Queen of Likes didn't answer to handlers. The Queen of Likes had staff. Had security. Had people who managed logistics while she focused on content creation.

Kyle's expression flickered with surprise that quickly transformed into something darker. Calculation. Understanding. A shift in their dynamic that both recognized but neither named.

"Sure," Kyle said slowly. "I'll handle Sherman. You do your... content review."

"Perfect!" Grace beamed at him, then turned her smile on Sherman. "Welcome to the Portland operation. I think you're going to love what we're building here. Very authentic. Very revolutionary. Exactly the kind of post-apocalyptic platform that changes everything."

She walked past both men toward the stairs, her combat boots leaving small bloody prints across the lobby floor. Behind her, she heard Sherman's low voice addressing Kyle.

"That girl is going to get everyone killed."

"Or she's going to make us legends," Kyle replied.

Grace climbed the stairs humming tunelessly, scrolling through her dead phone, reviewing imaginary footage of the morning's execution. The metrics looked incredible. Her best performing content ever. The Queen of Likes delivering exactly what her followers craved.

In her mind, fifty thousand people celebrated her evolution. Praised her willingness to create authentic content. Recognized her platform's cultural significance.

In reality, she left a body cooling on the lobby floor and a group of survivors who now understood cooperation wasn't optional. It was survival.

Grace reached her room on the fifth floor, closing the door behind her with a soft click. She moved to the window, looking down at the street below where Sherman's trucks sat parked beside Kyle's. More resources. More crew. More opportunities for platform expansion.

Her phone buzzed in her hand. Impossible, but she felt it. A notification. Her followers responding to the morning's content with overwhelming enthusiasm. She pressed her thumb against the dead screen, reading comments that existed only in her fractured mind.

Queen of Likes is SERVING

This content is everything

She really said consequences and meant it

The validation flooded through her system like a drug. This was what she'd been working toward since that first viral post three years ago. Recognition. Power. A platform that mattered.

Grace caught her reflection in the window's glass. Hollow cheeks. Sharp bones. Blood on her sequined top and pink camo pants. The pink pistol visible at her waist. She looked dangerous. She looked powerful. She looked like exactly what her platform needed.

Behind her reflection, the hotel room showed worn furniture and water-stained walls. But Grace saw a production studio. A content creation headquarters. The nerve center of a revolutionary platform that would rebuild civilization in her image.

She raised her phone, taking a selfie with the window behind her, Portland's ruined skyline visible in the background. Her influencer smile locked into place, practiced and perfect despite everything. She checked the shot, adjusting the angle, making sure the blood spatter looked intentional rather than accidental.

"Today's look," she narrated to her imaginary audience. "Post-execution aesthetic. Very raw. Very authentic. Remember, followers, true influence means being willing to make the hard decisions that other creators won't touch."

A knock on the door made her lower the phone. "Come in!"

Jennifer entered, the woman Kyle assigned as Grace's wardrobe coordinator. Her eyes stayed fixed on the floor, shoulders hunched like she was trying to make herself smaller. Behind her, Carol and Amy followed, the production team Grace assembled from prisoners who showed the right combination of competence and terror.

"You asked for wardrobe options for this afternoon," Jennifer said, her voice carefully neutral. "We pulled some pieces from the latest acquisitions."

"Excellent!" Grace moved to the bed where Jennifer laid out clothing. Silver sequined top. Gold shimmery top. Black leather jacket. Pink camo pants. White camo pants. Everything shimmered and caught light, turning survival gear into performance costume.

Grace's vision flickered. Jennifer's face rippled, became ghoulish and threatening. Skin pulled tight. Eyes sunken. Mouth stretched too wide. Then normal again. Just a tired woman trying to survive.

"The gold top," Grace decided, touching the fabric. "Very aspirational. Shows growth and evolution. And the white camo pants. Fresh start energy for the new organizational structure."

"New organizational structure?" Carol's voice came out small and frightened.

Grace turned to face her production team, her smile brightening. "We have new management joining the operation. Sherman and his crew. Which means expanded resources, larger audience potential, more opportunities for content creation. This is huge for the platform."

Amy's hands twisted together, her bruised face showing fresh fear. "What does that mean for us?"

"Opportunity!" Grace spread her arms, the bloody sequined top throwing light across their faces. "More crew means more content needs. More roles to fill. More chances to prove your value to the platform." Her voice dropped slightly, losing some of the forced brightness. "Or more chances to demonstrate your failure if you're not contributing to the vision."

The threat landed. Grace saw it in the way their shoulders slumped, in the way their eyes dropped to the floor, in the way they accepted her insanity as the new baseline for survival.

"Carol, I need you training more people on hair and makeup. Sherman's crew will need camera-ready preparation. Jennifer, expand the wardrobe coordination to accommodate larger team sizes. Amy, you're moving to full production assistance. I need someone managing lighting and shot composition for multiple filming locations."

She moved between them, her combat boots still leaving faint bloody prints on the carpet. Their faces flickered. Ghoulish. Hungry. Threatening. She blinked it away and raised her phone, filming their reactions.

"And this is what authentic leadership looks like," she narrated to her imaginary followers. "Clear delegation. Structured roles. Professional standards maintained even in crisis conditions. Very effective organizational management."

Jennifer looked up briefly, her expression showing something Grace's fractured mind couldn't quite interpret. Pity maybe. Or horror at what she witnessed evolving in real time.

"Is there anything else?" Jennifer asked quietly.

Grace checked her phone, scrolling through imaginary metrics from the morning's execution. "Actually, yes. I need you to coordinate with Kyle's crew. Find out Sherman's arrival timeline, crew size, supply inventory. I want a full briefing before this afternoon's integration meeting."

"Integration meeting," Jennifer repeated slowly.

"With Sherman's people. We're merging operations, which means merging crews, which means establishing clear hierarchy and expectations." Grace's voice took on that enthusiastic pitch again. "This is exactly the kind of expansion content my followers have been waiting for. Platform growth. Organizational scaling. Revolutionary community building."

The three women exchanged glances loaded with meaning Grace didn't see. They understood something she didn't. That Sherman's arrival changed the dynamic. That more predators in the territory meant more danger for everyone. That Grace's delusions were about to collide with someone who saw her clearly and might decide she was more liability than asset.

But Grace only saw opportunity. Content. Growth.

"Get started on those tasks," she said, already turning back to the window. "I need prep time before Sherman's official welcome orientation."

Amy stepped forward with a tray. "Miss… Uh, Grace? Kyle says you need to eat and sent this food for you."

Grace smiled widely, accepting the tray and saying, "See how he really cares about me?"

They left without responding, the door closing softly behind them. Grace stood alone in her room, scrolling through her dead phone, planning her afternoon's content strategy. The Queen of Likes preparing for her next performance.

Below, in the stairwell, Kyle and Sherman talked. Their voices carried up the stairwell, muffled but clear enough for Grace to catch fragments.

"She's completely insane." Sherman's voice.

"She's useful." Kyle's response.

"She's going to get everyone killed."

"Or she's going to make us legends."

Grace smiled at her reflection in the window. They were talking about her. Recognizing her value. Understanding her platform's revolutionary potential.

She was going to make them legendary.

Grace stood on the hotel roof at dawn, her phone pressed against her ear like she was on a call. Below, the Portland streets stretched empty and broken, smoke rising from a dozen fires scattered across neighborhoods that once housed families with routines, mortgages and arguments about whose turn it was to take out the trash.

"So here's the thing about expansion," she said to her invisible audience, her voice carrying that tone of enthusiasm that came so naturally now. "You can't just maintain. You have to grow. You have to reach new demographics, explore new markets, create content that resonates with broader appeal."

The pink pistol pressed against her hip, tucked into the waistband of her neon pink shorts. She'd paired them today with a camo mesh crop top over an identical neon pink bra. Her pink camo hiking boots in stark contrast to the shorts worked with the mesh camo crop top. She felt professional. Polished. Camera-ready with her new line of apocalypse wear.

Sherman's integration into their operation went smoothly over the past week. His crews merged with Kyle's people, doubling their numbers. Grace insisted on calling it a *strategic content partnership* while Sherman called it whatever men like him called violent consolidation of power. The words didn't matter. The platform expansion did.

Behind her, the roof access door opened. Grace didn't turn around. She knew Kyle's footsteps by now, the particular way his boots scraped against concrete.

"Planning something?" he asked.

"South Portland." Grace lowered her phone, scrolling through blank screens like she was reading intelligence reports. "There's a settlement there. Organized. Probably fifty, sixty people. They've fortified a neighborhood, established perimeter defenses, resource management protocols. Very impressive community infrastructure."

"How do you know this?"

"Sherman's scouts brought back reports yesterday." Grace turned to face him, her smile bright despite the darkness in her eyes. "They're calling it Crestview. Very suburban. Very defensive. Perfect for our next expansion content."

Kyle leaned against the doorframe, his rifle slung across his back. Three weeks working together taught Grace to read his expressions. Right now he wore calculation mixed with caution, the look he got when her ideas straddled the line between brilliant and catastrophic.

"That's a significant operation," he said. "Organized resistance means casualties. Our people aren't ready for that level of… engagement."

"Our people are ready for whatever I tell them they're ready for." Grace moved past him toward the stairs. "Besides, this isn't about difficulty. It's about narrative payoff. We've been hitting small targets, easy wins, low engagement potential. We need something bigger. Something that shows we're not just raiders. We're building something revolutionary."

She descended the stairs with Kyle following, her mind already framing shots, planning angles, constructing the story she would tell her followers about liberation and community transformation and authentic resource sharing.

The second floor hallway reeked of cigarette smoke and unwashed bodies. Kyle's crew occupied rooms along the corridor, weapons leaning against walls, gear scattered across floors. Sherman's people took the third floor, maintaining careful territorial separation that Grace found tedious but Kyle insisted was necessary for operational stability.

Grace pushed into the room she'd claimed as her planning space. Maps covered one wall, stolen from a hiking store during an early raid. She'd marked them with colored markers, tracking their expansion, noting settlements, plotting routes. Pink dots represented successful integrations. Black X's marked locations she called *creatively resolved.*

"I want to do this right," Grace said, tapping South Portland on the map. "Full coordination. Multiple entry points. Overwhelming force followed by immediate community restructuring. We go in hard, secure the territory, then shift into integration mode." She turned to face Kyle, her expression shifting into something that looked almost earnest. "I need you to trust me on this."

Kyle studied the map, his jaw working. "Why South Portland specifically? There are easier targets."

Because Hannah is from somewhere near there, Grace's fractured mind whispered. Because they sabotaged everything in Portsmouth and they're probably hiding somewhere close. Because revenge tastes better when it's served with production values.

But she said none of that. Instead, Grace smiled with warmth. "Strategic positioning. South Portland gives us control of the southern approach to Portland proper. We consolidate there, we control major supply routes. Plus, Sherman's scouts reported organized leadership. Take out the leaders, the rest fold. Classic integration strategy."

The lie came easily. Everything came easily now. Performance, manipulation, violence dressed up in lifestyle branding terminology. Grace moved through the apocalypse like she'd moved through the rest of her imagined influencer career, everything filtered through engagement metrics that only she could see.

"When?" Kyle asked.

"Tonight. We hit them after midnight when their guard is weakest." Grace pulled colored markers from her pocket, beginning to sketch approach vectors on the map. "Sherman's people take the western perimeter. Your crew comes in from the north. I'll coordinate from mobile command, documenting everything for post-production review."

"You mean you'll hide in a truck while we do the actual work."

Grace's smile never wavered. "I prefer strategic positioning for optimal content capture. But sure, your interpretation works, too."

Kyle watched her mark up the map, his expression unreadable. Three weeks taught Grace that he found her useful, maybe even valuable, but never quite safe. Good. Safety was for people who wanted to survive. Grace wanted to transcend.

"Meeting in one hour," Kyle said finally. "You present the plan to both crews. They need to hear it from you."

"Absolutely." Grace capped her markers with flourishes, each click precise. "This is going to be our most ambitious collaboration yet. My followers are going to be so invested in this expansion arc."

Kyle stepped closer, pressing himself against her and pinning her between him and the table. She liked it when he showed his possessiveness but sometimes he just couldn't see her vision. His finger came up under her chin lifting her face to meet his, his eyes darting back and forth looking into hers.

Searching her. Grace tried to put on her sultry face but he just smirked and left without responding. Grace turned back to her map, her fingers tracing the streets of South Portland, her mind already constructing narratives about liberation and community transformation and authentic content creation through overwhelming force.

She didn't notice her hands shaking. Didn't register the cold sweat forming along her spine. Didn't acknowledge the small voice in the back of her fractured psyche that whispered warnings. This was exactly what monsters did when they convinced themselves they were heroes.

That voice got quieter every day. Soon it would disappear completely.

Grace picked up her phone, pressing it against her ear. "So here's what I'm thinking for tonight's content," she said to the empty room. "We open with dramatic night-vision shots. Very authentic, very gritty. Then we cut to the action sequences, really highlight the tactical coordination. And the finale, the big reveal, that's where we introduce the integration process. Show the transformation from resistance to acceptance. My followers are going to love this character development."

Below, in the hotel lobby, sounds of movement and preparation filtered up to her. Sherman and Kyle began assembling the crews. The crew checked the weapons, distributed ammunition, and gave assignments. Grace's plan was taking shape; her insane vision translated into tactical reality by men who understood violence in ways she never would.

She stood at her map, pink pistol pressed against her hip, phone clutched in trembling fingers. The Queen of Likes preparing her next performance.

Three hours later, Grace descended to the lobby wearing tactical gear over her crop top. Black cargo pants replaced the pink shorts, though she kept the pink pistol visible. Compromise between operational necessity and brand consistency. Her followers would be into the style choices.

Forty-three men filled the space, a mix of Kyle's original crew and Sherman's absorbed forces. They wore mismatched tactical gear, carried weapons ranging from hunting rifles to stolen police equipment. Some looked professional, former military or law enforcement. Others looked like what they were—opportunistic predators dressed in apocalypse camouflage.

Grace moved to the center of the room, phone held high, framing her shot. Every eye tracked her movement, some with respect, most with barely concealed contempt. She was the crazy girl who talked to a dead phone and treated raids like reality television. Useful, maybe. Valuable, perhaps. But not quite human anymore.

"Good afternoon, team!" Her voice cut through the murmured conversations, bright and sharp. "Thank you all for joining today's strategic planning session. We're about to undertake our most significant expansion operation yet, and I wanted to make sure everyone understands their role in this exciting collaboration."

Someone snorted. Grace ignored it.

"South Portland's Crestview settlement represents everything we've been working toward." She moved to a wheeled whiteboard she'd had stolen from a school, flipping it to reveal a hand-drawn map of the target neighborhood. "Organized resistance, established infrastructure, approximately fifty to sixty individuals with defensive capabilities. This isn't a simple resource acquisition. This is a statement operation."

Kyle stood to her left, arms crossed, watching her perform. Sherman leaned against the wall to her right, his expression flat and unreadable. Between them, Grace commanded the room through sheer manic charisma, her delusions giving her a confidence that bordered on supernatural.

"We're dividing into three teams," she continued, tapping sections of her map with a pointer she'd found in a supply closet. "Alpha team under Sherman takes the western approach, securing the perimeter and cutting off retreat routes. Bravo team under Kyle comes in from the north, pushing toward the central residential area. Charlie team, that's our mobile reserve under Nate's command, positions here for rapid response."

She circled key intersections, drew arrows showing approach vectors, marked defensive positions the scouts reported. Every detail memorized, every variable calculated. Grace might be insane, but her intelligence remained razor-sharp when focused.

"Timing is critical," she said, moving to a second board showing a timeline. "We hit them at oh-two-hundred. Alpha moves first, secures the perimeter quietly. Bravo waits for my signal, then pushes hard and fast. We want shock and awe, overwhelming force that breaks their resistance before they can organize."

"What about civilians?" someone asked from the back. "Women and kids?"

Grace's smile never wavered. "We're liberating them, not harming them. Anyone who doesn't resist gets integrated into our community. Anyone who fights back gets…resolved. Simple community guidelines, really. Cooperate and thrive, resist and face accountability."

The euphemisms rolled off her tongue like she was discussing content moderation policies instead of life and death. Several men exchanged glances. Kyle's expression remained neutral, but something flickered in his eyes that looked almost like concern.

"What about leadership?" Sherman asked, his voice carrying the weight of someone who'd done this before. "Organized settlements always have someone calling shots. We take them out, the rest fold."

"Exactly!" Grace pointed at him with genuine enthusiasm. "Identify and neutralize leadership first. The scouts reported a man named Mitchell running the place. Former engineer, mid-fifties, commands respect from the community. He's priority target alpha. We remove him, their defensive structure collapses."

She didn't see Kyle's slight flinch at her casual discussion of assassination. Didn't register the uncomfortable shifting among some of the newer recruits. Grace existed in a bubble of performance where violence was just another tool for platform growth.

"Any questions?" She looked around the room, phone still held high like she was capturing every moment for her invisible followers.

"Yeah," a man named Dennis called out. "What's your role in all this, princess? You going to be doing any actual fighting, or just filming us while we risk our necks?"

Grace's smile hardened into something with sharp edges. "I'll be in mobile command, coordinating all three teams, ensuring tactical cohesion, and documenting this operation for…" She paused to glance at Kyle. "For strategic review. Command and control are crucial for operations of this scale. Someone needs to maintain the big picture perspective while you all handle ground-level execution."

"So you're hiding in a truck," Dennis said, his contempt obvious.

The room temperature dropped several degrees. Grace's expression shifted into something that made several men step back despite themselves. She lowered her phone slowly, her other hand moving to rest on the pink pistol at her hip.

"I prefer strategic positioning for optimal operational oversight," she said, her voice losing its performative brightness. "But if you'd like to challenge that decision, Dennis, we can resolve your concerns right now. I'm always open to feedback, though I prefer it in proper format rather than disruptive comments during team briefings."

Dennis held her gaze for a long moment, then looked away first. Grace's smile returned, bright and terrifying.

"Wonderful! Any other questions? No? Perfect. We deploy at twenty-three hundred hours. Get your gear ready, rest up, and remember: we're content creators building something revolutionary. Every action tonight contributes to our larger narrative. Make it count."

She turned back to her whiteboard, effectively dismissing the assembled crews. Men filed out in small groups, their conversations low and tense. Some looked excited. Others looked disturbed. A few looked at Grace like she was a bomb with an invisible timer, dangerous and unstable and absolutely capable of taking everyone down with her when she finally detonated.

Kyle remained after the others left, studying her whiteboard, his finger tracing the approach vectors she'd drawn.

"You're good at this," he said finally.

"Thank you!" Grace's enthusiasm returned, the brief darkness evaporating. "I've always been good at strategic planning. It's basically the same skill set as content calendars and engagement optimization, just applied to tactical operations instead of social media metrics."

"That's not a compliment." Kyle turned to face her, his expression serious. "You're good at convincing people to do terrible things. You're good at making murder sound like community building. That's a dangerous skill, Grace."

She met his eyes, her smile never wavering. "I prefer to think of it as leadership through authentic communication. But sure, your interpretation works, too."

Kyle shook his head, something between admiration and disgust in his expression. "You really don't see it, do you? What you've become. What we've all become by following your lead."

For just a moment, just a flash, Grace's mask cracked. Her smile faltered. Her eyes cleared of their manic brightness, showing something raw and terrified underneath. She saw herself reflected in Kyle's expression, saw the monster wearing her face, saw the blood on her hands that her mind kept insisting was just part of the authentic survival aesthetic.

Then her phone buzzed against her palm. Impossible, but she felt it. A notification. Her followers responding with overwhelming support. The validation she needed to keep performing, keep pretending, keep descending into whatever darkness waited at the bottom of her fractured psyche.

The moment passed. Her smile returned. The mask locked back into place.

"I see exactly what I need to see," Grace said softly. "And tonight, South Portland is going to see it, too."

Kyle left without responding. Grace turned back to her planning boards, her fingers tracing routes on the map, her mind already composing the narrative she would tell about tonight's operation. Liberation. Transformation. Authentic community building through necessary force.

She didn't let herself think about Mitchells, about the man, her friend's father, whose life she'd just casually marked for termination. Didn't acknowledge that somewhere in South Portland, families were eating dinner, children were getting ready for bed, people were living whatever version of normal they'd managed to construct in the apocalypse's wreckage.

Those details didn't fit her narrative. So, Grace simply edited them out, the way she'd edited out anything that complicated her performance since the moment Earl pulled her from the water.

The Queen of Likes preparing for her most ambitious content yet. The monster convinced she was the hero. The girl who drowned in more ways than one, now dragging everyone else down into the same dark water that claimed her sanity.

The sun set over Portland. Grace watched from her window, the blank screen of her dead phone catching the dying light. She scrolled through imaginary comments, narrating her plans to followers who would never hear her voice.

Below, forty-three men prepared for violence. Above, Grace prepared for content.

None recognized that the real horror wasn't what they were about to do to South Portland.

It was how easily they'd all convinced themselves it was justified.

Grace rode in the passenger seat of Kyle's truck, sandwiched between assault vehicles that carried men with weapons and intentions that would have terrified her in the before-times. Now she just adjusted her crop top's fit, making sure she caught the moonlight correctly.

"This is so exciting," she said, filming the convoy with her dead phone. "Strategic deployment at scale. Multi-team coordination. Comprehensive operational planning. This is exactly the kind of sophisticated content that separates amateur operations from professional platform development."

Kyle kept his eyes on the road, his hands tight on the steering wheel. Behind them, five trucks followed in loose formation. Sherman's convoy approached from a different route, maintaining radio silence. Everything coordinated with precision, Grace's insane vision transformed into tactical reality.

The South Portland neighborhood emerged from the darkness, residential streets that looked almost normal in the pre-dawn quiet. No fires here. No obvious destruction. Just the regular empty silence of suburbs where everyone stayed inside after dark, where survival meant avoiding attention.

Crestview Lane sat at the neighborhood's heart, a cul-de-sac development that probably cost a fortune before the world ended. Now it was a fortress, cars and debris barricading the entrance, defensive positions visible even in the dim light. Grace counted at least three guards on visible patrol, probably more in concealed locations.

"Alpha team in position," Sherman's voice crackled over Kyle's radio. "Perimeter secure. Ready on your signal."

Kyle glanced at Grace. She nodded, her smile bright despite the darkness.

"Execute," Kyle said into the radio.

Sherman's team moved first, shadows flowing through the streets, surrounding the barricaded neighborhood. Grace watched through her phone's camera, framing shots she would never actually capture, narrating action that only she could see.

"Notice the tactical precision," she whispered. "The coordinated movement. This is what happens when you invest in proper team development and establish clear operational hierarchies. Very professional. Very authentic."

Three minutes of tense silence. Then Sherman's voice again: "Perimeter secured. No alarm raised. Ready for Bravo deployment."

Kyle's truck rolled forward, engine idling low. Behind them, the other vehicles followed. They approached the barricade slowly, headlights off, using moonlight for navigation.

Grace's phone buzzed in her hand. Impossible, but she felt it. Her followers sending encouragement, praising her tactical genius, celebrating this moment of expansion. She smiled at the blank screen, reading comments that existed only in her fractured mind.

Fifty yards from the barricade, a shout rang out.

"CONTACT! VEHICLES APPROACHING!"

The settlement erupted into motion. Flashlights blazed to life. Figures ran to defensive positions. Someone fired a warning shot that cracked across the quiet night.

"Go!" Kyle barked into the radio.

His truck accelerated hard, the engine roaring. Behind them, the convoy surged forward. Grace grabbed the dashboard, her phone pressed against her face, capturing nothing, narrating everything.

"And here we see the initial engagement phase! Notice how the element of surprise has been compromised, forcing immediate adaptation." She squealed with excitement like it was some kind of amusement park ride. Almost giddy, she spoke to the blank phone. "Watch for some really compelling content development!"

Kyle's truck smashed through the barricade, metal screaming against metal, debris flying. He spun the wheel hard, positioning the truck to provide cover for the vehicles behind them. Men poured out, weapons raised, shouting commands that mixed with screams from the settlement.

Grace stayed in the truck, her phone raised, her eyes wide with manic excitement. Through the windshield, she watched Kyle's crew advance efficiently. Flashlights blazed. Gunfire cracked. People ran between houses, some toward cover, others toward defensive positions.

"Engaging target!" someone shouted over the radio.

Grace's attention snapped to the center of the settlement where a man organized the defensive response. Mid-fifties. Gray beard. It was him, priority target alpha.

"Kyle!" Grace shouted through the open window. "Center house! Gray beard! That's the leader!"

Grace bounced in her seat nodding enthusiastically.

Kyle redirected his team, pushing toward Mitchell's position.

For a moment, just a flash, Grace saw him clearly. Not a target. Not an obstacle to her expansion plans. Just a man trying to protect his community, his family, the people who trusted him to keep them safe. A father. A husband. A human being who deserved to live. Sudden clarity slammed into her and she felt crushed beneath the weight of it. Hannah's dad… Not a threat or a leader. Just a dad… her friend's dad.

Then her phone buzzed again. Validation flooding through her fractured mind. Her followers celebrating this moment, praising her strategic genius, confirming that everything she did was justified because it served the platform, because it created content, because her metrics were climbing even if only she could see them.

The moment passed, and he became a target again.

"Take him down," Grace said, her voice cold despite her bright smile. "Remove the leadership. Break their resistance."

Kyle's team advanced on their position but something was off. The people of the settlement had dispersed and were trying to run.

Around the settlement, resistance crumbled. Without Mitchell's coordination, defenders fell back in disorganized retreat. Some tried to flee. Sherman's perimeter team intercepted them. Others barricaded themselves in houses.

Sherman approached with a couple who'd tried to escape into the woods, forcing them to their knees on the street.

Grace climbed out of the truck, her combat boots crunching on broken glass and spent shell casings. She moved toward, her phone raised, documenting the tactical victory.

"This is the so-called leader?"

"I'm not…" Thomas Mitchell started but Grace waved him off.

"Listen, Grace. You know me. I'm Hannah's dad… Do you remember?"

The very mention of the name Hannah, her nemesis who tried to tear down her platform, it infuriated her and she spun back at him screaming, "You're in on it! You orchestrated it. Hannah couldn't have done it alone… it was YOU!"

She pulled out her pink handled pistol and emptied the magazine into the man on his knees begging her to come back. She didn't want to come back. She was viral. She was the star of her own reality media channel and he was not going to ruin that.

"Tom! TOM! Oh, God, no, please, no, TOM!" The screams were shrill and filled with raw emotion.

That's when she saw the woman.

Kyle's men restrained her, forcing her to stay on her knees. She continued struggling, her eyes locked on her husband's body, her screams becoming wordless animal sounds of loss.

Grace approached slowly, her phone camera focused on the woman's face. Mid-forties. Dark hair. Eyes filled with pain that went beyond physical. This was his wife. His widow now.

For a moment, the woman's face rippled. Skin pulled tight. Eyes sank into shadowed sockets. Mouth stretched too wide, showing too many teeth. A ghoul reaching for Grace with skeletal fingers, trying to drag her down into whatever hell she'd created through her actions.

Grace blinked hard. The vision cleared. Just a woman. Just a widow. Just another piece of collateral damage in Grace's expansion plan.

"Who are you?" Grace asked, lowering her phone slightly.

The woman looked up, her expression transforming from grief to pure hatred. "Grace, it's me, Rebecca. Rebecca Mitchell. What have you done?" Her sobs racked her body as she reached for the body on the ground before her.

Grace watched her with curiosity, her head tilting as she took in the scene. Her voice was quiet. It lost its earlier enthusiasm, taking on a somber tone. "Here we have it, my friends. The raw emotion you've all been asking for. Only here can you find content such as this."

She turned to the woman who was vaguely familiar, but her fractured mind couldn't grasp how she fit other than as a performer on the channel. "You're going to make for excellent ratings," she said flatly.

"And you're going to burn in hell for what you've done," she screamed at her.

Rebecca Mitchell. The name meant nothing to Grace's fractured mind. Just another civilian. Just another integration challenge.

"I'm Grace Reynolds," she said with false sympathy. "Community integration coordinator. I know this is traumatic, but we're here to help transition your settlement into our larger operation. Resistance only makes things harder for everyone. Cooperation leads to positive outcomes." Her eyebrows raised in feigned placation.

Rebecca spat at Grace's boots. "Go to hell."

Grace studied the woman's face, something tugging at the edges of her fractured memory. Something about those eyes. That bone structure. A familiarity she couldn't quite place.

Then it hit her with a force that took her breath away.

Hannah.

Rebecca Mitchell looked like Hannah Mitchell. Same eyes. Same cheekbones. Same defiant expression Grace remembered from Portsmouth, from the day Hannah and Maddie sabotaged her big break with those reality TV scouts.

"Oh, my God," Grace breathed, her eyes widening with sudden understanding. "You're Hannah's mother."

Rebecca's hatred intensified, confirming Grace's recognition. "You know us Grace. Don't you remember Hannah, my daughter? You spent many nights here through high school. What are you doing?"

Grace's smile spread across her face, wide and terrible and filled with manic joy. Her phone rose again, capturing this moment, this perfect unexpected gift that fate dropped into her lap.

"Know her?" Grace laughed, the sound high and brittle. "We were friends. Best friends. Until she betrayed me. Until she and Maddie destroyed everything I worked for. Until they sabotaged my big opportunity and left me to drown."

Rebecca's expression shifted from hatred to confusion to growing horror as she realized what Grace had become. "You suffered a break, Grace. They tried to save you. Can't you see?"

"All I can see is they thought they destroyed my break!" Grace's voice rose to a shriek, the imagined grievances flooding out. "I was about to go viral! Those scouts were going to make me famous! And Hannah and Maddie ruined it! They sabotaged me! They left me to die in that river!"

She moved closer to Rebecca, her phone shaking in her hand, her other hand moving to the pink pistol at her hip.

"But now," Grace's voice dropped to something almost tender, almost loving. "Now I have you. Hannah's mother. The perfect co-host for my revenge content."

Rebecca's face went pale. "They saved you. They stopped those men from—"

"THEY RUINED MY LIFE!" Grace screamed, spittle flying. "And now I have the perfect leverage! When I find them, when they see what I have, they'll understand what they did to me! This is perfect! This is exactly the kind of dramatic plot development my followers have been waiting for!"

Kyle appeared beside Grace, his hand on her shoulder, trying to pull her back from whatever edge she was racing toward. "Grace, we need to finish securing—"

"Get Sherman!" Grace interrupted, her eyes never leaving Rebecca's face. "I need him to build something. A cage. Mobile. Reinforced. Big enough for one person. I want it mounted on the lead truck where everyone can see it."

"What? Why—"

"Because Rebecca Mitchell is coming with us!" Grace's smile returned, bright and terrible. "She's not a prisoner. She's my co-host! She's going to help me create the most authentic revenge content my platform has ever seen!"

Rebecca lunged at Grace despite the men restraining her, her hands reaching for Grace's throat. "I'll kill you! I'll rip you apart with my bare hands!"

Grace just laughed, dancing back from Rebecca's grasping fingers. "That's exactly the kind of authentic emotional engagement I need! Yes! This passion! This rage! My followers are going to be so invested in your character development!"

She turned to Kyle, her expression manic and triumphant. "We're taking her. She goes in the cage. No exceptions. This is non-negotiable."

Kyle studied Grace's face, seeing something there that made even his hardened features show concern. "She's just a civilian. We don't need—"

"I NEED HER!" Grace grabbed Kyle's shirt, her face inches from his. "Don't you see? She's Hannah's mother! Hannah Mitchell from Portsmouth! The girl who destroyed my big break! This is fate! This is destiny! This is perfect narrative symmetry!"

She released him, spinning back to Rebecca, her phone raised again. "We're going to be such good friends, Rebecca. I'm going to tell you all about your daughter. About how she and Maddie sabotaged me. About how everyone will see what they did to me when I post this content. About how the truth always comes out… eventually!"

Rebecca's expression crumbled into despair, understanding finally settling in. This wasn't a random raid. This was something far worse, and there would be no reasoning with insanity this profound.

"Your day will come," Rebecca whispered, her voice carrying cold certainty despite her tears. "Somehow. And when it does, God help you."

Grace's smile widened impossibly. "I hope it does! That's the whole point! This is exactly the kind of dramatic content my platform needs! Hannah and Maddie finally seeing what their betrayal cost! Finally understanding what they did to me! It's perfect! It's beautiful! It's exactly what my followers deserve!"

She turned to address Kyle's crew, her voice carrying across the settlement. "Find Sherman! I want that cage built by morning! And someone secure the rest of the civilians! Anyone who resists gets creatively resolved! Anyone who cooperates gets integrated! Simple community guidelines!"

Men scattered to follow her orders, some with visible reluctance, others with the cold efficiency of those who'd stopped questioning their commander's sanity and found this apocalypse fun. The settlement's resistance broke completely, survivors emerging from houses with their hands raised, children crying, women begging for mercy.

Grace didn't see them. She only saw Rebecca, Hannah's mother, the perfect hostage, the ultimate revenge prop. Everything she'd worked toward since Earl pulled her from the water culminated in this moment.

She crouched before Rebecca, her phone between them, her smile bright despite the darkness in her eyes.

"You're going to help me tell my story," Grace whispered. "When I find Hannah and Maddie, when I finally get justice for what they did to me, you'll be there. The perfect witness. The perfect proof that I'm not the villain they made me out to be."

Rebecca spat in Grace's face. Grace just giggled, wiping the saliva away with her sleeve, her laughter high and broken and completely insane echoing into the early dawn.

Around them, South Portland burned with small fires. Bodies lay cooling in the street. Survivors huddled in terrified groups. Kyle's crew began the grim work of sorting the living from the dead, the useful from the expendable.

And Grace Reynolds, the Queen of Likes, stood in the center of the carnage she'd orchestrated, filming through her dead phone, narrating victory to followers who would never hear her voice, convinced she was the hero in a story where everyone else could see she was the monster.

The sun rose over South Portland, painting the sky in shades of orange and red that looked almost like blood. Grace stood beside Thomas Mitchell's body, her phone raised, her smile bright, her sanity shattered beyond any hope of recovery.

"Don't forget to like and subscribe," she whispered to the corpse at her feet.

Then she walked away to supervise Rebecca's cage construction, humming tunelessly, her combat boots leaving bloody prints across streets where families once lived in peace.

The Queen of Likes preparing for her ultimate content drop. The monster wearing an influencer's smile. The girl who drowned in the harbor and dragged her humanity with her into the dark water.

Behind her, Rebecca Mitchell wept for her murdered husband, for her endangered daughter, for the world that ended, not with nuclear fire, but with the quiet breakdown of a college girl's fragile mind.

And Grace just kept filming, kept performing, kept descending into whatever hell she'd constructed in the ruins of her psychosis.

Her followers understood. They loved her, and the likes flooded her feed with furious intensity.

They loved her!

Grace woke to sunlight streaming through the hotel window, her body tangled in sheets that smelled like sweat and Kyle. He was already gone, probably downstairs coordinating the morning patrols. Always working. Always on top of the production needs. But last night, pressed against the wall with her nails in his back, he'd been something else entirely.

She rolled over, reaching for her phone on the nightstand. The screen stayed black when she pressed the power button, but her followers' responses scrolled through her mind with perfect clarity.

The Queen is THRIVING

This relationship content is everything

#welovekyle

Power couple goals

Grace smiled, scrolling through imaginary comments while Rebecca Mitchell's distant weeping filtered through the window from the parking lot. In the days since South Portland. She'd had the cage mounted to the lead truck and used Rebecca for authentic hostage content that showed real psychological deterioration, but she had not yet broken to tell her where Hannah went.

Professional production values required commitment.

She dressed carefully, selecting the pink camo cargo pants and a black crop top that showed the bruises Kyle's fingers left on her ribs. Her fingers brushed against the tender area and she breathed deep running last night's intimate moments through her mind. She knew how much he loved her and their passion was always volatile. She wanted nothing more than to show everyone that he was hers and she was his.

"Sorry boys, I'm off the market," she said to the blank screen with a smirk.

Visual storytelling. Her followers appreciated attention to detail. The combat boots came next, laced tight, then the pink pistol tucked into her waistband where it pressed against her hip bone.

Camera ready.

Grace descended to the lobby, phone raised to capture the morning's opening shot. Sherman stood at the registration desk with Kyle, both men leaning over maps spread across the counter. They looked up as Grace approached, and something passed between them that made her pause.

Competition? She was pretty sure that's what it was. Two alpha males establishing hierarchy in her presence.

"Good morning, gentlemen." Grace moved between them, her body deliberately brushing Kyle's arm. Ownership. Territory. The apocalypse stripped away pretense. "Strategic planning session?"

"Discussing next steps," Kyle said, his voice neutral but his eyes tracking the bruises on her ribs. "We've cleared the immediate area. South Portland's integrated. We need new objectives."

Sherman's expression stayed carefully blank. "I have a suggestion, if *Her Majesty* is interested."

Grace turned to face him fully. The days of watching Sherman adapt taught her valuable lessons about reading people. He wanted something. Wanted it badly enough to play her game, use her titles, feed her platform in exchange for whatever goal drove him.

Smart man. Dangerous man. Not like Kyle, who burned with something raw, more honest in its brutality.

"I'm listening," Grace said.

"Cornish." Sherman tapped the map. "Town about thirty miles to the northwest. About a hundred people, maybe twenty fighters. They've fortified around a farm complex. Good resources. Water. Food. Medical supplies. Infrastructure that could support a larger operation."

Grace's heart rate accelerated. "You know this place?"

"Grew up there. Left after a skirmish when this all… uh when some rabble rousers closed down the feed store." Sherman's face remained neutral, but Grace caught the tightness around his eyes. "I know every road. Every defensive position. Every weakness."

"Why'd you leave?" Grace asked, her influencer instincts sensing story potential.

"Political disagreement." Sherman's smile held sharp edges. "The community leadership and I had different visions for survival strategy. They chose wrong. I chose to live."

Grace studied his face, reading between the words. Sherman was run out. Exiled. Humiliated. Now he was offering her the information to destroy the place that rejected him. Revenge wrapped in tactical information.

Beautiful narrative symmetry.

"Tell me more," Grace said, leaning forward.

Sherman's finger traced routes on the map. "The Thompson farm sits here, north of town. Main house, barn complex, multiple outbuildings. They've organized around it because the family spent years preparing for collapse. James Thompson runs operations. Other family, including son-in-law. He's former military. But mostly just farmers and town folk."

Grace studied the map, her mind racing. "And the town itself?"

"Small. Hardware store. Meeting hall. Residential neighborhoods." Sherman's finger moved. "The Foster family owns the hardware store."

Grace's breath caught. "Maddie Foster?"

Sherman glanced up, catching her reaction. "You know her?"

"Maddie Foster destroyed my platform." Grace's voice dropped to something cold and focused. "Her and Hannah Mitchell. They sabotaged my big opportunity. They tried to cancel me. They left me to drown in Portsmouth."

The memory flooded back with visceral intensity. The reality scouts. The intervention. Hannah and Maddie's concerned faces telling those producers Grace was unstable. The river. The dark water. Earl pulling her out and changing everything.

"Is she there? At the Thompson farm?" Grace asked, her hand moving to her phone.

"If she made it home after the collapse, she'd be in town at the hardware store or at the farm." Sherman watched her carefully, feeding information like kindling to fire. "Thompson's place is the stronghold. Protected by people who think they're secure."

Grace turned to Kyle, her smile widening impossibly. "We have to take Cornish."

"Grace." Kyle's voice carried a warning. "That's a significant operation. A fortified position. This isn't like the farmhouses we've been hitting."

"I don't care!" Grace grabbed Kyle's arm, her nails digging into his skin. "Don't you understand? Maddie Foster is there! Hannah Mitchell's probably there too, trying to warn them about us! They think they escaped! They think they're safe! This is perfect narrative convergence!"

Kyle pulled his arm free, but Grace caught the flicker of something in his eyes. Not quite concern. More like fascination with her intensity.

"Sherman," Kyle said, still watching Grace. "How current is your intelligence?"

"Several months old. Things change." Sherman straightened. "I'd need to scout it. Confirm defenses. Check population. Identify changes since I left."

"Do it." Grace's voice allowed no argument. "Take whoever you need. Get me current intelligence. I want to know everything about Cornish. And I want confirmation that Maddie Foster is there."

Sherman nodded, already calculating. "I'll need five men. Three days minimum."

"Two days," Grace countered. "I can't wait longer than that. My platform needs momentum. My followers expect regular content drops. Two days, then you report back with everything I need to plan the assault."

"Your Majesty." Sherman's use of the title came smoothly now. "Proper reconnaissance takes time. If we rush—"

"Two days." Grace's hand moved to her pistol. "You know Cornish. You know the terrain. You can get in and out fast. I want current intelligence in forty-eight hours."

Sherman glanced at Kyle, who gave a barely perceptible nod. "Two days. I'll leave tonight after dark."

"Good." Grace turned back to Kyle, her voice shifting to something lighter. "That gives us prep time. Team coordination. Equipment checks. All the essential pre-production content."

Sherman moved away to select his reconnaissance team, leaving Grace and Kyle alone at the desk. She stepped closer, her body pressing against his, her phone between them like a barrier that meant nothing.

"You think I'm crazy," she said, looking up at his face.

"I think you're obsessed." Kyle's hand found her hip, fingers pressing into the bruise he'd left there last night. "There's a difference."

"They tried to destroy me." Grace's voice came out raw. "They looked at me like I was broken. Like I needed fixing. Like my platform, my followers, my entire life meant nothing. They treated me like I was the problem."

"Maybe you were." Kyle's other hand moved to her throat, not squeezing, just resting there. "Maybe you still are. But you're my problem now."

Grace's breath quickened. Around them, men moved through the lobby on various errands, studiously ignoring their commander's increasingly volatile relationship with the Queen.

"Tonight," Grace whispered. "After Sherman leaves. I want you in my room."

"Demanding little thing." Kyle's thumb pressed against her pulse point. "What if I have other plans?"

"You don't." Grace's smile turned predatory. "You never do."

Kyle's answering smile held edges that excited and terrified her in equal measure. Then he released her and stepped back, his expression shifting to calculation. "I need to brief the men about perimeter security while Sherman's gone. You going to film Rebecca's suffering for a while?"

"Morning content session." Grace raised her phone like a camera. "Hostage diary day three. My followers need to see authentic emotional deterioration. Long-term character development requires commitment."

She moved toward the lobby doors, her combat boots loud against the tile floor. Behind her, Kyle watched with an expression that mixed disgust, desire, and a darker expression that Grace chose not to examine too closely.

The parking lot baked under the July sun. Rebecca's cage sat in the middle of the asphalt, no shade, no shelter from heat that made the metal bars burn to touch. Rebecca huddled in the corner, her clothes stained with sweat and worse. Three days of exposure left her sunburned, dehydrated, hollow-eyed.

Grace approached with her phone raised, filming from multiple angles. "Good morning, Rebecca! How are we feeling today? Any messages for your daughter?"

Rebecca didn't respond. She'd stopped responding yesterday, retreating into silence as her only remaining defense.

"The strong, silent treatment is very dramatic," Grace continued, circling the cage. "My followers appreciate authentic emotional responses, but stoic suffering works too. Very martyrdom-adjacent. Good character choice."

Grace crouched beside the cage, her face level with Rebecca's. "Hannah's time is coming, you know. She's probably already in Cornish by now. Warning them about the Queen. Trying to prepare defenses. Playing the hero, but it won't matter."

Rebecca's eyes flickered. A crack in the silence?

"Oh, that got your attention!" Grace's smile widened. "Yes, Hannah thinks she's so smart. Running to Cornish. Finding Maddie. Organizing resistance. But she doesn't know I have you. She doesn't know her mother is in a cage, waiting to be the centerpiece of my ultimate content drop."

"You're insane," Rebecca whispered, her voice raw from dehydration.

"I prefer *visionary*." Grace stood, phone still raised. "But we can agree to disagree. That's what makes good content. Conflicting perspectives. Authentic disagreement. Real stakes."

She walked away, leaving Rebecca to bake in her cage. Professional content creation required calculated cruelty. Grace's followers understood. They appreciated her commitment to authentic storytelling.

The next two days blurred together in a haze of preparation and waiting. Grace filmed everything. Equipment checks became content about operational readiness. Team briefings became behind-the-scenes footage of revolutionary planning. Rebecca's deterioration became a daily vlog documenting authentic suffering although she noted a young girl bringing her food and water. She decided not to stop her for the moment, because Rebecca was getting too weak for good content. Besides, she figured catching the dissent might make for a good livestream at a later time.

Kyle came to her room both nights, and their encounters grew more savage each time. Grace collected bruises like merit badges, wore them visible beneath her crop tops, documented them as proof of her platform's intensity. Kyle didn't talk about feelings or relationships or whatever had been between them. He just pressed her against walls, bit marks into her shoulders, turned her body into evidence of his own descent into darkness.

It worked for both of them. Two broken people breaking each other further.

On the afternoon of the second day, Sherman's vehicle returned. Grace stood on the hotel roof with her phone, filming the arrival, narrating the moment when her reconnaissance team brought back the intelligence she needed.

Sherman climbed out looking exhausted but triumphant. Grace descended the stairs three at a time, meeting him in the lobby where Kyle already waited.

"Report," Grace demanded, phone raised to capture every detail.

Sherman spread fresh maps across the desk, his finger tracing updated positions. "Cornish is more organized than when I left. The Thompson farm is the primary stronghold. Multiple defensive positions. Overlapping fields of fire. They've established patrol rotations, supply distribution networks, communication and medical. James Thompson runs operations. He's fortified the perimeter, cleared sight lines, positioned fighters at key locations."

"Population?" Kyle asked, leaning over the map.

"I was right at about a hundred total, but only twenty or so capable fighters. Mix of families, individuals, some former law enforcement."

Grace barely heard the tactical details. "Did you see her? Did you see Maddie Foster?"

Sherman nodded slowly. "Confirmed visual on a female matching your description. Dark hair, mid-twenties, working at the hardware store. Can't guarantee identity without closer observation, but timing and location match."

Grace's hands trembled. "What about Hannah? Hannah Mitchell?"

"Nothing concrete on that."

The room tilted. Grace grabbed the desk for balance, her phone clattering to the floor.

"Grace?" Kyle's hand found her elbow, steadying her. "You okay?"

"I'm perfect." Grace retrieved her phone, her smile returning with manic intensity. "This is perfect. We know Maddie is there, and if Hannah is going there, we'll be waiting."

She turned to face both men, her voice climbing with excitement. "We assault tomorrow night. I think we need to hit them full force. Coordinated teams. We take the whole town, capture Maddie and Hannah, bring them back here to the cage. Then they get to watch while we systematically dismantle everything."

"Tomorrow?" Kyle's voice carried doubt. "That's fast. We need more time to—"

"We don't have more time!" Grace grabbed his shirt, pulling him close. "Every hour we wait is an hour they prepare. An hour they organize. An hour they build defenses. We hit them tomorrow. While they think they're secure."

Sherman cleared his throat. "The teams aren't fully prepared for—"

"The teams are ready enough." Grace released Kyle, spinning to face Sherman. "You grew up there. You know every road, every position, every weakness. Guide us in. We hit them fast, hit them hard, take what we need before they can mount effective resistance."

She saw the calculation in Sherman's eyes. The revenge fantasy playing out behind his careful expression. He wanted Cornish to burn as badly as she wanted Maddie and Hannah to suffer.

"It's tactically viable," Sherman admitted. "If we move at night. Multiple assault teams. Coordinated strikes. The element of surprise multiplies our effectiveness."

Kyle studied both of them, recognizing he was outvoted. "Why are you trying to get our Queen killed? This isn't a rampage. It's an operation."

"What?" Sherman stepped back.

"There is no way we can properly mobilize and be there by tomorrow night. Why would you jeopardize our precious queen?"

Grace looked at Kyle, his face twisted with concern for her safety. "What do you mean?"

"Grace," Kyle said, stepping closer to her and shooting a look at Sherman. "We can't risk you. You're too important. We need to take our time, make sure we have everything in place and can move forward with fully rested resources. This needs to be a precision operation, babe."

Babe? He called her babe? Her safety was his first concern. She was sure of it. "Of course." Grace's smile widened. "Professional execution with authentic emotional stakes. That's what separates amateur content from platform-defining work.

"I'm sorry, Sherman… this time I think Kyle is right. I know you only want to press the platform to new heights, but we have to be strategic."

"Of course, my queen." Sherman's head dipped, but his eyes, contemptuous, never left Kyle.

She picked up her phone, immediately scrolling through imaginary responses from her followers.

Queen is READY

This content is going to be legendary

Can't wait for the Cornish arc

Grace spent the rest of the day filming preparation content. She interviewed team leaders about their assault roles. She documented equipment checks and ammunition distribution. She filmed Kyle coordinating defensive positions while Sherman poured over maps looking for staging areas.

As evening approached, Grace stood on the roof watching the sun set over Portland. Soon everything she'd worked toward would culminate. Maddie Foster. Hannah Mitchell. Both in cages. Both forced to watch their survival fantasy crumble. Both finally understanding what they'd done when they tried to cancel the Queen of Likes.

Rebecca's weeping drifted up from the parking lot, a soundtrack that never stopped.

Grace raised her phone to capture the sunset, the orange and red light painting the sky like blood. "Tomorrow, my beautiful followers," she whispered to the dead screen. "Tomorrow I start the new segment to give you the content you deserve. The finale. The climax. The moment when everything breaks."

Behind her, the roof access door opened. Kyle emerged, rifle slung across his back, exhaustion carved into his face.

"You should rest," he said. "Tomorrow's going to be brutal."

"I can't rest." Grace turned to face him. "I'm too excited. Too focused. Everything's finally coming together exactly how I envisioned."

Kyle moved closer, his hand finding her waist, pulling her against him. "You're going to get us all killed."

"Maybe." Grace's arms wrapped around his neck. "But at least it'll make incredible content."

His mouth found hers, brutal and claiming. They fell together against the roof access structure, Grace's phone clattering to the concrete, Kyle's hands leaving fresh bruises to match yesterday's marks. The sun set over Portland while they destroyed each other on the hotel roof, two broken people spiraling into darkness together.

When they finally pulled apart, Grace retrieved her phone and scrolled through blank screens showing imaginary engagement metrics from followers who would never see this content.

"Very soon," she whispered. "Cornish burns."

Kyle adjusted his rifle, his expression shifting back to tactical calculation. "Soon. Get some sleep. You'll need it."

He left her on the roof, descending into the hotel where armed men prepared for violence. Grace remained, watching the lights of the aurora, peppered with stars, emerging in the darkening sky, planning her ultimate performance.

The Queen of Likes preparing for her magnum opus. Maddie and Hannah would finally understand what happened when you tried to cancel someone's platform. Grace would deliver exactly what she promised. Authentic content. Real stakes. Genuine consequences.

Her followers would love it. They always loved her.

Grace smiled at the stars and whispered her sign-off to the darkness: "Don't forget to like and subscribe."

Grace woke to the smell of rotting food and human waste. The stench crawled through the hotel's ventilation system like something alive, invading every room, every hallway, every breath. She pressed her face into the pillow, trying to block it out, but the fabric reeked of mildew and sweat.

Three days since the rooftop water tanks stopped working. Three days since anyone could flush a toilet or wash properly. The gravity-fed system that made the hotel livable now sat empty, the pipes dry, the building transforming into something uninhabitable.

Grace rolled onto her back, staring at water stains spreading across the ceiling. Her phone lay against her chest, the screen black, the weight of it somehow comforting. She pressed the power button knowing nothing would happen, then held it against her ear anyway.

"Infrastructure challenges are just growth opportunities," she whispered to her invisible audience. "This is what authentic survival documentation looks like. Very educational. Very engaging for our community."

Kyle's voice drifted up from the lobby below, sharp with frustration. Someone else responded, words indistinct but tone angry. Grace sat up, her crop top sticking to her skin, her hair matted with grease she couldn't wash away. The pink camo pants felt stiff with accumulated dirt and dried sweat.

She moved to the window, pulling back curtains that left dust coating her fingers. Portland spread below, empty streets and gutted buildings and smoke rising from scattered fires. Her empire. Her platform. Her revolutionary community transformation project.

Except the building stank like an open sewer and people were starting to talk about leaving.

Grace grabbed her phone and descended the stairs, each step releasing new waves of stench from floors below. The lobby gathered maybe twenty-five people, Kyle at the center with Sherman beside him. Pete and Nate stood near the entrance, rifles held casually but ready. The three women from upstairs, Jennifer, Carol, and Amy, huddled together near the reception desk, their faces showing exhaustion beyond anything sleep could fix.

A new group clustered near the door. Five men Grace didn't recognize, their clothes cleaner than most, their weapons better maintained. The one in front stood there like a chubby mafia king, late forties maybe, salt-and-pepper hair cut short, pontificating some grand gesture on some insignificant detail Grace was sure.

"The building's done," Kyle was saying as Grace reached the bottom stair. "We can't stay here. The smell alone will make us a target from miles away."

"So we move." Sherman's voice carried authority that made Grace's spine stiffen. "Push north. Find somewhere with working infrastructure."

"Or we split up," someone else suggested. Grace recognized him as Monroe, one of the earlier recruits. "Smaller groups survive better than big targets."

"Nobody's splitting up." Grace's voice cut through the conversation, making heads turn. She moved into the center of the lobby, phone raised like a talisman. "This is a strategic operational adjustment, not a crisis. We're not scattering. We're expanding."

The new men turned to face her. The one in front studied Grace with an expression that made her pause. Not dismissive like most men looked at her. Not hungry, like Kyle sometimes got. Just calculating, like he was assessing a piece of equipment for usefulness.

"You must be Grace," he said, his voice carrying the kind of calm that came from years of giving orders. "Frank Wilson. Sherman told me about your operation here. Impressive work, from what I hear."

Grace's pulse quickened. New blood. New resources. New content potential. She moved closer, phone angling to capture his face even though nothing recorded.

"Sherman talked about you, too," she said, trying to remember what exactly Sherman had mentioned during yesterday's meeting. "You know the area northwest of here?"

"Know it better than I know my own reflection." Frank's smile held sharp edges. "Spent twenty years around Cornish before things went to hell. Know every road, every property, every farm worth taking."

"Taking." Grace rolled the word around her mouth. Direct. Honest. Not pretending to be something softer than what it was. She appreciated that.

Frank gestured to the men behind him. "These are my people. Davis, Lucas, Wrench, and we call the kid Rabbit. We've been working the territory between here and Cornish for weeks. Gathering intel. Making connections. Staying alive. Sort of…"

Grace studied the crew. Davis looked solid, built like someone who'd done physical labor his whole life. Lucas had that twitchy energy of someone always scanning for threats. Wrench stood quiet, hands resting on a rifle like it was an extension of his body. The nickname felt earned somehow, like the man could fix anything or break it with equal efficiency. The kid, Rabbit, couldn't have been more than twenty, all nervous energy and darting eyes.

"What brings you to Portland?" Grace asked, her influencer instincts sensing story potential.

"The smell, mostly." Frank's tone stayed deadpan. "Could catch wind of this place from five miles out. Figured anyone living in this stench was either desperate or organized. Wanted to see which."

"Maybe both," Kyle said, his voice holding a warning.

Frank's attention shifted to Kyle, recognition flickering across his face. "You must be the organizational person here. Sherman mentioned you. Said you know how to run operations without getting everyone killed."

"I try." Kyle's rifle stayed casual but ready. "What's your play here, Frank? You didn't come just to comment on our plumbing situation."

"Smart man." Frank moved to the reception desk, pulling a folded map from his jacket. "My play is survival. Your play is apparently empire building in a rotting hotel. Thought maybe we could help each other out."

Grace felt electricity shoot through her exhausted body. Empire building. He understood. He saw what she was creating. Not just random violence. Not just survival. Something bigger. Something revolutionary.

"Tell me more," she said, moving beside him as he spread the map across the counter.

Frank's finger traced routes north and west. "There's a farm here, just outside a town called Cornish. Thompson place. They've got wells, generators, food production, defensive positions. It's the most fortified location within fifty miles."

"Fortified means defended," Kyle said, his tone careful.

"They may be families and kids, but taking it head-on would be bloody."

"But?" Grace heard the unspoken word.

"But I know their patterns. Their weaknesses. Their blind spots." Frank looked up, meeting Grace's eyes directly. "And I've still got friends inside who'd open doors if the situation was right."

The room went silent. Grace scrolled through her dead phone, her mind already spinning content angles. Permanent base of operations. Real infrastructure. Sustainable resources. This was exactly what her platform needed to move beyond Portland's temporary staging.

"What do you want in return?" Kyle's voice cut through her excitement.

"Position in your operation. Resources for my crew. And a guarantee that when you take the farm, nobody gets hurt… At least, none who don't need to be." Frank's tone stayed level. "I'm not looking to massacre my former neighbors. Just replace leadership that's too weak to survive long-term."

Grace's phone buzzed in her hand. Not really. The vibration existed only in her mind. But the imaginary notification made her smile anyway.

Your followers love strategic expansion content!

Permanent base acquisition streams are trending!

The Queen knows opportunity when she sees it!

"We have a deal," Grace said before Kyle could object. "You provide intel and inside support. We provide the force to take the farm. Everyone wins except weak leadership that was going to fail anyway."

Frank extended his hand. Grace took it, feeling calluses and strength and the weight of commitment. This was real. This was happening. She was actually building something that could last beyond Portland's failing infrastructure.

"One condition," Frank added, his grip tightening slightly. "We move out fast. The longer you sit in this stinking building, the more people you lose to desertion or disease. We need to be mobile within days."

"Agreed." Grace pulled her hand back, already turning to address the room. "New operational directive. We're relocating to establish a permanent base of operations. Sherman, you're now working with Frank for reconnaissance. I want complete intelligence on the target location."

"Grace, wait." Kyle's hand closed around her arm, pulling her aside. His voice dropped to something only she could hear. "We don't know this guy. He shows up convenient, offers exactly what you need, and you're buying it without question?"

"He's useful," Grace said, echoing Kyle's own logic back at him. "And he's motivated by the same things that motivate everyone. Power. Position. Resources that don't smell like a sewer."

"Or he's playing you. Leading you into a trap. Using your need for permanent staging against you."

Grace pulled free, meeting his eyes directly. "Then we verify his information. Send Sherman with him. They scout together. Either Frank's intel is good, or we know he's lying. Either way, we're better informed than staying here breathing shit."

Kyle studied her face for a long moment. "You're not going to let this go, are you? The permanent base idea. Even if the scouting comes back negative."

"Why would I let it go?" Grace gestured around the lobby, at the stench, at the water stains, at the deteriorating infrastructure. "This place is dying. We need somewhere sustainable. Somewhere we can build something that lasts beyond just surviving another day."

Kyle's expression shifted into something between concern and resignation. "Fine. But we plan it right. No rushing in blind."

"Obviously." Grace turned back to the room, raising her voice. "Frank, Sherman, Kyle. Tactical planning sessions start now. Everyone else begins convoy preparation. We move in three days maximum."

The lobby exploded into activity. People scattered to their assigned tasks, relief visible on faces that no longer had to breathe the building's stench for much longer. Frank and his crew moved toward the reception desk where Kyle was already spreading detailed maps. Sherman joined them, his expression showing satisfaction that Frank's arrival validated his earlier suggestions about moving.

Grace stood in the center of it all, phone raised, filming the organized chaos through her dead camera lens. This was content. This was empire building. This was exactly what her followers craved.

A scream cut through the activity. Female. Desperate. Coming from the basement.

The room froze. Grace's head snapped toward the stairwell leading down. The basement where they kept prisoners. Where people who resisted integration waited to either comply or die.

Kyle moved first, rifle coming up, already heading for the stairs. Grace followed, her phone still recording, her heart rate accelerating with anticipation. Something was happening. Something was wrong. Something that would create compelling dramatic content.

The basement reeked worse than the upper floors. No windows. No ventilation. Just concrete walls and makeshift cells created from storage cages and chain-link fencing. Five prisoners huddled in various states of compliance, their faces showing the progression from defiance to defeat that Grace found so satisfying to document.

Except one cage sat empty. Door hanging open. Chain cut.

"What happened?" Kyle's voice cracked like a whip.

Pete stood near the empty cage, his face pale, blood running from a cut above his eye. "Two of them got out. Maybe twenty minutes ago. They had a knife. Grabbed it off Nate when he came down to check on them."

"Which prisoners?" Grace's voice came out steady despite the rage building in her chest.

"Mrs. Henderson and that teenage girl Zoe. Both from the South Portland raid."

Grace's breath caught. Mrs. Henderson. The other woman captured during the Crestview operation. Older, maybe fifties, defiant even in restraints. And Zoe. A teenage girl swept up in the raid, maybe sixteen, dark hair, quick eyes. Not Rebecca Mitchell. Hannah's mother still sat in her cage outside in the parking lot where Grace could monitor Rebecca's deterioration. But two prisoners from the same raid. Escaped. No doubt running to warn Cornish of what was coming.

"How?" The single word emerged cold enough to make Pete flinch.

"The younger one, Zoe, distracted Nate. Mrs. Henderson moved fast for someone her age. Grabbed his knife, cut through the zip-tie locking them in, and they ran." Pete gestured to the basement's exterior access, a metal door that led to the alley behind the building. "They went out that way. By the time we realized what happened, they were gone."

Grace moved to the empty cage, her fingers trailing over the cut piece of plastic. This happened recently. Maybe the women were still close. Maybe they could be recovered.

"Which direction?" Kyle asked, already moving toward the exterior door.

"North. Nate saw them heading toward the bridge." The woman who'd come to bring the meal and screamed made him wince when she pressed a rag against his bleeding scalp. "They moved fast."

"Toward that farm." Grace's voice stayed flat, her mind already calculating implications. "They're running somewhere they think will protect them. Somewhere organized."

Kyle's expression shifted into something between concern and calculation. "If they reach organized settlements before we're ready, they'll spread word about your operation. Make every target between here and Cornish defensive instead of vulnerable."

"Then we catch them." Grace turned to face the assembled group, her phone rising to capture everyone's reactions. "Go! I want those women found and brought back. Alive if possible. Dead if necessary. But I want proof they didn't reach anywhere that matters."

"Grace." Kyle's hand caught her arm again. "We don't have resources for a manhunt. We need everyone focused on convoy prep and planning."

"We make resources." Grace pulled free, moving toward the stairs. "Frank, your crew is freshest. Take them and sweep the route. Sherman, you know the territory. Coordinate with Frank. Find those women before they reach anywhere organized."

Frank exchanged a glance with Sherman, something passing between them Grace couldn't quite read. Then he nodded, already gesturing to his crew. "We'll need vehicles. Weapons. Maps of the route."

"Take whatever you need." Grace climbed the basement stairs, her mind already spinning scenarios. "Bring them back within twenty-four hours and I'll double your position in the new operation. Fail, and you explain to me why I should trust your intel about the farm when you couldn't even catch two unarmed women."

The threat hung in the air. Frank's expression tightened but he nodded, recognizing the test being presented. Prove his value or lose his place in Grace's expanding operation.

The group dispersed, Frank and Sherman organizing the pursuit while Kyle coordinated convoy preparations. Grace stood in the lobby, scrolling through imaginary engagement metrics.

"Temporary setback," she whispered to her invisible followers. "Content interruption. But every good narrative needs complications. This just makes the resolution more satisfying when it comes."

Someone coughed behind her. Grace turned to find one of the basement prisoners being hauled upstairs by Nate. A younger man, maybe mid-twenties, his face bruised from resisting capture during some earlier raid Grace barely remembered.

"He's talking," Nate said, shoving the prisoner forward. "Wants to make a deal."

Grace studied the man with cold assessment. "What kind of deal?"

"Information for release." The prisoner's voice shook but held determination. "I know things about the women who escaped. Things you need to hear."

"I'm listening." Grace moved closer, phone angling to capture his face.

"Mrs. Henderson, the older woman. She's not just some random survivor from South Portland." The prisoner swallowed hard. "They spoke of someone named Maddie and a town called Cornish. Planned to find another girl. Don't recall the name but began with an H. Hillary maybe or Hailey?"

"Could it be Hannah?"

"Yeah, maybe. I will do whatever you want. Can I get out?"

"Integrate him into the production crew," she said, waving him and Nate away.

The information clicked into place in Grace's mind. Mrs. Henderson wasn't just a random prisoner. Letting her escape wasn't just losing a hostage. It was creating an enemy who could organize resistance.

Grace felt the rage building again, hot and consuming. Two women. Two escaped prisoners. Creating problems that could undermine everything she'd built.

"He's right, you know. Mrs. Henderson reaching Cornish changes everything. Makes your permanent base target into an active threat instead of passive opportunity," Kyle said.

"Then Frank and Sherman catch them." Grace moved to the windows, staring out at Portland's dead streets. "Or we adjust our timeline. Hit the farm before they can organize proper resistance."

"That's rushing. Rushing gets people killed."

"Everything gets people killed." Grace turned to face him, seeing concern in his expression. "At least this way, we control the timing instead of letting escaped prisoners dictate our strategy."

Kyle studied her for a long moment. "You're spiraling. I can see it. This obsession with permanent infrastructure, with controlling every variable, with building something that can't fall apart. It's consuming everything else. Making you sloppy."

"I'm not sloppy." But even Grace heard the weakness in her voice. The doubt creeping in around the edges of her delusion. "I'm strategic. I'm building something revolutionary. I'm creating content that will define apocalypse survival narrative."

"You're building something." Kyle's hands moved to her face, forcing her to meet his eyes. "I'm just not sure it's what you think it is."

The words should have triggered anger. Should have made her defensive. Instead, they just made Grace tired. Tired of performing. Tired of maintaining the delusion. Tired of the constant energy it took to filter reality through engagement metrics that didn't exist.

"I need them found," Grace whispered, her forehead dropping against Kyle's chest. "I need to know escaped prisoners can't just run to Cornish and warn everyone about my operation."

"They're two women on foot with no supplies." Kyle's arms wrapped around her, his voice rumbling against her ear. "Even if they reach settlements, who's going to believe their stories? Two random survivors showing up claiming some crazy girl in Portland is building an army? Sounds like paranoid fantasy."

Grace pulled back enough to see his face. "Unless Mrs. Henderson convinces them in Cornish. Convinces them she's someone whose word carries weight."

"Then we adapt." Kyle's smile held sharp edges. "Frank's scouting mission becomes pursuit and reconnaissance. Two objectives instead of one. Either they catch the women or they gather enough intel to make their warnings irrelevant."

The logic penetrated Grace's spiraling thoughts. Kyle was right. Frank would prove his value by either catching the escaped prisoners or providing intelligence that made their advance knowledge meaningless. Either way, Grace's operation could stay on track.

"Okay." Grace stepped back, adjusting her crop top, trying to reclaim some composure despite the setting. "Frank and Sherman leave within the hour. Timeline is three days maximum. They either return with Mrs. Henderson and Zoe or at the very least a new staging location."

"Agreed." Kyle's hands moved to her hips, pulling her closer despite the sweat and dirt and stench coating both of them. "And Grace? When they get back, when we have solid intelligence, we plan this right. No rushing. No letting rage or fear drive decisions."

"When have I ever let rage drive decisions?" But Grace's smile held recognition of the lie even as she spoke it. "I'm perfectly rational. Perfectly strategic. Perfectly in control."

"Sure you are." Kyle's mouth found her neck, teeth scraping against her pulse point. "That's why you're shaking right now."

Grace realized he was right. Her hands trembled. Her breathing came too fast. The escaped prisoners triggered something deeper than just concern. Triggered the fear that everything she'd built was fragile. Temporary. One escaped warning away from collapse.

"Make me stop thinking about it," she whispered against Kyle's shoulder.

"That's what I'm here for." Kyle's hands tightened on her hips, guiding her toward the stairs.

His body pressed her against the wall of her room with the building's stench surrounding them. Grace clawed at Kyle's shoulders, his back, anywhere she could reach. He moved with the kind of rough possession that left marks, left bruises, left evidence that this wasn't romance but collision.

Neither of them spoke. Neither of them needed to. They were both chasing the high that came from someone seeing your madness and wanting you anyway.

When it was over, they stayed pressed together, both breathing hard, both covered in sweat and dirt and each other. Kyle's hand moved to Grace's face, his thumb tracing her cheekbone with surprising gentleness.

"They'll find them," he said quietly. "Frank and Sherman. They'll either catch the women or verify they didn't reach anywhere that matters. Either way, your operation stays secure."

Grace wanted to believe him. Wanted to trust that two escaped prisoners couldn't undermine everything she'd built. But the doubt lingered. The fear that Mrs. Henderson and Zoe were already miles north, spreading stories about the Queen of Likes and her army of the damned.

"What if they don't?" Grace's voice came out small. Vulnerable. "What if the women reach settlements before we're ready? What if they organize resistance? What if everything falls apart?"

"Then we adapt." Kyle's grip tightened on her face. "We find a different target. Build a different base. Your operation isn't dependent on one specific farm. It's dependent on you. Your vision. Your ability to keep performing even when everything goes sideways."

The words should have been comforting. Should have reinforced Grace's sense of control. Instead, they just highlighted how much of her empire existed only in her fractured mind. How much depended on delusion and performance and people willing to enable her madness.

"I'm tired," Grace whispered. "I'm so tired of performing. Of filtering everything through engagement metrics. Of pretending my followers exist."

Kyle pulled back, studying her face with concern. "Grace. Listen to me. You can't afford clarity right now. Not with Frank's crew watching. Not with the convoy move coming. You need to stay in character. Stay functional. Can you do that?"

Grace felt the familiar pull. The handlers pulling her back from the edge of sanity before she broke completely. Kyle doing what Pete and Nate did. What all of them did. Keeping her crazy enough to be useful but not so broken she became a liability.

"I can do that." Grace's voice strengthened. "I'm fine. Just momentary weakness. Content creator burnout. Very common in high-pressure production environments."

"That's my girl." Kyle's smile held relief but his eyes held doubt. "I'll send up some wash water for you. Now get cleaned up. Frank and Sherman leave in thirty minutes. You need to brief them personally. Show them you're in complete control."

Grace nodded, already moving toward the scattered clothes on her floor. Kyle was right. She couldn't afford to break down right now. Couldn't let escaped prisoners and failing infrastructure and the building's overwhelming stench crack the performance she'd maintained since Portsmouth.

She was the Queen of Likes. The revolutionary leader. The platform that would redefine apocalypse survival content.

And if that required pretending two escaped women didn't terrify her? Required filtering doubt through engagement metrics? Required performing confidence she didn't feel?

Well. That's what she'd been doing since Earl pulled her from the harbor anyway.

Grace descended to the lobby thirty minutes later, her crop top changed, her hair pulled back, her phone held like a weapon. Frank and Sherman stood by the entrance with their assembled pursuit team. Davis, Lucas, Wrench, and Rabbit, along with Sherman's best guys.

"Operational briefing," Grae announced, moving to stand before them. "Your mission has two objectives. Primary is prisoner recovery. Mrs. Henderson and the girl, Zoe, must be located and returned or confirmed neutralized. Secondary is target reconnaissance. I want complete intelligence of the farm. Defenses. Personnel. Weak points. Everything."

Frank nodded, his expression professional. "Timeline?"

"Three days maximum. You either return with prisoners or return with intelligence that makes prisoners irrelevant." Grace's voice stayed level. "Fail both objectives and you're no longer part of this operation."

"Understood." Frank gestured to his crew. "We'll move fast. Cover maximum territory. Either catch them or verify they didn't reach anywhere organized."

Sherman stepped forward, maps already spread across the reception desk. "Northern route has three possible destinations. Small settlements at intervals. The farm location is here." His finger tapped the map. "Thirty miles. Two women on foot could make it in three days if they pushed hard and knew the territory."

"Then you move faster." Grace moved closer to the map, studying the routes. "Vehicles give you an advantage. Use it. Catch them before they reach Cornish."

The pursuit team gathered their gear, checking weapons, loading vehicles. Grace filmed everything through her dead phone, narrating the deployment for her imaginary followers, but her enthusiasm was weakening.

"Strategic pursuit operations," she whispered to her invisible audience. "Professional rapid response. This is what revolutionary platform security looks like."

Kyle appeared beside her, his presence solid and grounding. "They'll find them. Or they won't. Either way, we move forward."

Grace nodded, watching the pursuit team disappear into Portland's empty streets. Two vehicles. Seven men. Hunting two women who represented everything Grace feared.

The building's stench wrapped around her like a physical presence. Reminding her that nothing was permanent. Nothing was secure. Everything she'd built could collapse with one escaped warning reaching the wrong ears.

"Three days," Grace said quietly. "In three days we either have prisoners or intelligence or a completely new strategy."

"In three days we're out of this stinking building either way." Kyle's hand found the small of her back. "That alone makes it worthwhile.

Grace leaned against him, feeling the exhaustion that came from constant performance. From filtering reality through delusion. From building empires in her mind that barely existed in the world around her.

But she was the Queen of Likes. And queens didn't break. Didn't falter. Didn't let escaped prisoners undermine revolutionary platforms.

So Grace raised her phone, scrolling through imaginary metrics, and smiled for the followers who existed only in the broken spaces of her mind.

The industrial park sprawled across cracked asphalt like a graveyard for machinery. Rusted shipping containers stacked in uneven towers. Gutted warehouses with walls tagged in faded graffiti. Vehicle husks stripped for parts scattered across the lot. Everything coated in dust and bird shit and the particular decay that came from abandonment.

Grace stood in the truck bed, phone raised, filming the convoy's arrival through her dead camera lens.

"Location scouting is so important for platform development," she narrated to her invisible audience. "This automotive graveyard aesthetic is absolutely perfect. You literally could not hire set designers to create anything this authentic. Very gritty. Very wasteland chic."

The convoy rolled to a stop, five vehicles arranged in a defensive semicircle around the lot's center. Kyle killed the engine, stepping out with his rifle already scanning the perimeter. Pete and Nate moved in behind him, establishing defensive positions, checking sight lines, securing the area.

Grace jumped from the truck bed, her combat boots crunching on broken glass. "Defensive perimeter establishment," she continued filming. "Professional operations. This is what revolutionary platform security looks like."

But Grace's attention fixed on the flatbed truck at the convoy's center. On the cage welded to its bed. On Rebecca Mitchell's crumpled form inside.

The cage mounted where everyone could see. Maximum visibility. Maximum psychological impact. Grace approached slowly, phone capturing every angle. Rebecca didn't move. Didn't respond. Just lay curled in the cage's corner, her clothes stained with sweat and waste, her skin burned raw by July sun, her lips cracked and bleeding from dehydration.

For a moment, just a flash, Grace saw her clearly. Not a hostage or leverage against Hannah. Just a woman. A mother. Someone's wife. Someone who deserved basic humanity even in the apocalypse's wreckage.

Then Grace's phone buzzed. Not really. But the sensation felt real enough to chase away the moment of clarity. Her followers responding. Praising her commitment to authentic content. Celebrating the revolutionary nature of her platform.

"Morning check-in with our community integration participant," Grace said brightly, circling the cage. "Rebecca's been with us about a week now. Experiencing firsthand what authentic survival lifestyle looks like. Very immersive. Very method."

Rebecca's eyes opened. Red. Swollen. Filled with hatred that transcended words. She tried to speak but her throat produced only a rasping croak.

"Hydration is so important," Grace continued, her tone cheerful. "Nate! Bring water! We need Rebecca functional for today's content."

Nate appeared with a bottle, his expression carefully neutral. He'd stopped questioning Grace's decisions weeks ago. Just executed orders. Kept his head down. Like most of the others, he survived by not thinking too hard about what they'd become.

He passed the bottle through the cage bars. Rebecca grabbed it with trembling hands, drinking in desperate gulps that made her choke and cough. Water ran down her chin, wetting her filthy shirt, washing pale streaks through the grime coating her skin.

"Excellent engagement," Grace filmed the scene. "Real emotional authenticity. This is the kind of raw human experience my followers crave."

Kyle appeared beside her, his voice low enough only Grace could hear. "She's not going to last much longer like this. Another day or two and she'll be dead."

"Then we better start on her integration today." Grace's smile never wavered. "I need her functional. Compliant. Ready to help create content when we reach Hannah."

"Grace." Kyle's hand found her elbow, pulling her away from the cage. "Listen to me. Rebecca's not going to break. She's not going to help you. She's Hannah's mother. She'd rather die than cooperate."

"Everyone breaks eventually." Grace pulled free, her voice rising with manic certainty. "It's just a matter of finding the right approach. The right incentive structure. The right community building exercises."

She turned back to the cage, addressing Rebecca directly. "Here's how this works. I'm going to let you out for integration sessions. We're going to have conversations. Build rapport. Establish mutual understanding. And you're going to learn that cooperation leads to positive outcomes while resistance just makes everything harder."

Rebecca spat bloody water at Grace's feet. "Go to hell."

Grace's smile widened. "Perfect! That defiant energy is exactly what makes a great reel. But trust me, Rebecca. By the end of this week, you'll be thanking me for these opportunities. You'll understand that I'm not the villain. I'm the hero who's been misunderstood."

She gestured to Pete. "Get her out. Clean her up. Make her presentable. We start our first session in an hour."

The cage door opened. Rebecca tried to stand, collapsed immediately, her legs unable to support her weight after days of confinement. Pete caught her, half-carrying her toward one of the warehouses where Kyle's crew established makeshift living quarters.

Grace filmed the whole thing, narrating for her imaginary followers. "Community member transition from orientation to integration. This is such an important phase. Very transformative. Very authentic journey content."

She turned to survey the industrial park, already planning. The warehouse could serve as production space. The containers provided storage. The open lot offered perfect staging for future content. This was temporary. Just a waypoint before Cornish. But Grace would make it work.

Her phone buzzed again. Grace scrolled through imaginary metrics, checking engagement rates that existed only in her fractured mind. The numbers climbed. Comments flooded in. Her followers loved this direction. Loved the gritty aesthetic. Loved watching Rebecca's authentic struggle.

They loved her.

"Okay!" Grace raised her voice, addressing the assembled followers. "Production briefing! Kyle, establish perimeter security. We don't need any fans crashing our content. Nate, inventory supplies. Pete, prepare the warehouse. Everyone else, time to set up camp. We're here for at least a week so make it comfortable."

People scattered to their tasks, some with visible relief at having something concrete to do, others with the hollow-eyed exhaustion of those who'd stopped questioning where this convoy was heading or why.

Grace moved toward the warehouse, her phone still raised, filming everything. Professional documentation. Revolutionary platform development. Content that would define apocalypse survival narrative.

Inside, the warehouse stretched vast and empty. Broken windows let in dusty afternoon light. Graffiti covered concrete walls. Old machinery sat rusted in corners. The space smelled like oil and decay and pigeons that nested in the rafters.

"Perfect production environment," Grace narrated, spinning in a slow circle. "Raw. Unfiltered. Authentic wasteland aesthetic that you literally cannot manufacture. My followers are going to eat this up."

Kyle appeared in the doorway, backlit by the setting sun. "Grace. We need to talk about the plan."

"The plan is perfect." Grace lowered her phone, moving to where sunlight caught her best angle. "We wait for Frank and Sherman to return with intelligence on Cornish. We use that week to integrate Rebecca. Then we move on the farm with maximum force and Hannah's mother as leverage. Simple. Effective. Revolutionary."

"And if Frank doesn't come back?" Kyle's voice held

something Grace couldn't quite identify. Concern maybe. Or resignation. "If Mrs. Henderson reached Cornish already? If they know we're coming?"

"Then we adapt." Grace's smile returned, bright and terrible. "That's what makes it good. The unpredictability of things—complications, obstacles. Rising tension leading to climactic resolution. My followers understand narrative structure."

Kyle studied her face for a long moment. "You know they don't exist, right? Your followers. Your platform. It's all in your head."

The words should have triggered rage. Should have made Grace defensive. Instead, they just slid off her fractured psychosis like water off glass. Of course her followers existed. She saw their comments. Felt their engagement. Heard their validation with every decision she made.

"You're just jealous," Grace said, moving closer to him. "Because I have something you don't. A purpose. A vision. A platform that matters beyond just surviving another day."

"I have you." Kyle's hand moved to her face, his thumb tracing the line of her jaw. "And you're more exciting and terrifying than anything the apocalypse could throw at me."

Grace rose on her toes, pressing her mouth to his. The kiss was rough, desperate, tasting like dust and violence and the particular madness they'd built together. Kyle's hands moved to her hips, pulling her closer, his fingers finding the bruises he'd left two nights ago and pressing until she gasped against his mouth.

"Not here," Kyle said, his voice rough. "People are watching."

"Let them watch." Grace's hands worked at his belt. "Let them see what a power couple looks like. This is exactly the kind of authentic relationship content my followers crave."

But Kyle pulled away, his expression shifting back to the calculating leader she appreciated. "Later. Tonight. After you deal with Rebecca. Right now, we have a convoy to secure."

He left before Grace could protest, disappearing into the industrial park's gathering shadows. Grace stood alone in the warehouse, her phone in hand scrolling through imaginary notifications that praised her commitment to content creation even in the apocalypse's wreckage.

Outside, the convoy settled into camp mode. Fires started. Food cooked. People moved through routines that found their way into everyday life now. Grace watched through the broken windows. The phone raised, filming the authentic survival community she'd built.

A vehicle approached from the south, engine noise carrying across the empty lot. Grace tensed, hand moving to the pink pistol at her hip. But Kyle waved the truck through, recognizing whoever drove.

Two men climbed out. Brothers maybe, based on the similar build and features. Both in their twenties. Both carrying rifles casually slung over their shoulders. They looked at ease and it intrigued Grace. She descended from the warehouse, phone raised, moving to intercept them.

"Hello! Welcome to our community staging area! I'm Grace Reynolds, platform director and content coordinator. You are?"

The taller one spoke first. "Sean… Sean Burke. This is my brother Tommy. We heard that you were building some kind of community and thought we could help."

Grace's pulse quickened. New blood. New resources. New content potential. She moved closer, phone angling to capture their faces.

"Cornish intel is exactly what we need right now. Do you know anything about the area? What's your background? Military experience? Tactical training? Previous apocalypse survival credentials?"

Tommy Burke shifted uncomfortably. "We're from there. Know the territory. Know the layout. That information valuable?"

"It's absolutely valuable!" Grace's enthusiasm ramped into that manic pitch her followers loved. "Strategic partnership opportunities! Collaborative content creation! This is exactly the kind of authentic community building my platform requires!"

She circled the brothers, phone filming from multiple angles. "Okay, so first things first. We need to work on your aesthetic. That whole generic raider look is so last season. Very derivative. We need to establish personal branding that distinguishes you from standard wasteland survivors."

Sean and Tommy exchanged glances. Kyle appeared beside Grace, his expression warning her to slow down, but Grace was already spinning with possibilities.

"Strategic Planning with the Burke brothers!" she announced. "Exclusive tactical content! Military consultant energy meets apocalypse lifestyle branding! My followers are going to eat this up!" She hopped around them and squee'd.

"We're not consultants," Sean said carefully. "We just thought we might join your operation. Help if we can."

"It helps tremendously!" Grace grabbed Sean's arm,

pulling him toward better light. "Stand here. No, three inches left. The backlight is wrong. We need authentic yet cinematic wasteland vibes for your introductory content."

Tommy cleared his throat. "Ma'am, we're not here for photos. I don't understand what is—"

Grace lowered her phone slightly, actually listening for once. "Photos? Is that what you think we're doing? Taking photos?"

Grace studied both brothers with calculating assessment. They knew Cornish. Knew the terrain. Offered exactly what her operation needed. But something in Tommy's voice made her pause. Guilt maybe. Or regret. Like he was confessing something rather than just providing tactical intelligence.

"Why help us?" Grace asked. "What's your angle?"

Sean and Tommy exchanged another look. Some silent communication passed between them. Then Sean spoke, his voice flat.

"We killed someone in Cornish. George Miller. During a raid on the pharmacy. Thompson's people have been hunting us ever since. Figured joining up with you might… Well, helping you take the farm might earn us protection."

The confession hung in the dusty air. Grace's phone rose again, filming their faces, capturing this moment of authentic vulnerability that made such compelling content.

"George Miller," Grace repeated. "Who was he?"

"Pharmacy owner. Old guy. Tried to stop us from taking medical supplies." Tommy's voice held something broken. "Sean shot him. I helped carry the supplies. We're both responsible."

Grace's smile widened. "That's perfect! Authentic moral

complexity! Real consequences for survival decisions! This is exactly the kind of character development my followers crave!"

She turned to Kyle. "We're keeping them. The Burke brothers bring tactical knowledge plus authentic emotional stakes. This collaboration is going to break all engagement metrics!"

Kyle studied the brothers. "You understand what you're signing up for? Grace's operation isn't standard raiding. It's something else entirely." He tilted his head toward her and raised his eyebrows.

"We need protection," Sean said. "If taking Cornish earns that, we're in."

"Excellent!" Grace grabbed her phone, immediately planning content angles. "We'll do promotional shoots tomorrow. Behind-the-scenes tactical planning. Exclusive interviews about the Miller killing. Very authentic. Very raw. My followers appreciate moral ambiguity in apocalypse narratives."

She turned back to the warehouse where Rebecca was being cleaned up for integration sessions. "But first, community building exercises. Kyle, bring the Burke brothers. I want them to see authentic integration methodology. Very educational. Very professional development content." She paused and looked back at them a moment. Eyeing them up and down before spinning on her heel and heading into the warehouse. "Kyle, remind me that we need to send these two to wardrobe for a makeover."

Grace strode toward the warehouse, phone raised, narrating her approach for imaginary followers. Behind her, the Burke brothers followed with visible reluctance, already regretting whatever deal they'd just made.

Inside, Pete had Rebecca sitting on a makeshift chair. Someone found clean clothes. Gave her water. Let her wash the worst of the filth from her skin. She still looked half-dead. Sunburned. Dehydrated. Hollow-eyed with exhaustion and despair. But conscious. Functional enough for Grace's purposes.

"Rebecca!" Grace's voice echoed through the warehouse. "Looking so much better! Ready for our first integration session?"

Rebecca's eyes tracked Grace with pure hatred. "I'll never help you."

"That's what they all say at first." Grace moved closer, phone filming from multiple angles. "But integration isn't about force. It's about building authentic community connections. About finding shared values. About transforming resistance into engagement."

She gestured to the Burke brothers. "See, I'm not a monster. I'm a community builder. These men just joined our operation. Tomorrow they'll be creating exclusive tactical content. Next week they'll help us take Cornish. That's what positive engagement looks like."

Rebecca spat at Grace's feet. "You murdered my husband. You keep me in a cage like an animal. You're building an army to attack innocent people. And you call that community building?"

Grace laughed an uneasy laugh. "Perspective is so important," Grace replied, circling Rebecca's chair. "Thomas Mitchell tried to resist inevitable change. That's poor engagement strategy. You're experiencing intensive integration protocols. That's immersive learning methodology. And Cornish represents territorial expansion opportunities. It's all about framing."

She crouched before Rebecca, phone between them. Her voiced dipped into a dark tone. "But here's what you need to understand. It is possible that Hannah is in Cornish right now. Your daughter. Probably terrified. Probably organizing defenses. Probably preparing for the Queen of Likes to arrive with overwhelming force."

Rebecca's face crumbled. "Leave her alone. Please. She's never done anything to you."

"She sabotaged my Portsmouth opportunity!" Grace's voice rose to a shriek. "She and Maddie destroyed my big break! Made me look crazy in front of those reality TV scouts! They're the reason everything fell apart!"

"They tried to save you!" Rebecca's voice cracked. "Those weren't scouts, Grace! Those were men trying to hurt you! Hannah stopped them! She saved your life!"

The words crashed into Grace's fractured psychosis like waves against rocks. For just a moment, doubt flickered and a flash of that moment burst through, shattering her illusion if only for a moment. What if Rebecca was telling the truth? What if Hannah and Maddie really were trying to help? What if everything Grace believed about Portsmouth was wrong?

Then her phone buzzed. Validation flooding through her system. Her followers reassuring her. Confirming her narrative. Reminding her that she was the victim. That Hannah and Maddie were the villains. That everything she did was justified.

"That's exactly what a saboteur would say," Grace replied, her voice calm again. "Classic gaslighting. Trying to make me doubt my own experiences. But I know what I saw. I know what they did. And I know that you're going to help me show them the consequences."

She stood, addressing the assembled group. "This is integration methodology. Building rapport through authentic dialogue. Establishing shared understanding through consistent messaging. Rebecca will come around. They always do."

Grace moved toward the warehouse exit, phone still raised. "Tomorrow, we continue sessions. Work on compliance training. Develop cooperative frameworks. By the end of the week, Rebecca will understand that resistance is futile but engagement brings rewards."

She paused at the doorway, looking back. "Oh, and Rebecca? If you cooperate, if you help me create the content I need, I'll make sure Hannah survives what's coming. But if you resist, if you continue this defiant performance, I'll make you watch while I destroy everything she loves. Simple incentive structure. Very standard community guidelines."

She spotted the young girl she'd seen bringing her water in the cage with a protein bar standing in the doorway. She wanted to scold her for betraying the group and giving her comfort then shifted her mindset. "Oh, good, I see you've brought her something to eat. Make sure you help get her cleaned up for tomorrow."

Grace glanced at Rebecca, her look shifting from confusion to hope and back to confusion. She smirked and left before Rebecca could respond, her phone buzzing with imaginary notifications praising her professional integration methodology. Behind her, Rebecca wept silently while the Burke brothers watched with growing horror at what they'd just joined.

Outside, night fell across the industrial park. Fires burned. People ate. The convoy settled into temporary existence while waiting for Frank and Sherman's return with intelligence on Cornish.

Grace found Kyle near the perimeter, his rifle across his lap, watching the darkness for threats that might materialize. She sat beside him, close enough to feel his warmth but not quite touching.

"The Burke brothers bring good intel," Kyle said without looking at her. "But they're dangerous. Killers running from consequences. We need to watch them."

"Everyone here is dangerous," Grace replied. "That's what makes good content. Authentic, complex and at times… even morally gray. Real survival decisions. Revolutionary platform development."

"Grace." Kyle's hand found hers in the darkness. "You know this ends badly, right? All of it. The convoy. The assault on Cornish. Your revenge against Hannah. It's all building toward something catastrophic."

"Catastrophic makes great content. Something the television execs will want to pick up. We're almost there, I promise." Grace said, squeezing his hand. "Climactic moments. Dramatic reveals. Revolutionary content that redefines apocalypse survival narrative."

Kyle pulled her closer, his mouth finding her neck. "Then let's make the most of it while we can."

The encounter was savage even by their standards. Kyle pressed Grace against the shipping container, rough metal cold against her back, his hands leaving new bruises over old ones. Grace clawed at his shoulders, her nails drawing blood, both of them seeking oblivion in the collision of their broken pieces.

When it was over, they stayed pressed together in the darkness, both breathing hard, both covered in sweat and blood and each other. Kyle's hand moved to Grace's face with surprising gentleness.

"I love you," he said. "Whatever that means anymore. Whatever we've become. I love the monster you are."

Grace should have said it back. Should have acknowledged the twisted bond they'd built. Instead, she just kissed him again, tasting blood where her teeth caught his lip, and whispered against his mouth.

"Then help me finish this. Help me reach Cornish. Help me show Hannah what betrayal costs."

"Always," Kyle replied.

The next five days blurred together in a haze of integration sessions and tactical planning. Grace worked on Rebecca daily, using every manipulation technique she could think of. Isolation. Reward cycles. Inconsistent treatment. Building false rapport. Creating dependency.

And slowly, Rebecca began to break.

Not really. Not in the way Grace believed. But Rebecca was smart enough to recognize that survival required performance. Required playing along. Required making Grace believe the integration was working.

So, Rebecca stopped resisting. Started cooperating. Answered Grace's questions about Hannah. Participated in "community building exercises." Played the role of grateful convert to Grace's revolutionary platform.

Grace filmed everything, creating content about transformation and redemption and authentic community building that existed only in her fractured mind.

The Burke brothers integrated into the operation, providing tactical intelligence, helping Kyle plan approach vectors, contributing their knowledge of Cornish's layout. Tommy seemed haunted by the George Miller killing. Sean showed no remorse at all. Both brothers added authenticity to Grace's content that made her followers' engagement metrics soar.

On the third day, a man named Travis made the mistake of mocking Grace.

He was one of the earlier recruits. Mid-twenties. Sarcastic. Smart enough to see through Grace's delusions but not smart enough to keep his mouth shut. He interrupted one of Grace's "broadcasts," laughing at her dead phone, calling her crazy in front of everyone.

Grace shot him without hesitation. She spun around to look at him and without hesitation, or even a blip in the narrative, while she livestreamed with one hand she pulled the gun from her waistband with the other. The pink pistol barked once. Travis dropped, blood spreading across his chest, his expression frozen in surprise. Grace stood over his body, phone raised, filming his death for her imaginary followers.

"Accountability content," she narrated calmly. "Sometimes you have to remove toxic influences to maintain positive platform engagement. Very necessary. Very professional community management."

Kyle appeared beside her, Travis's phone in his hand. He passed it to Grace without a word. Understanding what she needed. What she'd always need. Validation. Performance. The ritual that made killing bearable.

Grace took the phone, adding it to her collection. Travis's screen stayed as black as all the others. But in Grace's mind, the notifications scrolled. Her followers praising her decisive leadership. Her engagement metrics climbing. Her platform growing stronger with each necessary execution.

That night, lying in her sleeping bag in the warehouse, Grace heard a voice.

"You're losing control." Travis's voice. Clear as day. "Your engagement numbers are down. People are starting to question the platform."

Grace sat up, heart pounding. The warehouse stretched empty in the darkness. No one there. Just shadows and moonlight through broken windows.

"Hello?" Grace whispered.

"I'm here." Travis appeared beside her sleeping bag. Pale. Translucent. Blood staining his chest. "Someone had to tell you. Your content strategy is failing."

Grace should have been terrified. Should have recognized this as her psychosis fragmenting further. Instead, she just felt relieved. Travis understood now. He saw the platform's potential and could help her create better content.

"What do I need to change?" Grace asked the ghost only she could see.

"Rebecca's playing you," Travis replied. "She's not really broken. She's performing compliance. Planning rebellion. You need to watch her closer."

Grace nodded, pulling out her phone, taking notes that would never save. Travis offered strategic advice. Content suggestions. Engagement optimization strategies. All of it existing only in Grace's fractured mind but feeling absolutely real.

When morning came, Grace descended from the warehouse with renewed purpose. Travis walked beside her, invisible to everyone else, offering commentary on follower dynamics and platform development that Grace accepted as gospel.

The Burke brothers watched her talking to empty air with growing concern. Kyle just sighed, recognizing another crack in

Grace's sanity but too far gone himself to care. Rebecca saw the ghost conversations and filed the information away, recognizing that Grace's deterioration created opportunities for escape.

On the sixth day, dark clouds gathered on the horizon. Thunder rumbled in the distance. The air grew thick and heavy with the approaching storm. Grace stood in the center of the industrial park, phone raised, filming the dramatic sky.

"Weather event incoming," she narrated. "Natural disaster aesthetic that you literally cannot manufacture. Very authentic. Very apocalypse lifestyle branding."

Rebecca stood beside her now, out of the cage, playing the role of loyal assistant. Grace believed she'd won. Believed the integration was complete. Believed Rebecca would help her create the ultimate revenge content when they reached Hannah.

But Rebecca's eyes tracked the Burke brothers. Especially Tommy. The one who showed guilt. The one who might be turned. The one who exchanged a brief glance with her when Grace was too busy with content to care.

Grace registered none of the nuances. She only saw her platform growing and revolutionizing apocalypse survival narrative. The Queen of Likes stood at the center of her empire, completely insane and completely certain of her ultimate victory while thunder rolled across the industrial park. Lightning flickered in the distance. The storm was coming.

And Grace couldn't wait to film it.

14

Grace woke in the warehouse office Kyle claimed for them. Morning light slanted through the window they'd covered with a tarp. She rolled onto her side, reaching for her phone on the box used as a makeshift nightstand. The screen stayed black. Dead. But to her, it was perfect for filming content that lived only in her fractured mind.

Kyle was already up. His side of the bed already cold.

Grace stretched in the sheets Kyle scavenged from somewhere, actual linens because the Queen deserved better than rough blankets. The black crop top she slept in clung to her skin. She pulled on her pink camo pants and tucked the ever present pink pistol into her waistband before descending the metal stairs.

Kyle stood near one of the trucks with Sherman, both men bent over route maps. Pete and Nate flanked the perimeter. Throughout the lot, maybe twenty people moved around doing morning routines, each one hyperaware of Grace's presence.

Rebecca Mitchell sat on a crate near the warehouse entrance, hands folded in her lap. Clean clothes. Hair pulled back. Blank expression. Days in that cage followed by Grace's intensive integration sessions taught her that survival meant compliance and Grace felt sure of that.

"Good morning, Rebecca!" Grace called out. "Ready for another productive day?"

Rebecca nodded and stood without speaking. Perfect. Grace's methods worked.

Jennifer, Carol, and Amy clustered near the entrance. The production team. Grace's handlers for wardrobe, makeup, and general content coordination. All three women looked exhausted.

"Jenniferrrr!" Grace sang out as she moved closer, phone already framing imaginary shots. "I need the gold sequin top for today's content. Very aspirational energy. And Amy, I'm thinking smoky eye makeup with that coral lip we tried yesterday. Camera-ready in thirty minutes."

The three women exchanged glances. Jennifer moved first, heading toward one of the containers where they'd stashed supplies. Carol followed. Amy stayed frozen, her hands twisting together, her bruised face showing fresh fear.

"Amy." Grace's voice dropped lower. "Did you hear me?"

"I heard you." Amy's voice came out small. "I just. Grace, I don't think the coral worked yesterday. It looked wrong in certain light. Maybe we should try—"

"Are you questioning my aesthetic vision?" Grace moved closer, phone between them like a barrier. "Because yesterday's content performed incredibly well with my followers. Engagement metrics were through the roof. So, when you say it 'looked wrong,' what you're really saying is that you don't understand platform optimization."

"No, I just meant—"

"You're sabotaging me." The words came out flat. Certain. "Just like Hannah and Maddie did. Just like everyone who couldn't handle my success. You're trying to make me look bad. Trying to undermine my brand."

Amy backed against the warehouse wall. "Grace, no. I swear I'm not. I'm just trying to help—"

Grace's hand moved to the pink pistol. The lot went silent. Every person in the space froze, reading the shift in atmosphere.

Kyle looked up from his maps. "Grace."

"She's negative content." Grace pulled the pistol free. "Bringing down metrics. Creating friction in the production pipeline. That's unacceptable."

"Grace." Kyle's voice stayed level, but he moved away from the truck, putting himself between Grace and Amy. "Put the gun down. We can handle this differently."

"There is no other way." Grace's smile returned. "Performance reviews are essential for maintaining platform quality. Amy failed hers. Now she gets to experience creative consequences."

"Please," Amy whispered. "Please, I have a sister. She's only fifteen. She's in the warehouse. Please don't—"

Grace fired.

The shot went deliberately low, catching Amy in the thigh. The young woman screamed, collapsing against the wall, blood spreading across her jeans. Grace adjusted her aim, firing again. This shot took Amy in the knee, shattering bone with a wet crack that echoed across the lot.

"Maiming is more effective than killing," Grace explained to her phone. "Creates a lasting psychological impact. Don't you think? Demonstrates consequences without removing potentially useful resources. Very strategic leadership decision." Her smile, ever present, didn't reach her eyes, her resolve was wavering, yet she could not stop herself.

Amy writhed on the ground, hands pressed against her ruined leg, blood pooling beneath her. Carol rushed forward with supplies, the need to help her overriding terror. Jennifer stayed frozen in the container doorway, the gold top falling from her numb fingers.

Kyle reached Grace in three strides, his hand closing around her wrist. Not gentle. Not quite violent. Just firm enough to break through the haze.

"What the fuck was that?" His voice stayed low, meant only for her, but rage burned beneath the control.

"Performance review." Grace looked up at him. "She was sabotaging my aesthetic. Creating negative content. I gave her chances to correct the behavior, but she kept undermining my vision."

"She made a makeup suggestion."

"She questioned my authority." Grace pulled her wrist free, tucking the pistol back into her waistband. "In front of everyone. That's the same thing Hannah did. The same thing Maddie did. Treating me like I'm crazy instead of recognizing my platform's revolutionary potential."

Kyle stared at her, something flickering behind his eyes that Grace couldn't quite read. His hand moved to her face, thumb brushing her cheekbone with surprising gentleness.

"You're losing it," he said quietly.

"I'm maintaining standards." Grace leaned into his touch. "That's what leaders do."

Behind them, Carol worked on Amy's leg with trembling hands. Amy's screams faded to whimpers, shock setting in. The lot stayed silent except for those sounds. Everyone watching. Everyone understanding that whatever thin line existed between Grace's delusions and outright murder was dissolving.

Grace pulled away from Kyle, moving toward the center of the lot, phone like a conductor's baton.

"Lesson learned, everyone!" Her voice climbed back into that bright tone. "Negative engagement gets negative consequences. But positive engagement gets rewarded! So, who wants to show me their value today? Who's ready to contribute to the platform in meaningful ways?"

No one spoke. Twenty faces stared back at her with expressions ranging from terror to disgust.

Grace's smile faltered. They weren't responding. Weren't engaging. Weren't giving her the validation she needed.

"I said," her voice dropped lower, hand moving back toward her pistol, "who wants to contribute?"

"We all do," Jennifer said quickly, stepping away from the container. "Everyone here wants to help. We're committed to the platform. To your vision. I'm afraid we're simply unable to do your vision justice on our own. We need your guidance, is all. Just tell us what you need."

The lie was obvious. But Grace's fractured mind reorganized it into truth.

"Good." Grace's smile returned. "That's what I like to hear. Professional attitudes. I understand your hesitation. It's hard to come up with content and not everyone is good at it. This is why we have a production team… Each of you has your own job to do. Silly me, this is team cooperation—platform dedication."

She turned back to Kyle, who watched her with an expression she couldn't quite decode. "I'm going to prep for today's content. Send someone to help Amy, but make sure she understands this was a teaching moment. Growth through consequences. Very effective management strategy."

Grace moved toward the warehouse before Kyle could respond, her combat boots loud on concrete, her phone pressed against her chest. Behind her, Amy's whimpers continued despite Carol's urgent whispers to stay quiet. The lot's shocked silence accentuated her steps that now echoed in the large building.

In the warehouse loft, she stood before a cracked mirror propped against the wall, examining her reflection. Sunken cheeks contrasting her wild eyes. The black crop top showed Kyle's bruises she loved to display as a symbol of possession. She raised her phone, taking a selfie, her smile locking into place.

"Today's lesson," she whispered to her imaginary followers. "Leadership requires difficult decisions and consequences matter. Quality control is essential for platform growth. Remember, true influence means being willing to do what others won't."

Her phone's dead screen reflected her face back at her. Grace scrolled through imaginary comments.

Queen knows what she's doing

Amy deserved it for being negative

This is what real leadership looks like

We love a decisive queen

A knock interrupted her scrolling. "Come in."

Jennifer entered, the gold sequin top recovered from below. She moved carefully, keeping distance, her body language screaming 'trapped animal'.

"The top you wanted," Jennifer said, laying it on a crate. "And Kyle said to tell you there's a situation developing with some of the crew. He needs you outside."

"What kind of situation?" Grace pulled off her crop top, reaching for the gold sequins. Modesty didn't matter anymore.

"Two of the men are talking about the platform." Jennifer's voice stayed carefully neutral. "Kyle said you should know."

Grace's pulse quickened. She pulled on the gold top, the sequins catching light, transforming her from gaunt survivor into a glittering beacon of hope. Jennifer helped her brush out her hair, and she spun around in a circle with her phone held high, allowing her strawberry blonde hair to fly out. "Readyyyyy," she said in a sing-song voice.

"Where?" Grace turned to Jennifer, phone in hand, and tone shifting so fast into an ominous threat she stepped back.

"Near the trucks. Kyle's keeping distance, but he thought you'd want to handle it."

Without another word, Grace descended to find Kyle near the perimeter, two voices carrying across the lot from between vehicles. She recognized them. Dice and Landry, both early recruits.

"I'm telling you, she's lost it completely." Dice's voice, low and tense. "Three people dead over the last few weeks. Amy's leg is destroyed. And for what? Bad makeup suggestions and disagreeing about content?"

Landry sighed loudly, saying, "This isn't content, this is insanity. Kyle has to see it. Everyone sees it. This chick is batshit crazy!"

Grace moved closer, staying behind a shipping container, phone capturing nothing, but her delusions fed on their words like fuel.

"Keep your voice down." Landry sounded nervous. "Someone'll hear you."

"I don't care if she hears me!" Dice's voice climbed. "Someone needs to say it! She's talking to a dead phone! Her followers don't exist! She's making us all participate in her delusions while we should be focusing on actual survival!"

"Kyle says she's useful," Landry said, but doubt crept into his voice. "Says she breaks people down psychologically. Makes prisoners compliant."

"Kyle's fucking her, so of course he says that!" Dice's laugh came out harsh. "But she's not useful. She's dangerous. She's unstable. She's going to get us all killed because we're too busy pretending her platform matters instead of actually surviving!"

Grace stepped into view.

Both men spun around. Dice's hand moved toward his rifle but froze when he saw Grace's pistol already drawn.

"You don't believe in the platform," Grace said softly.

"Grace, we were just—" Landry started.

"Just discussing how I'm… What did you say? 'Batshit crazy?'" Grace finished. "How my followers don't exist. How I'm dangerous and unstable. That's what you said, right Dice? That I'm making you participate in my delusions?"

"I didn't mean—" Dice's voice shook.

"You're negative energy," Grace said. "Bringing down metrics. Creating friction. Undermining platform credibility."

"Grace." Kyle's voice came from behind her. "Don't."

Grace pulled the trigger.

The shot caught Dice in the chest. He staggered backward, eyes going wide, mouth working but producing no sound. Blood spread across his shirt.

"One star review," Grace said, firing again. This shot took him in the throat. Dice collapsed against the truck, sliding down the door panel, leaving a red smear. His hands scrabbled at his neck, blood pulsing between his fingers.

Grace turned to Landry. "What about you? Do you believe in the platform?"

"Yes!" Landry backed away, hands raised. "Absolutely! I was trying to get Dice to stop! I believe in everything you're doing!"

"Are you sure?" Grace moved closer, pistol still raised. "Because you were listening to him. Agreeing with him. Maybe you're just telling me what I want to hear now that I have a gun pointed at you. Wasn't it just you that called me 'batshit crazy?'"

"No! I swear!" Landry's voice broke. "I think you're a genius! I think the platform is revolutionary! I think—"

Grace fired.

The shot took Landry in the face. His head snapped back, body crumpling. He hit the asphalt without sound, blood and worse things spreading beneath his skull.

Grace lowered the pistol, scrolling through her phone with her free hand.

"Two one-star reviews eliminated," she announced to her invisible audience. "Quality control is essential for maintaining platform standards. Remember, followers, true influence requires removing negative energy from your community. Very important content creation principle."

She turned to find everyone staring at her. Kyle. Pete. Nate. Sherman standing by his truck, expression somewhere between worry and fear. The rest of the convoy, maybe fifteen people, all frozen. Her fans were stunned with her excellent content, and they were right to pause earlier. None of them would have come up with such an amazing livestream.

"Clean this up," Grace said. "And someone find out if they had any personal belongings that might work for wardrobe purposes. We can't let quality materials go to waste."

She walked past the bodies stepping in a pool of Dice's blood without looking down, her combat boots leaving a trail of bloody prints.

Kyle caught up to her near the warehouse entrance. His hand closed around her arm, not rough but firm, guiding her away from where others could see. He pulled her into the shadowed space between shipping containers.

"Grace." His voice stayed low. "Look at me."

She looked up.

"You just killed two men," Kyle said, his hands moving to her face, forcing her to focus on him. "Do you understand that? Two people are dead because they questioned you."

"They questioned the platform," Grace corrected. "That's different."

"It's not different." Kyle's thumbs pressed against her cheekbones. "You're spiraling. You're losing control. And I can't. Grace, I can't keep you functional if you're executing people for having opinions."

"You need me," Grace said, confusion creeping into her voice. "You said so. You said I'm useful for breaking people down. For creating psychological pressure. That's exactly what I'm doing."

"I know what I said." Kyle's forehead pressed against hers. "But this is beyond that. This is beyond using fear as a tool. You're killing people because you can't tell the difference between disagreement and betrayal anymore."

"They were betraying me." Grace's voice climbed. "Just like Hannah did. Just like Maddie did. They called me insane. They said my followers don't exist. They said—"

"Because your followers don't exist." Kyle's words came out gentle despite their brutality. "Grace, baby, you're talking to a dead phone. Your platform is in your head. And I've been enabling it because you're right, you are useful. But now you're dangerous in ways I can't control."

The words should have triggered rage. Instead, they just slid off her fractured psychosis.

"I'm dangerous because I'm effective," Grace whispered. "And you love me for it. You said so. Whatever monsters we are."

Kyle pulled back, studying her face with an expression caught between horror and resignation. "I do love you. God help me, I do. But Grace, you have to give me something to work with here. You have to show me you can still think clearly instead of just reacting to every perceived slight."

"I am thinking clearly," Grace insisted. "I'm maintaining platform standards. Removing negative influences. Creating an environment where people understand consequences."

"You're creating an environment where everyone's terrified to breathe." Kyle's grip softened, his hands sliding down to her shoulders. "But I get it. I understand what you're doing. Just. Just let me help you do it smarter. Can you do that?"

Grace looked up at him, reading the concern, the genuine fear that she was slipping beyond even his ability to manage. Something in her fractured mind recognized that Kyle was her anchor.

"I can do that," she said quietly. "I can be smarter."

"Good." Kyle pulled her close, his mouth finding hers in a kiss. "Good girl. Now come on. We need to establish order before people start thinking about running."

He guided her back to the lot, his hand steady on her lower back. Grace leaned into the contact.

The afternoon sun beat down on the industrial park. Grace stood near the trucks, phone capturing organized activity. Rebecca Mitchell moved through the space with careful steps, carrying water bottles to various crew members. She had been released from the cage two days ago after finally breaking, finally agreeing to cooperate, finally playing the role of grateful convert.

Grace watched her with satisfaction. Proof that her methods worked.

Kyle stood with Sherman near the lead truck, both men examining route maps. Pete and Nate worked on vehicle maintenance. Throughout the lot, maybe fifteen people moved through various tasks, each one hyperaware of Grace's presence.

Grace lowered her phone, scrolling through imaginary engagement metrics.

"Grace."

She turned to find Sherman approaching. He'd been quiet since the morning executions. Watching. Calculating. Probably rethinking his integration into Grace's operation.

"We need to talk," Sherman said, stopping a careful distance away. "About the killings."

"Performance reviews," Grace corrected. "Very effective management strategy. Creates accountability. Establishes standards. Motivates remaining team members to maintain quality output." Her head bobbed up and down, agreeing with her own words.

"You shot three people this morning for disagreeing with you."

"Two people. Amy's still alive. That was strategic maiming, not execution." Grace moved closer, filming Sherman's face. "And they weren't disagreeing. They were creating negative content. Undermining platform credibility. That's completely different."

Sherman glanced past Grace toward where Kyle stood watching their conversation with sharp attention.

"Kyle," Sherman called out. "Can we talk? All three of us?"

Kyle moved down from the truck, joining them near the container. Grace caught sight of Rebecca who stirred at the sound of new voices but didn't shift her gaze up.

"What's this about?" Kyle asked, his hand resting on his rifle.

"This is about the fact that Grace is unstable," Sherman said flatly. "She's killing people for minor infractions. Maiming them for making a suggestion about lipstick. C'mon man… Lipstick? She's creating an environment where everyone's terrified to breathe wrong. That's not leadership. That's psychosis. We can't go up against any kind of organized force if they're all terrified."

Grace's vision flickered. Sherman's face rippled, became ghoulish. Skin pulling tight. Eyes sinking. Mouth stretching too wide.

She blinked. His face returned to normal. Just a man. Just someone who didn't understand her vision.

"She's… She's maintaining standards," Kyle said, but his voice lacked conviction.

"She's murdering people!" Sherman's voice climbed. "And you're enabling it because you think she's useful for breaking prisoners down. But she's breaking everyone down. Including you. She's going to get us all killed or scattered or… or worse. Me and my men are outta here, man. This is nuts."

"That's negative content," Grace said softly.

Sherman turned to face her fully. "What?"

"Negative content. Undermining morale. Creating friction in the command structure. That's exactly the kind of toxic behavior that destroys cohesion, cooperation." Grace's hand moved toward her pistol. "I thought you understood the platform. Thought you were committed to the vision."

"I'm committed to survival," Sherman said. "And right now, you're the biggest threat to that. You're completely insane, Grace. You're talking to a dead phone. Your followers don't exist. You're killing people over imaginary engagement metrics. That's not leadership. That's delusion."

The words felt like slaps to her face. Insane. Delusion. The same words Hannah used. The same words Maddie used.

Grace's smile widened.

"Kyle," Sherman continued, never taking his eyes off Grace. "You need to do something about this. Before she kills someone we actually need. Before she destroys everything we've built."

"I'm handling it," Kyle said, but uncertainty crept into his voice.

"You're not handling anything." Sherman's voice hardened. "You're fucking her and pretending that makes her your problem instead of everyone's problem. But she's dangerous. She's unstable. She needs to be removed before—"

Grace pulled the pistol.

Sherman saw it. Started to react. Started to reach for his own weapon.

Grace moved faster.

She crossed the distance between them in three strides, pressing the pink pistol's barrel against Sherman's temple. His eyes went wide. His mouth opened. His hand froze halfway to his holster.

"Negative content gets creative resolution," Grace said, her voice bright and cheerful, her smile widening impossibly. "Remember? That's platform policy."

"Grace." Kyle's voice came sharp, filled with warning. "Don't."

Grace's smile grew wider. "He questioned my metrics. Undermined my authority. Called me insane. That's exactly the kind of toxic behavior that requires elimination."

"Grace, please." Sherman's voice shook. "I was just trying to help. Just trying to protect the operation. Just—"

Grace pulled the trigger.

The shot was loud. Impossibly loud inside the warehouse. The sound echoed through the building and across the lot, bouncing off containers, making birds scatter from gutted structures. Sherman's body dropped like a puppet with cut strings, crumpling to the asphalt, blood seeping from the ruin of his skull.

Grace lowered the pistol, her smile never faltering, scrolling through her phone with her free hand.

"One-star review eliminated," she announced to her invisible audience. "Sometimes leadership requires difficult decisions. Removing negative influences. Maintaining platform standards. Very important content creation principle."

She turned to face the convoy, raising her voice so everyone could hear. "Pete! Nate! Display Sherman on the hood of the lead truck. I want everyone to see what happens to negative content. What happens when people undermine the platform. This is a teaching moment for the entire community. Just think about the apocalypse aesthetic this will be." She giggled excitedly.

Pete and Nate exchanged glances. They moved toward Sherman's body without speaking.

Grace turned to Kyle, who stood frozen.

"He was bringing down metrics," Grace said brightly. "Creating friction. Undermining my authority. But don't worry. The platform is secure now. Leadership is maintained. You know he was trying to take your place. We couldn't have that, but now everything's fine."

Kyle didn't respond. Just stared at Sherman's body, at the spreading blood, at the proof that whatever thin control he'd maintained over Grace was now completely shattered.

"Kyle?" Grace moved closer, confusion creeping into her voice. "You're not mad, are you? I was protecting the operation. Protecting us. He was dangerous. He was going to destroy everything we built."

Kyle's hands moved to her shoulders, not pushing her away this time, but pulling her close. He guided her toward the warehouse, his grip firm but not violent, his body shielding her from the stares of everyone in the lot.

They climbed to the loft in silence. Kyle pushed her against the far wall, closing the distance between them. The metal was cool against her back.

"Grace." His voice came out low, dangerous, but underneath it she heard something else. Fear maybe. Or exhaustion. "You just executed Sherman in front of everyone. Without consultation. Without considering operational consequences. You just pulled your gun and blew his brains out."

"I protected the platform!" Grace's voice climbed. "He was dangerous! He was trying to turn you against me! Trying to make you think I'm crazy instead of recognizing my value!"

Kyle moved closer, his hands finding her face, forcing her to look at him. "You are crazy. But that's not the point. The point is that I can't control you anymore. Can't predict you. Can't manage what you're going to do next."

"You never controlled me," Grace whispered. "I let you think you were handling me. Let you believe you were keeping me functional. But—"

"Stop." Kyle's grip tightened on her face. "Just stop. Listen to me. Really listen. You're spiraling beyond anything I can manage. Sherman was right about that. You're killing people for minor infractions. You're creating an environment where everyone's terrified of you. And I… Grace, I can't keep you safe. From our people or even from yourself anymore."

The words should have hurt. Instead, Grace felt something crack inside her chest. Something that recognized Kyle was her anchor, and that anchor was slipping.

"Don't leave me," she whispered, her hands finding his chest. "Please. You're the only one who understands. The only one who sees me and stays anyway. If you leave, I'll have nothing."

Kyle's forehead pressed against hers. "I'm not leaving. I can't. Because you're right. I do love the monster you are. I do see you clearly. But Grace, you have to help me here. You have to show me you can still be coherent instead of just reactive. Can you do that?"

Grace nodded, her phone falling from her hand, clattering to the concrete floor. "I can do that. I can be... I can be whatever you need."

"Then prove it." Kyle's mouth found hers in a kiss that was not the usual rough and desperate kind. It was soft and gentle and a tear escaped, rolling down her cheek. Kyle reached up and gently brushed it aside saying, "Show me you can still think past the next execution. Show me there's something left in there besides rage and delusion. Show me because you love me and trust that I know what we need."

Grace responded with ferocity, her hands fisting in his shirt, pulling him closer. The kiss was rough, claiming, a collision of their broken pieces seeking something that felt like connection. "I do love you, Kyle. I can be what you need."

When they broke apart, Kyle's expression showed someone wrestling with the knowledge that he'd enabled this, created this, turned a broken girl into something far worse.

"Sherman's death changes everything," he said quietly. "Morale is destroyed. People are terrified. And you're the cause of all of it. But we can work with that. Fear is useful if we channel it right. Can you let me help you channel it?"

"Yes," Grace whispered. "Yes. I trust you."

Kyle pulled her close, his arms wrapping around her, his chin resting on top of her head. "Then we do this together. No more solo executions. No more killing people without telling me first. We make decisions as a team. Can you give me that?"

Grace nodded against his chest, feeling his heartbeat, feeling the solid reality of someone who saw her madness and stayed anyway.

"Good girl," Kyle murmured. "Good. Now let's go down and establish order. Show them that Sherman's death wasn't chaos. Show them it was strategy."

Outside, Pete and Nate positioned Sherman's body across the lead truck's hood, arranging him like a gruesome ornament. Blood dripped down the grille. His ruined head lolled at an unnatural angle.

Grace moved closer, filming from multiple angles.

"Visual deterrence is so important," she explained to her phone. "Creating lasting psychological impact. Demonstrating consequences in ways that resonate with community members. Very effective leadership strategy."

Around the lot, people watched with expressions ranging from terror to disgust. Jennifer stood near the warehouse with Carol, both women's faces showing pure horror. Amy lay somewhere inside, her ruined leg bound with inadequate supplies.

And Grace just kept filming, kept performing, kept scrolling through imaginary comments that praised her leadership, her decisiveness, her revolutionary approach to community management.

The sun moved lower, painting the lot in shades of orange and red that looked almost like it was the blood she'd shed today. Grace watched from the warehouse entrance, phone raised, scrolling through imaginary metrics that validated every terrible choice she'd made.

Her followers understood. They loved her. They always would.

Because she was the Queen.

And queens did whatever they wanted.

Because she was the Queen.

And queens did whatever they wanted.

The sky turned green.

Grace stood in the warehouse doorway, phone raised, filming clouds that twisted into shapes that in her mind began looking like a cheering audience. The air pressed down with a weight that made breathing difficult and static electricity crawled across her skin, making the sequins on her gold top look to her as though they sparked and shimmered.

"This is incredible," she whispered to her phone. "Atmospheric phenomena that literally defines the apocalypse aesthetic. My followers are going to lose their minds."

We already are, Travis said from somewhere behind her left shoulder. *This is perfect content. Natural disaster narrative. Very trending.*

Queen of disaster porn, another voice added. Dice maybe. Or Landry. Grace couldn't quite place which of the voices spoke, but their validation flooded through her like warmth.

Thunder rolled across the industrial park, so deep it vibrated in her chest. The sky darkened from green to black. Wind picked up, carrying debris across the lot and empty containers groaned against their moorings.

"Grace." Kyle appeared beside her, his hand closing around her elbow. "We need to secure the vehicles. Get everyone inside. This is going to be bad."

"Bad makes great content." Grace pulled free, moving further into the doorway to capture better angles. "Crisis situations. Authentic survival challenges. Revolutionary platform development? What could be better?"

"Grace." Kyle's voice hardened. "Inside. Now."

She turned to argue, but the look on his face stopped her. Not anger. Fear. Real fear that cut through her manic haze for just a moment. Kyle was afraid of the storm.

"Okay," she said quietly. "Okay."

The first drops hit like bullets. Fat and cold and driven by wind that went from nothing to everything in seconds. Grace stumbled backward into the warehouse, Kyle pulling her by her arm. Outside, the convoy scrambled. Men securing vehicles. Tying down loose equipment. Pete and Nate herding people toward shelter.

Rebecca appeared in Grace's peripheral vision, moving through the chaos with careful steps. She carried supplies toward the warehouse, her face blank, her movements mechanical. The perfect little helper. Grace's trained pet performing her assigned tasks.

She's playing you, Travis whispered. *Planning something. I can see it in her eyes.*

"I know," Grace murmured back. "I'm watching her."

Kyle shot her a look. "What?"

"Nothing. Just thinking out loud." Grace raised her phone, filming Rebecca through the warehouse doorway. "Look how well integration works. Three days ago, she was defiant, even hateful. Now she's contributing to community operations. Now, she understands my effective methodology."

Kyle grabbed Grace's wrist, lowering her phone. "Listen to me. That storm is going to be catastrophic. Category five winds, maybe worse. We need everyone secured in the warehouse. No phones. No filming. Just survival. Can you do that for now?"

Grace stared at him. His face so close to hers. His grip tight enough to hurt. Behind him, the sky opened up and rain poured down in sheets so thick she couldn't even see the vehicles twenty feet away.

"I can do that," she said.

Kyle kissed her. Hard and desperate, then released her and moved toward the entrance, shouting orders Grace couldn't hear over the roar of wind and rain.

The warehouse filled with people. Twenty bodies pressed into the space that felt vast and empty hours ago. The Burke brothers secured the main doors. Pete and Nate covered the windows with whatever they could find. Carol and Jennifer moved through the crowd, checking on the terrified faces.

Amy sat against the far wall, her ruined leg stretched in front of her, pain etched into every line of her face. Grace felt a flicker of something. Not quite guilt but more like recognition that Amy existed outside Grace's content narrative. That she was real and suffering, and Grace caused it.

She deserved it, one of the ghosts said. *Negative content gets negative consequences.*

"That's right," Grace whispered. "She undermined the platform."

Rebecca moved past Grace, carrying blankets. Their eyes met for just a moment. Rebecca's expression stayed carefully blank, but something flickered underneath. Grace grabbed her arm.

"Stay close to me," Grace said. "When this gets bad, I want you where I can see you."

"Of course." Rebecca's voice came out soft. Compliant. "Whatever you need."

She's lying, Travis insisted. *Can't you hear it in her voice?*

But Grace didn't hear lies in her voice. She heard broken acceptance and the sound of someone who'd finally understood that resistance was futile. Rebecca was hers now. Her project. Her proof that integration methodology worked.

Kyle returned, soaked through, his hair plastered to his skull. "That's everyone. Doors secured. We ride this out."

The wind hit.

Not gradually. There was no building of the storm. It was just suddenly there with a force that made the warehouse groan. Metal sheeting screamed as it tore free somewhere outside. The sound of crashing filled the air. Vehicles shifting. Containers toppling. The world outside tearing itself apart.

Grace pressed against Kyle's side, phone clutched to her chest. Around them, people prayed. Cried. Held each other. But Grace's mind raced with content possibilities. The authentic fear. The real danger. The survival narrative unfolding in real time.

Film it, the ghosts urged. *Document everything.*

This is once in a lifetime content, another voice added. Maybe the man from the settlement. Or the woman she'd threatened. Grace's ghost audience had grown, all of them offering advice, all of them validating her choices.

She raised her phone, filming the terrified faces around her.

"Grace." Kyle's hand closed over her phone, lowering it. "Not now."

"But the content—"

"Not. Now." His voice left no room for argument.

Grace lowered her phone but kept scrolling through imaginary metrics. Her followers understood even if Kyle didn't. This was revolutionary documentation. Crisis coverage that would define her platform.

The warehouse shook. A window exploded inward, glass spraying across the concrete floor. Grace felt something hot slash across her cheek. Warm blood ran down her jaw. She touched it, her fingers coming away red.

"I'm bleeding," she said, staring at the blood. "I'm actually bleeding."

The sight of it triggered something in her separate from fear. A sudden overwhelming sense that her reality was collapsing. That the barrier between her delusions and actual truth was shattering like that window. Her blood was real and the glass was real. Even the storm was real.

But her followers. Her platform. Her carefully constructed narrative about being the hero, the victim, the revolutionary leader.

None of it was real.

"No," Grace whispered. "No… no, no, no."

Don't break now, Travis said urgently. *You're so close. The platform needs you.*

We need you, the chorus of ghosts agreed. *You're the Queen. Stay strong.*

Grace's breathing came too fast. Her vision tunneled and the warehouse walls pressed in with all those terrified faces staring at her. Kyle's hand on her shoulder stopped the world from spinning. She noticed Rebecca watching from across the space with something that might have been concern or might have been calculation.

"I need air," Grace gasped. "I need to get out."

"You can't go out there." Kyle pulled her close, his arms wrapping around her. "Grace, baby, look at me. You're having a panic attack. Just breathe. I've got you."

But Grace couldn't breathe. Her lungs wouldn't work. Blood dripped from her cheek onto her gold sequined top, dark stains spreading across the glittering fabric. Everything was falling apart. The storm. Her mind. The careful performance.

"Make it stop," she whispered against Kyle's chest. "Please make it stop."

Kyle tilted her face up, his thumbs wiping blood from her cheek. "Listen to my voice. Focus on my voice. You're safe. I'm here. The storm will pass."

"My followers—"

"Fuck your followers." Kyle's voice cut through her panic. "There are no followers. There's just you and me and this moment. That's all that exists. Can you feel that? Can you feel me holding you?"

Grace nodded, her fingers digging into his wet shirt. She could feel him. Solid and real, he was here. He was the only anchor in a world that was tearing itself apart.

Another window exploded. More glass rained down. People screamed. The moved to cover the opening with shipping pallets. Wind howled through the gaps, carrying rain that soaked everyone within ten feet of the breach.

"I've got you," Kyle murmured against her hair. "I've got you. Just stay with me."

Don't listen to him, Travis warned. *He's trying to break your connection to the platform.*

The platform is everything, the other ghosts agreed. *Don't let him take it away.*

But Grace couldn't hear them over the sound of her own gasping breaths and Kyle's heartbeat against her ear and the storm trying to tear the warehouse apart around them.

Kyle pulled her to a corner beneath a catwalk where no windows were near and pulled her down to the hard cold floor.

Holding her against his chest, they waited for the storm to pass. Time lost all meaning. Minutes or hours passed in darkness broken only by lightning that turned the warehouse into a strobe. Grace stayed pressed against Kyle, her phone forgotten, her followers silent for the first time since Earl pulled her from the harbor.

She felt Kyle's hands in her hair. Felt his breath on her forehead. Felt the steady rhythm of his breathing and realized she'd synced her own breathing to match his. In. Out. In. Out. Simple and real and completely divorced from content metrics and engagement rates.

"That's it," Kyle said softly. "That's my girl. Just stay here with me."

Grace looked up at him, blood drying on her cheek, sequins dark with rain and sweat. "I'm scared."

"I know."

"What if I'm actually crazy?"

Kyle's laugh came out harsh. "Baby, you are crazy. Completely and totally insane. But you're mine, and I'm not letting go."

The words should have hurt. Should have triggered defensive rage. Instead they felt like relief. Someone saw her clearly and stayed anyway, naming the truth. And that truth was she'd spent weeks hiding behind delusions and performance.

"I killed people," Grace whispered. "I hurt Amy and tortured Rebecca. I'm a monster."

"I know," Kyle said again. "I'm a monster too. We're monsters together. That's what this is."

A massive crack split the air. This wasn't thunder. One of the shipping containers outside toppled over, and crashed into the side of the building. The warehouse shuddered and dust rained down from the rafters.

Grace buried her face against Kyle's chest, squeezing her eyes shut. If the warehouse collapsed, at least she wouldn't die alone. At least Kyle would be there with her when it ended.

But the building held.

The storm raged for hours. Wind screaming. Rain hammering. Lightning revealing terrified faces in brief flashes. Grace stayed pressed against Kyle, his arms around her, his body between her and the broken windows and the storm trying to kill them all.

Rebecca moved through the warehouse during a brief lull, checking on people. She stopped near Grace and Kyle, offering a water bottle. Grace took it with shaking hands.

"Thank you," Grace said quietly.

Rebecca's expression flickered. Surprise maybe. Or calculation. But she just nodded and moved on to check on Amy.

She's dangerous, Travis insisted. *I can see her planning. Plotting. Waiting for you to break completely so she can escape.*

But Grace was too exhausted to care. Too wrung out from panic to maintain the paranoia. Rebecca was just a woman trying to survive, just like everyone else in this warehouse. Just like Grace herself.

Another window exploded. Another section of metal sheeting tore free with a shriek. The storm showed no signs of stopping. If anything, it was getting worse.

"This is the big one," Pete said from somewhere in the darkness. "Hurricane. Cyclone. Whatever you want to call it. This is apocalypse level shit."

"Everything's apocalypse level now," Nate replied. "That's the whole point."

Grace felt Kyle's laugh vibrate through his chest. "He's not wrong."

"Is this my fault?" Grace asked suddenly. "Did I cause this? Some kind of punishment for what I've done?"

"Grace." Kyle tilted her face up again, forcing her to meet his eyes. "It's a storm. Just a storm. You didn't cause it. You're not that powerful."

But Grace wasn't sure. The timing felt too perfect. The storm of the century hitting right when her sanity was fracturing. When her careful delusions were collapsing. When she'd killed Sherman and was planning to assault Cornish.

Maybe the universe was trying to stop her. Trying to tear apart her operation before she could hurt more people. Her mind was consuming itself in panic and self doubt. Thoughts racing uncontrolled. Were it not for Kyle holding her she felt she might fly apart. The universe itself was against her.

That's not how this works, one of the ghosts said. *The storm is content. Just content. Use it.*

Documentary footage, another agreed. *Crisis narrative development.*

But Grace couldn't raise her phone. Couldn't perform. Could only hold onto Kyle and hope the building didn't collapse and bury them all.

Hours passed into the wee hours of the morning and the storm was still raging. Grace dozed fitfully against Kyle's chest, jolting awake every time something crashed or exploded outside. Each time she woke, Kyle was there. Solid. Real. Still holding her.

Rebecca brought food at some point. Protein bars and water distributed through the warehouse. When she came to Grace and Kyle, she lingered for just a moment.

"Are you okay?" Rebecca asked Grace.

Grace touched the cut on her cheek, feeling dried blood flake away. "I'm fine."

"You're bleeding."

"It's just a scratch."

Rebecca pulled out a small first aid kit, kneeling beside Grace. She dabbed at the cut with antiseptic that stung like fire. Grace flinched but didn't pull away.

"Why are you helping me?" Grace asked.

Rebecca's hands paused. Her eyes met Grace's in the dim light. "Because you're human. Despite everything. You're still human."

She's manipulating you, Travis warned. *Building false rapport. Planning rebellion.*

But Grace didn't hear manipulation. Just tired resignation. Rebecca had truly broken. Or at least, broken enough to survive in Grace's world.

"Thank you," Grace said quietly.

Rebecca finished bandaging the cut and moved on. Kyle who watched the interaction with narrowed eyes.

"I don't trust her," Kyle said once Rebecca was out of earshot.

"She's fine. Look at her. She's helping. Cooperating. Integration worked."

"She's too cooperative. Too helpful. It's an act."

"Everything's an act," Grace said. "I act. You act. Everyone here is performing survival. At least Rebecca's performance is useful."

Kyle studied Grace's face in the lightning flashes. "You actually care about her."

"What?"

"Rebecca. You care about her. In some twisted way."

Grace opened her mouth to deny it, but couldn't. She did care. In a strange, fractured way that had nothing to do with hostages or leverage or Hannah. Rebecca was hers. Her project. Her proof that broken people could be integrated, controlled, made useful.

She was like her pet.

The thought should have disgusted Grace. Should have made her recognize how completely warped her mind had become. Instead it just felt true. Rebecca belonged to her now, and Grace took care of her belongings.

"She's my responsibility," Grace said finally.

"That's not the same as caring."

"Maybe not. But it's close enough."

Kyle shook his head but didn't argue. They lapsed into silence, listening to the storm rage outside. More crashes, structural groaning and rain, but the warehouse held, barely.

Grace pulled out her phone, scrolling through blank screens out of habit. Her fingers moved through familiar patterns even though nothing would ever appear. No notifications. No comments. No followers.

Just ghosts.

Still here, Travis assured her. *We never left.*

Always watching, the others agreed. *Your platform is eternal.*

Grace almost laughed. Her followers were dead people and delusions. Her platform existed only in her fractured mind. Her revolution was just madness dressed up in sequins and filtered through engagement metrics.

But they were all she had besides Kyle. And Kyle scared her sometimes with how clearly he saw her. How completely he understood the monster she'd become. At least her ghost followers loved her unconditionally. Praised every choice. Validated every terrible decision.

Maybe madness was easier than truth.

"What are you thinking about?" Kyle asked.

"How I'm going to die in this warehouse surrounded by people who hate me."

"No one's dying, the storm will pass. Don't worry my dear, we'll survive. That's what we do."

"And then what? We assault Cornish? Kill more people? I keep performing until someone puts a bullet in me?"

Kyle's arms tightened around her. "Then we figure it out. One day at a time. One decision at a time. We don't have to plan the whole future right now."

"But I'm supposed to have a plan. That's what leaders do. That's what the Queen does."

"The Queen can take a damn break during a hurricane." Kyle pressed his mouth to her hair. "Just be Grace right now. Not the Queen. Not the platform. Just Grace."

But Grace didn't know how to be just Grace anymore. That girl drowned back in Portsmouth. The thing that crawled out was something else entirely. Reality had crept in and shattered her delusions. All she had was violence, and a desperate need for validation from followers who didn't exist.

The storm howled. The warehouse shuddered. Grace closed her eyes and tried to remember what it felt like to be normal. To have real friends instead of hostages. To create actual content instead of imaginary broadcasts and exist without filtering everything through engagement metrics.

She couldn't.

That girl was gone. Dead. Replaced by whatever Grace had become.

"I'm tired," she whispered against Kyle's chest.

"I know."

"I don't know how much longer I can keep this up."

"Then don't. Just rest. I've got you."

Grace wanted to believe him. Wanted to think she could stop performing, killing to build this imaginary empire, built on delusions and blood. But the ghosts were already whispering and planning. They were pushing her toward Cornish and Hannah and the ultimate revenge content that would justify everything.

Soon, Travis promised. *Very soon you'll show them all.*

The platform demands it, the others agreed. *Your followers are waiting.*

Grace squeezed her eyes shut tighter, trying to block out the voices. But they were inside her head. They would always be inside her head. There was no escaping them. No escaping what she'd become.

The storm raged through the night and died down to just rain as the sky began to lighten. When dawn finally came, and the sun peeked through scattered rain clouds, it revealed devastation. The warehouse doors opened onto a landscape transformed, where shipping containers scattered like toys amidst vehicles crushed under fallen trees. The industrial park flooded with standing water two feet deep.

Grace stepped into the doorway, phone raised by instinct, filming the destruction. The sky hung low and gray. Rain still fell, but lighter. Softer now that the worst had passed.

"My God," someone whispered behind her.

The convoy was destroyed. Three of the five vehicles totaled. Equipment scattered. Supplies ruined by water. Everything they'd built over weeks of raiding and killing, wiped out in one night.

Grace should have felt despair. Instead she just felt numb. Empty. The storm inside her mind raged louder than the hurricane ever did.

Kyle appeared beside her, surveying the damage with grim silence.

"Can we salvage anything?" Grace asked.

"Maybe. Two vehicles might still run. Some supplies survived in the warehouse. But Grace." He turned to face her fully. "This is a sign. A chance to stop. To walk away from Cornish and find somewhere quiet where we can just survive."

"Walk away." Grace repeated the words like they were foreign. "From Hannah. From Maddie. From everything."

"Yes. From all of it. We could head north. Find some isolated place. Build something that isn't based on violence and delusion. Don't you want that? You and me, Grace."

Grace laughed. The sound came out broken and wrong. "Kyle, I can't walk away. You know that. The platform demands resolution. My followers need closure. Hannah and Maddie have to pay for what they did."

"What followers?" Kyle grabbed her shoulders, forcing her to look at him instead of the devastation. "Grace, there are no followers. There never were. It's just you talking to yourself in your delusions. You need to let it go before it kills you."

But Grace couldn't let it go. The ghosts were already screaming. Travis and the others demanding she continue. Demanding she finish what she started. The platform required sacrifice and blood. It needed Grace to keep performing until the narrative reached its conclusion.

"I can't," she whispered. "I can't stop."

Kyle stared at her, resolve breaking behind his eyes. A sad resignation. Like he'd known all along that Grace couldn't be saved. The girl who drowned was really dead, and what remained was just a monster in sequins, filming her way toward inevitable destruction.

"Then I'll stay with you," he said finally. "Until the end. Whatever that looks like."

Grace leaned into him, her phone still clutched in one hand, the devastated industrial park stretching before them. Behind them in the warehouse, people were stirring. Assessing damage. Rebecca moved among them, still playing her role of compliance.

The storm had passed, but Grace's madness remained.

Grace woke to voices coming from the warehouse floor below. The tone was urgent, even tense.

She rolled out of bed, her body aching from yesterday's storm and terror. The office window showed gray dawn light filtering through clouds that still hung heavy and threatening. Water covered everything outside. The industrial park was now a lake with debris islands.

Kyle was already gone. His side of the bed cold again.

Grace crawled out of bed slowly, her mind unable to focus on what she was doing. She quickly dressed in the same clothes she'd worn for the past week and descended the metal stairs, phone already in hand.

She walked up to see Frank standing near the warehouse entrance, soaked through with his crew behind him looking exhausted and rattled. Kyle faced them with arms crossed, and Pete and Nate flanked him in the doorway.

"When did you get back?" Kyle asked.

"Three hours ago." Frank's voice came out rough. "Drove through the worst of the storm. Nearly lost the truck twice."

Grace moved closer, filming their faces through her dead camera. "Did you find them?"

Frank's eyes shifted to Grace. Something flickered across his expression. Not quite fear. More like recognition that he'd made a terrible mistake joining this operation.

"The women reached Cornish," Frank said flatly. "Mrs. Henderson and the girl. They made it to the Thompson farm. They're talking. Warning everyone about what's coming."

The warehouse went silent. Grace's phone stayed raised, capturing everyone's reactions. Her followers would love this. The dramatic reveal. The escalating tension.

Perfect content, Travis whispered. *This makes everything better. Higher stakes. Greater payoff.*

"They know we're coming," Kyle said slowly.

"They know everything." Frank pulled out a soggy notebook, flipping through pages. "I got close enough to gather intel. The farm's on full alert. Armed patrols. Reinforced positions. They're expecting us. Mrs. Henderson gave them numbers, vehicles, names. They know about the Queen."

Grace's smile widened. "They know about me?"

"Everyone in Cornish knows about you now." Frank's voice carried something between contempt and exhaustion. "The crazy girl who thinks she's an influencer. Who keeps her phone charged with delusions and kills people for content. Mrs. Henderson told them everything."

Kyle shot Grace a warning look, but she didn't care. Her followers were buzzing. The comments flooding faster than ever.

They're scared of you, one ghost said.

The Queen's reputation precedes her, another agreed.

Fear is the best engagement metric, Travis assured her.

"Good," Grace said, her voice climbing with manic energy. "Let them be afraid. Let them prepare. It makes better content when we break them anyway. Revolutionary platform development requires authentic resistance."

"Grace." Kyle's hand found her elbow. "Not now."

But Grace pulled free, moving to Frank. "What else?"

"There's more," he said hesitantly. "Others arrived with them. A young woman and her brother." His eyes shot toward Rebecca in the corner.

"Oh? And this concerns me how?"

"The young woman is friends with Maddie Foster. Does that help?" He cringed slightly after saying it.

"Fabulous, now we know where Hannah is as well. This is perfect actually." She spun around, her eyes and phone bearing down on Rebecca. "Right, Rebecca."

Rebecca's eyes remained on the floor, but Grace could see the small satisfaction in this information. It wouldn't last long.

Frank stared at her like she'd lost her mind. Which she had. But Grace didn't care anymore. The ghosts loved her. The platform demanded resolution. Hannah and Maddie waited in Cornish, probably laughing about how they'd beaten her again.

"They have about eighty people," Frank said carefully. "Maybe twenty with any kind of hunting or gun experience. The Thompson farm is pretty well set up. Wells, generators, stored food, defensive positions, multiple buildings. Taking it will cost lives."

"Everything costs lives." Grace scrolled through her phone, checking imaginary metrics. "That's what makes it meaningful. Authentic consequences. Real stakes. This is exactly the content my followers have been waiting for."

The warehouse stirred. People started waking up and assessing storm damage, some coming to hear the news after realizing Frank had returned during the night. Rebecca remained near the back, her face carefully neutral, watching Grace with those blank eyes.

She's still plotting, Travis warned. *I can see it.*

But Grace ignored him. Rebecca was her pet now. Broken and trained and completely loyal. Kyle was just being paranoid.

"We move out in two hours," Grace announced, her voice carrying across the warehouse. "Frank's intelligence confirms target location. Storm delayed us, but we're still on schedule. Everyone pack up. We push to Cornish today."

"Grace." Kyle's voice hardened. "We need to discuss this. Plan, remember? Not just react?"

"I'm not reacting. I'm executing the mission." Grace turned to face him, her smile bright despite the dark circles under her eyes. "You said we'd do this together. Was that a lie?"

Kyle stared at her. Behind his eyes, she saw the war. The knowledge that Grace was spiraling beyond anything he could manage. The choice between stopping her or staying with her until the end.

"Two hours," Kyle said finally. "But we do this smart. Okay?"

"Of course." Grace's smile widened. "Very professional. Very tactical."

She moved through the warehouse, filming the aftermath of the storm. Water damage. Broken equipment. The remaining vehicles they'd need to salvage. Sherman's body still displayed across the lead truck's hood, now rain-swollen and grotesque.

Beautiful composition, one of the ghosts praised. *The decay. The symbolism. Very artistic.*

Grace zoomed in with her dead camera, capturing Sherman's ruined face. Days on the hood through July heat and yesterday's storm, he barely looked human anymore. Just meat and a warning.

"Memento mori content," Grace narrated softly. "Reminder that all platforms eventually end. But the Queen's platform is eternal. Revolutionary and unstoppable."

Rebecca approached with breakfast. Protein bars and bottled water distributed through the warehouse. When she reached Grace, she paused.

"Are you okay?" Rebecca asked quietly.

"I'm perfect." Grace took the food without looking at her. "Why wouldn't I be perfect? We're finally moving on Cornish. Finally getting closure. Finally showing Hannah what betrayal costs."

Rebecca's expression flickered. "Hannah tried to help you. They all did."

Grace's head snapped up. "What did you say?"

"Nothing." Rebecca backed away. "I'm sorry. I shouldn't have spoken."

She's turning against you, Travis hissed. *I told you she was playing.*

But Grace just smiled. "It's okay, Rebecca. You're confused. The integration isn't complete yet. But it will be. After Cornish. After you see what I'm capable of. Then you'll understand."

Rebecca nodded and moved on. Kyle appeared at Grace's side.

"She's right, you know," Kyle said quietly. "Hannah and Maddie. They tried to help you in Portsmouth. The intervention. Trying to stop those scouts. They saw you breaking and tried to save you."

"They destroyed me." Her voice cracked and turned high pitched.

"They tried to save you from yourself." Kyle's hand found her face, forcing her to look at him. "And I'm trying to save you now. But Grace, baby, you have to let me. You have to give me something to work with."

Grace leaned into his touch. "I can't stop now. You know that. The platform demands resolution. My followers need closure. If I stop, if I walk away, then what was it all for? All of it will be meaningless if I don't finish what I started."

"What if it's all meaningless anyway?"

The words hung between them. Grace's phone buzzed. Her followers screamed disagreement. The ghosts insisted the platform mattered. That everything she'd done was justified. That Kyle was trying to break her connection to her audience.

"It matters," Grace whispered. "It has to matter."

Kyle kissed her. "Then we finish it. Together. But Grace, when this is over, we need to talk about what comes next. About whether there's anything left of you worth saving."

"There isn't." Grace pulled away, adjusting her crop top. "That girl drowned in Portsmouth. What's left is just the Queen. And queens don't get saved. They rule or they die."

Two hours later, the convoy moved out.

Three vehicles left the lot. The lead truck with Sherman's body still displayed across the hood, attracting flies that swarmed despite the rain. The cage Rebecca lived in for days now sat empty, moved to the front of the second truck to make room for salvaged supplies in the bed. Behind it, one of Frank's trucks, loaded with the remaining crew and equipment.

Grace rode in the passenger seat of the lead truck. Kyle drove. Behind the trucks walked those who didn't fit on a vehicle The number dwindled significantly from the day she executed Sherman. Some snuck away that night, and others scattered during the storm or died in the building collapse.

The industrial park disappeared behind them. Grace filmed it through the rear window.

"And here we document our departure from the staging area," she narrated. "Moving toward final confrontation. Revolutionary content arc reaching climax. My followers understand narrative structure."

We've been waiting for this, Travis said from the back seat. Invisible to everyone except Grace.

The ultimate content drop, another ghost agreed.

Queen versus betrayers, a third voice added. *This is what we came for.*

Grace smiled at the ghosts crowding the truck bed. There were dozens now. Everyone she'd killed. Everyone who'd died in her operation. All of them validating her choices. Praising her vision. Loving her unconditionally.

The roads flooded worse than Grace expected. Water covered everything. Trees down everywhere. Power lines tangled across streets. The storm had torn the world apart and left it drowning.

Kyle navigated carefully, the truck pushing through water that sometimes reached the doors. Behind them, Frank's vehicle followed at a distance, staying in their tracks.

They drove for hours through devastation barely making any headway and even having to backtrack around obstacles. Grace filmed everything. The authentic apocalypse aesthetic. The genuine disaster content.

Late afternoon brought them to a river.

Not a river, but a torrent. What should have been a modest stream now raged across the road, brown water churning with debris. Trees. Parts of buildings. Things that might have been bodies, but no one wanted to look too closely. The bridge that once crossed it collapsed, twisted metal jutting from the water like broken teeth.

Kyle stopped the truck, climbed out and walked to the water's edge.

Grace followed, phone raised, capturing his face as he stared at the impossible crossing.

"We can't cross this," Kyle said.

"We have to." Grace moved closer to the water, feeling spray on her face. "Cornish is on the other side. Hannah is on the other side. We can't stop now."

"Grace, look at it. The current would flip the trucks. We'd all drown."

"Then we find another crossing."

"There isn't one for twenty miles. And that one's probably worse." Kyle turned to face her. "We camp here tonight. Wait for the water to go down. Cross tomorrow when it's safer."

But Grace's followers were screaming. Demanding she push forward. Insisting she prove her commitment to the platform. The ghosts grew louder, drowning out Kyle's reasonable voice.

You can't stop now, Travis urged. *Not when you're so close.*

The Queen doesn't let rivers stop her, another agreed.

Test the crossing, a third voice suggested. *Send someone across first.*

Grace's smile widened. "That's brilliant."

"What's brilliant?" Kyle asked.

"We test the crossing. Send someone across first to prove it's possible." Grace turned to survey the group gathering near the trucks. "Who wants to volunteer?"

Silence. Everyone stared at the raging water. At the debris spinning past. At the collapsed bridge that proved the river's power.

"Come on," Grace said, her voice climbing with manic energy. "Someone has to go first. Someone has to prove the Queen's platform doesn't stop for natural disasters. Who's brave enough to make history?"

More silence. People backing away. Even Frank's crew looked disturbed by the suggestion.

"Fine." Grace's hand moved to her pistol. "Then I'll choose."

She scanned the faces. Landed on a man and woman near the back. Mid-thirties maybe. Grace barely remembered their names or where they'd come from. Just two faces in the crowd. Two people who'd contributed nothing memorable to her content.

"You two." Grace pointed. "Mike and Jenny, right?"

The couple exchanged terrified glances. The man, Mike, stepped forward slightly. "Ma'am, I don't think—"

"You don't think what? That you should contribute to the platform? That you should prove your value?" Grace moved closer, pistol drawn now, pointing casually at them. "I've been very patient. Very accommodating. But everyone needs to carry their weight. And right now, the platform needs someone to test this crossing."

"Grace." Kyle's voice came sharp. "Don't do this."

"Why not?" Grace spun to face him. "They're expendable. Barely contributing. No real value or unique skills. Just two more mouths to feed. If they drown, we lose nothing. If they make it, we know the crossing is possible."

"If they drown, we're murderers."

"We're already murderers!" Grace's laugh came out high and brittle. "We've killed dozens of people! What's two more? Especially when it serves the platform's needs?"

Jenny started crying. Mike put his arm around her, both of them frozen in terror.

Grace raised her phone, filming their fear. "Look at this authentic emotional content. Raw terror. Genuine despair. My followers are eating this up."

They are, the ghosts confirmed. *Engagement metrics are through the roof.*

This is revolutionary content, Travis agreed.

Do it, the chorus urged. *Send them across.*

"Get in the truck," Grace said, gesturing with her pistol. "Drive across. Prove the crossing is possible."

"Please," Jenny whispered. "Please don't make us do this."

"I'm not making you do anything." Grace's smile widened. "You're volunteering. You're choosing to contribute to the platform and prove your value. To create meaningful content that will define this moment."

Mike's face hardened. "And if we refuse?"

Grace shot him in the foot.

The crack of the pistol made everyone flinch. Mike screamed, collapsing to the muddy ground, blood mixing with rainwater. Jenny dropped beside him, her hands pressing against the wound.

"Then I shoot the other foot," Grace said calmly, filming their agony. "Then the knees. Then eventually, you crawl to the truck and drive across anyway. Or I kill you both right here and find someone else to volunteer. Your choice. But someone is testing this crossing."

Kyle grabbed Grace's wrist. "Enough."

"It's not enough!" Grace pulled free, spinning on him. "Nothing's ever enough! I lost everything! Hannah and Maddie destroyed my platform! My followers abandoned me! My phone died! The world ended! And now this fucking river thinks it can stop me from getting the revenge I deserve?"

Her voice climbed to a shriek. Spittle flew. The ghosts roared approval.

"So yes," Grace continued, her pistol swinging back to Mike and Jenny. "Someone is crossing this river. Even if I have to shoot every single person here until someone volunteers. Even if I have to drive across myself. The platform demands it. My followers demand it. And the Queen does not back down!"

The silence that followed was absolute. Even the river seemed to quiet. Everyone stared at Grace. At the monster wearing sequins and madness like a crown.

Mike struggled to his feet, Jenny supporting him. Blood soaked his boot. He limped toward the lead truck.

"We'll do it," Mike said through gritted teeth. "We'll cross. Just don't hurt anyone else."

Grace's smile returned. "See? That's the spirit. Positive engagement. Willing contribution. This is exactly the kind of team cooperation the platform needs."

She filmed Mike and Jenny climbing into the lead truck. Filmed Kyle's horrified face. Filmed the ghosts dancing with glee in her peripheral vision.

Mike started the engine. Jenny sat in the passenger seat, crying.

The truck edged toward the water.

Grace moved to the bank, phone raised high, capturing every second. This was it. Revolutionary content. The moment that would define her platform forever. Either Mike and Jenny would make it across, proving the Queen's will conquered nature. Or they'd drown, creating authentic tragedy content that would break engagement metrics.

Win-win.

The truck's front wheels touched the water. Then the hood. The water reached the doors.

Mike accelerated. The truck pushed deeper. Water climbed the windows. The current hit the side like a hammer.

The truck tilted.

Grace gasped in delight.

"Oh my God," she breathed, filming as the truck twisted sideways. "This is incredible. Look at this. Look at the water pressure. The force. The authentic disaster content."

The truck flipped.

One moment it was upright, fighting the current. The next it rolled completely over, windows disappearing beneath brown water. Grace could see Mike crawl out, gripping the truck trying to save Jenny and buzzed with excitement.

Then the current took the truck. Swept it downstream. Smashed it against the collapsed bridge. Metal shrieked and the glass shattered.

Grace laughed.

The sound bubbled up from somewhere deep and broken. Pure, unfiltered delight at watching two people die in real time. She zoomed in on the submerged truck. On the windows where Mike and Jenny's faces no longer appeared. On the water pouring through broken glass to claim them.

"Yes!" Grace shouted over the river's roar. "YES! Did you see that? Did everyone see that? The current. The flip. The authentic drowning content. My followers are going insane right now!"

She spun to face the group, her phone still recording, her face split with the biggest smile anyone had seen since the apocalypse began.

"Wasn't that amazing? The way the truck just rolled? The way the water took them? This is exactly why we film everything. Why we document every moment. This is revolutionary content that will define apocalypse survival narrative forever!"

No one spoke. Everyone stared at Grace like they were seeing a demon wearing human skin.

Kyle walked away. Just turned and walked back to Frank's truck, his shoulders tight, his rifle gripped so hard his knuckles went white.

"Where are you going?" Grace called after him. "Kyle! We need to plan the alternate route! We need to coordinate the next attempt!"

But Kyle didn't respond. Didn't look back. Just kept walking.

Grace's smile faltered. "Kyle?"

Frank appeared beside her. His voice came out flat. "We camp here tonight. Find a crossing in the morning. And Grace? You stay the fuck away from everyone. Clear?"

"But the content—"

"I don't give a shit about your content." Frank's face was inches from hers. "You just killed two people for fun. Watched them drown and laughed. I've done terrible things in my life. Things that would make you sick. But I never enjoyed it. You're not a revolutionary. You're not a queen. You're just a psychopath with a dead phone and ghost audience that doesn't exist."

He walked away too. Left Grace standing by the river, phone still raised, filming the water rushing past with Mike and Jenny's bodies somewhere downstream.

They don't understand, Travis said softly. *They never will.*

That was beautiful content, another ghost agreed. *Perfect tragedy. Authentic death. Your followers loved every second.*

The Queen does what she must, a third voice added. *Never apologize for greatness.*

Grace lowered her phone slowly. Looked at the faces still watching her. Pete and Nate wouldn't meet her eyes. The Burke Brothers backed away like she was radioactive. Rebecca stared with an expression Grace couldn't quite read. Jennifer and Carol held each other, crying.

Amy sat on the ground, her ruined leg stretched in front of her, and laughed. A broken, bitter sound that cut through the river's noise.

"You're finally showing everyone what you really are," Amy said. "No more pretending. No more performing. Just pure, unfiltered monster."

Grace wanted to argue. To explain. To make them understand that Mike and Jenny's deaths meant something. Created something. Mattered in ways they couldn't comprehend.

But she was so tired of explaining. Tired of performing. Tired of filtering her madness through justifications that no one believed anyway.

So she just smiled. "I know what I am. The question is, do you know what you are? Accomplices. Enablers. Witnesses to greatness who'll tell stories about the Queen long after I'm gone."

She walked back to Frank's truck, climbed into the bed, and sat among the supplies and equipment. The ghosts crowded around her, offering praise and validation and unconditional love.

That was perfect, they assured her.

You're perfect, they promised.

The platform is eternal, they guaranteed.

Grace scrolled through her phone, reading imaginary comments from followers who loved her no matter what she did, understood her vision and celebrated her revolution.

And if everyone else thought she was a monster? Well. Monsters made the best content anyway.

Grace woke before dawn with the emptiness already gnawing at her chest. The high from yesterday's drowning had faded during the night, leaving behind a hollow ache that made her fingers twitch toward her phone. She scrolled through blank screens in the darkness, searching for the rush of validation that used to flood her system with warmth.

Nothing.

The comments weren't loud enough anymore. The imaginary hearts felt distant, muted. Mike and Jenny's deaths were beautiful content, maybe even revolutionary. The way the truck flipped, the water taking them to their watery grave, Grace's own delighted laughter echoing across the river only accentuated the horror in their eyes. But now, less than twelve hours later, the memory felt flat. Used up. A high that burned too fast and left her craving more.

You need bigger content, Travis whispered from somewhere near the tent flap. *Yesterday was good, but today needs to be better.*

"I know," Grace murmured, pulling on her pink camo pants in the pre-dawn gray. Her hands shook slightly. Withdrawal. That's what this felt like. Coming down from the most incredible rush only to find reality waiting with its teeth bared.

Kyle still slept beside her, one arm thrown across his face. Grace studied him in the dim light. He'd barely spoken to her after the drowning. Just walked away and set up camp on the opposite side of their small clearing. Later, after dark, he came to the tent and took her with a violence that left bruises, but he didn't say a word. Just used her body like he was punishing something, then rolled over and slept.

Grace liked it better when he was afraid of her.

She left the tent, with the phone already raised to film the sunrise. The river had dropped significantly overnight. What was a raging torrent yesterday now looked almost crossable. The current still moved fast, but the water level had fallen enough to expose rocks and the twisted remains of the collapsed bridge.

"Location update for my amazing followers," Grace narrated softly, capturing the pink and orange sky. "The algorithm blessed us with perfect conditions for today's crossing attempt. Very aspirational dawn aesthetic. One could almost say that nature really understands content creation."

The engagement numbers are still down from yesterday, Travis said, appearing beside her. He looked more solid this morning, his chest wound less apparent. *You need something to boost them back up.*

"I know." Grace lowered her phone, that hollow ache spreading through her chest again. "Yesterday was perfect. Why isn't it enough?"

Because content creation is about momentum, another voice added. Dice materialized on her other side, the hole in his face from her bullet somehow less disturbing in the morning light. *You can't coast on past successes. You need fresh material.*

Grace nodded, understanding blooming through her exhaustion. That's why she felt so empty. She'd created incredible content yesterday, but the platform demanded more.

Always more. The audience got bored quickly, needed constant stimulation, and required escalation to maintain their interest.

She was learning that with each execution. The first few gave her such an incredible high. Travis's death especially; the way everyone's faces changed when she pulled the trigger. The power flooding through her system like electricity. But the high faded faster each time. Sherman's execution barely lasted a day before she needed another fix. Amy's maiming gave her maybe six hours of satisfaction.

And Mike and Jenny? Beautiful, perfect content that should have sustained her for days. But here she was, less than twelve hours later, already craving more.

Diminishing returns, Landry said, appearing near the water's edge. *Classic addiction pattern. You need bigger doses to get the same effect.*

"I'm not addicted," Grace said sharply. "I'm building a platform. Creating revolutionary content. That's completely different."

The ghosts exchanged glances. Travis smiled. *Of course it is. We're just saying you need something special for today. Something that will really drive those engagement metrics.*

Grace's fingers tightened on her phone. They were right. Today's content needed to be bigger than yesterday's. Better. More dramatic. Something that would fill this gnawing emptiness in her chest and bring back that incredible rush of power and validation.

Behind her, the camp stirred. People emergede from tents and makeshift shelters, faces haggard from another night of terror and exhaustion. Grace filmed them, capturing their fear for her audience.

"Morning content featuring authentic survivor energy," she narrated. "Look at those raw emotional states. You can't fake this kind of material."

Rebecca appeared near the supply truck, moving with that careful efficiency Grace appreciated. The woman had become such a good assistant. Always anticipating Grace's needs, always supportive, always there with whatever props or materials the content required. Grace felt good in how she'd trained her perfectly.

She's planning something, Travis warned. *I can see it in her eyes.*

But Grace dismissed the concern. Rebecca was broken but loyal. The cage had done its job, the integration sessions worked exactly as planned. She was Grace's pet now, completely dependent on her Queen's approval.

Frank emerged from his tent, stretching and yawning. His crew followed. Davis, Lucas, Wrench, and Rabbit, all looking as exhausted as everyone else. Frank's face showed the strain of the past few days. The storm, the destruction, Grace's escalating violence. He looked like a man regretting his choices.

Grace raised her phone, filming his approach. "Guest intelligence update! Frank, tell our followers about today's crossing strategy."

Frank glanced at the river, then at Grace. Something flickered across his expression. Calculation maybe. Or concern. "Water's dropped enough. We can cross about a quarter mile upstream. There's a ford there, should be manageable now."

"Perfect!" Grace's enthusiasm felt forced even to her own ears. "Strategic planning from our expert consultant! This is exactly the kind of professional content that drives serious engagement!"

Frank's jaw tightened. "Grace, we need to talk about Cornish. About what we're actually walking into."

"We've been over this," Grace said, her smile straining. "You provided intelligence, Sherman confirmed it, the Burke brothers filled in details. We're completely prepared for the coming liberation content."

"That intelligence is wrong." Frank's voice carried an edge Grace didn't like. "Or at least incomplete. I've been thinking about it, and there's no way the Thompson farm is as lightly defended as we discussed. Not after Mrs. Henderson reached them. Not after the storm gave them time to prepare."

The emptiness in Grace's chest sharpened into something colder. Frank was creating negative content. Undermining her platform. Questioning her leadership in front of everyone.

He's tanking your engagement numbers, Travis said urgently. *Making you look weak.*

"Frank." Grace's voice dropped lower. "Are you questioning my strategic planning? In front of my entire community?"

"I'm trying to keep us alive." Frank stepped closer, lowering his voice. "Grace, listen to me. I know you think this is all some kind of show, but people are going to die today. Real people. And if we go into Cornish expecting light resistance, we're going to be the ones that get slaughtered."

Grace felt her parents' presence flickering. She turned, searching for them in the growing dawn light. "Mom? Dad? Where are you? Frank's being negative again."

But the spaces where her parents usually stood remained empty. Their voices, which normally provided constant encouragement, stayed silent.

"They're not here," Frank said quietly. "Grace, they've never been here. Your parents are in Boston, and they have no idea what you've become."

The words hit like ice water. Grace's vision flickered. For just a moment, she saw everything clearly. The terrified faces around her. Frank's genuine concern. The bodies they'd left behind. The trail of death and madness stretching back to Earl's cabin.

No, Travis said sharply. *Don't let him break your connection to the platform.*

He's sabotaging your content, Dice agreed. *Making you doubt yourself.*

The audience needs you strong, Landry added. *Confident. Not questioning everything.*

Grace blinked hard, forcing the moment of clarity away. Frank was right about one thing. Her parents weren't here. But not because they were in Boston. Because Frank had driven them away with his constant negativity. His toxic energy disrupted the connection between Grace and her followers, interfered with the algorithm, destroyed the engagement metrics she'd worked so hard to build.

"You're fired," Grace said softly.

Frank stared at her. "What?"

"From the platform. From the community. From my content creation team." Grace raised her phone, filming his confusion. "You've been consistently bringing negative energy to our operation. Questioning my strategic planning. Undermining community morale. That's unacceptable for someone in your position."

"Grace, for fuck's sake, I'm trying to help you."

"By telling me my parents don't exist?" Grace's voice climbed. "By saying my platform is imaginary? By contradicting the intelligence we've carefully gathered from multiple sources?"

She turned to face the assembled camp. Most people were awake now, watching the confrontation with varying expressions of fear and resignation. Kyle stood near his tent, arms crossed, face unreadable.

"Everyone needs to understand something," Grace announced, phone sweeping across the crowd. "This is a professional content creation operation. We have standards. We have expectations. And when someone consistently fails to meet those expectations, when they actively work to sabotage our platform, there are consequences."

Good, Travis approved. *Show them what happens to negative influences.*

Grace felt the emptiness in her chest begin to fill. Not with the validation she craved, but with something darker. Anticipation. The promise of that incredible high she'd been chasing since yesterday's drowning wore off.

"Frank has been fired from his consulting position," Grace continued, her smile returning. "But he still owes the platform for all the resources we've invested in him. Transportation. Food. Security. Protection from the consequences of his past actions."

Frank's face went pale. "Grace, don't do this."

"Strip," Grace said simply.

The camp went silent. Even the ghosts seemed to hold their breath.

"What?" Frank's voice came out strangled.

"You heard me. Everything off. Right now. You're not part of this community anymore, so you don't get community privileges. Including clothes."

Frank looked around desperately, searching for allies. His crew stepped back, unwilling to challenge Grace's authority. Kyle's expression never changed. Pete and Nate moved their hands to their weapons, making their positions clear.

"Grace, please," Frank said, his voice breaking. "I was trying to help. I just wanted to make sure we planned this right."

"Then you should have been more positive," Grace replied. Her phone stayed raised, capturing every moment of his humiliation. "You should have supported the platform instead of undermining it. But you made your choice, Frank. Now you experience the consequences."

The anticipation building in Grace's chest grew stronger. This was going to be good content. Not as dramatic as yesterday's drowning, but satisfying in a different way. Public humiliation. Complete power demonstration. The kind of thing that would remind everyone who was in charge.

Frank's hands shook as he began removing his clothes. His face burned with shame and rage, but he complied. Grace filmed every moment, narrating for her invisible audience about accountability and community standards.

When Frank stood naked in the morning light, Grace felt that familiar rush starting to build. Not quite the high she needed, but getting closer. The power flooding through her, the complete control over another human being's dignity and suffering.

Better, Travis said. *But you need more.*

Grace knew he was right. This wasn't enough. The emptiness still gnawed at her, demanding something bigger, something that would fill the void Mike and Jenny's deaths had temporarily satisfied.

"Bring rope," Grace ordered. "The good rope, not the fraying stuff. We're going to create some authentic accountability content that my followers will never forget."

Pete brought the rope. Grace directed him and Nate to tie Frank's wrists together, then attach the rope to the rear bumper of the lead truck. Frank tried to resist, but two armed men made resistance pointless.

"What are you doing?" Frank asked, his voice thick with terror and rage.

"Creating content," Grace said brightly. "Very authentic consequence demonstration. The kind of thing that really drives engagement metrics."

She positioned Frank behind the truck, making sure the rope was long enough that he could walk if he kept pace. But not so long that he could rest or slack.

"Here's what's happening," Grace explained, filming Frank's terrified face. "You're going to walk behind this truck all the way to Cornish. Every step of the way, you're going to think about how your negative energy brought you to this moment. How questioning the platform led to consequences."

"Grace, please," Frank's voice cracked. "Don't make me do this. The road is torn up. My feet will be shredded before we go a mile."

"Then you'd better keep up with the truck," Grace said sweetly. "Because if you fall, we're not stopping. The show must go on, Frank. Content creation doesn't wait for people who can't handle the pace."

Perfect, the ghosts chorused. *This is what the audience wants to see.*

Grace felt the high building stronger now. Not quite there yet, but close. Watching Frank's face cycle through terror and disbelief and desperate hope that this was somehow a joke. Seeing the moment when he realized she was completely serious.

That's when the rush hit. Not as powerful as yesterday's drowning, but satisfying in its own way. Frank's complete helplessness. The camp's horrified silence. The absolute proof that Grace controlled everything and everyone.

"Let's move out," Grace called, climbing into the passenger seat of the lead truck. Kyle took the driver's position without comment. "We've got a river to cross and a revolution to film."

The convoy assembled and people packed supplies, secured equipment, prepared vehicles. All of them carefully avoiding looking at Frank behind the lead truck.

Grace filmed everything through the rear window. Frank standing naked behind them, rope tight around his wrists, face showing the dawning horror of what the next few hours would bring.

"Behind the scenes content," Grace narrated softly. "Showing authentic consequences for platform sabotage. This is what real leadership looks like, everyone. Making hard choices that other content creators won't touch."

Kyle started the truck, moving slowly forward. The rope went taut. Frank stumbled, then found his footing, forced to walk or be dragged.

Grace watched him through the cracked rear window, phone pressed against the glass. Each step Frank took seemed to pump more of that precious high into her system. Not enough yet. Still not enough. But building. Growing. Promising that if she just pushed a little further, if she created content just a little more extreme, she'd finally fill this emptiness.

They moved toward the river crossing at a crawl, maybe five miles per hour. Fast enough to make Frank work to keep up, but slow enough that he could maintain the pace if he focused. The road was as bad as he'd feared. Broken asphalt, scattered debris from the storm, sharp rocks and twisted metal.

Grace filmed Frank's stumbling progress. His feet already bleeding. His face contorted with pain and exhaustion and rage. Every few minutes he'd try to stop, try to rest, but the moving truck gave him no choice. Walk, or be dragged.

Beautiful composition, Travis said, appearing in the passenger seat beside Grace. *Very authentic suffering. The engagement numbers are climbing.*

Grace checked her phone, seeing the imaginary metrics soaring. Hearts flooding in faster than ever. Comments praising her decisive leadership. Follower count jumping by thousands with each passing minute.

The high built stronger and Grace's breath came faster with each passing moment. This was working. This was filling the void. Frank's pain translating directly into platform growth, into validation, into that incredible rush that made everything else worth it.

They reached the ford after an hour of crawling progress. Frank collapsed behind the truck, his feet leaving bloody prints on the broken road. His body shook with exhaustion and pain, but Grace felt nothing but satisfaction. He'd questioned her. Undermined her platform. Now he paid the price.

The water here moved fast but shallow, maybe three feet deep at most. Rocky bottom visible through the brown current. Kyle studied it carefully.

"Should work," he said, his first words of the day. "Take it slow, stay in the truck's tracks. Should be fine."

Grace barely heard him. She was too focused on Frank through the rear window. On the way his chest heaved with exhausted sobs and the blood streaking his legs. She reveled in the complete defeat written across his face.

More, the ghosts whispered. *You need more. This isn't enough yet.*

They were right. The high had plateaued. Frank's suffering was good content, but it wasn't pushing her further up that slope toward the peak. She needed escalation. Needed something that would take this from good to revolutionary.

"Kyle," Grace said softly, an idea forming. "When we cross, keep the same speed. Don't slow down for the water."

Kyle's hands tightened on the wheel. "Grace. Frank can't swim while tied to the truck. If he falls in the current—"

"Then he'd better not fall," Grace interrupted. "This is consequence content, Kyle. Real stakes. Authentic danger. That's what drives serious engagement."

Kyle stared at her. For a long moment, Grace thought he might refuse. Might finally draw a line she couldn't cross. But then his jaw clenched and he nodded once, sharp and final.

"Your platform," he said flatly.

Grace's smile widened. Kyle understood. He always understood. Even when he was afraid of her, even when he questioned her methods, he never actually stopped her. Because he was addicted, too. To her madness, to the savage intimacy between them, to watching how far she'd go.

The lead truck rolled into the water. The current hit immediately, pushing against the side panels. Kyle kept the speed steady, wheels churning through the rocky bottom. Behind them, Frank scrambled to follow, stumbling into the water with a gasp.

Grace pressed her phone against the rear window, filming every second. Frank fighting to keep his feet. The current shoving at his naked body. His face a mask of terror as he struggled to maintain pace with the moving truck.

The high started climbing again. Grace's pulse quickened. This was it. This was the escalation she needed. Frank might drown. Might get swept away. Might die right there on camera while Grace filmed revolutionary content.

Yes, Travis breathed. *Yes, this is perfect.*

Frank went under. Just for a moment, his feet slipping on the rocks. He surfaced, gasping, the rope still connecting him to the truck. Kyle kept the speed steady. Frank fought harder, terror lending him strength.

Grace felt the rush building toward that peak: her breathing shallow and fast; her whole body trembling with anticipation.

This was almost as good as yesterday's drowning. Almost as satisfying as watching the truck flip with Mike and Jenny inside.

Frank made it across. Stumbled onto the far bank and collapsed, coughing up river water. Still alive. Still breathing.

Grace's high crashed hard and fast. The disappointment flooded through her system like poison. He'd survived. The content hadn't reached its full potential. She'd been so close to that incredible peak, and Frank ruined it by not drowning.

Tomorrow, the ghosts promised. *Tomorrow you'll get what you need.*

Grace lowered her phone slowly. The rest of the convoy crossed without incident, vehicles churning through the ford one by one. Nobody spoke. Everyone carefully avoiding looking at Frank's broken form behind the lead truck.

Kyle parked on the far bank, killing the engine. The sudden silence felt oppressive. Grace climbed out, moving to stand over Frank.

"Good job keeping up," she said brightly, filming his wheezing gasps. "That's the kind of dedication to the platform I like to see. Very professional attitude despite the challenging circumstances."

Frank raised his head, and Grace saw something in his eyes that sent a thrill through her. Pure, concentrated hatred. The kind of rage that came from complete helplessness. From being broken and humiliated and forced to endure something inhumane.

That look gave her a small hit of the high. Not enough to fill the void, but enough to ease the worst of the craving.

"We're almost to Cornish," Grace continued. "Just a few more miles. Then we'll set up camp, and you can rest. Isn't that exciting? We're so close to the finale content."

Frank said nothing. Just stared at her with those hate-filled eyes.

Grace patted his head like a dog. "Don't worry. Tomorrow's content is going to be incredible. Revolutionary. The kind of thing that breaks the internet. You're going to be such an important part of that."

She turned back to the convoy, phone raised high. "Everyone take thirty minutes to rest and regroup! Then we push to Cornish for tonight's camp! The finale is almost here, my beautiful followers!"

The camp moved along with all the people so numbed by Grace's escalating violence that Frank's treatment barely registered anymore. Just another atrocity in a long line of them.

Grace scrolled through her phone, reading imaginary comments. The numbers weren't as high as she'd hoped. Frank's near-drowning had given her a decent hit, but nothing like yesterday's actual deaths. She needed more. Needed bigger. Needed something that would finally, permanently fill this gnawing emptiness.

Tomorrow, Travis promised again. *A hanging will be perfect.*

Grace nodded, understanding with crystal clarity. Frank's suffering today was just setup. Appetizer content. The real meal came tomorrow when she turned his execution into performance art. When she made an example that would terrify everyone into compliance and drive her platform metrics through the roof.

She just had to make it through tonight. Had to endure the comedown, the craving, the empty ache that came from chasing a high that demanded more and more and more.

Kyle appeared beside her, handing her a water bottle. His face was carefully blank, but Grace saw the tension in his jaw. The way his hands wouldn't quite stay still.

"You're scared of me," Grace said. It wasn't a question.

Kyle's throat worked. "Yes."

"But you're staying anyway."

"Yes."

Grace smiled, feeling a small rush of validation. Even Kyle, who'd enabled her madness from the beginning, who'd taught her how to use fear as a weapon, who'd shaped her into the Queen she'd become. Even he was terrified now.

"I love you," Grace said. The words came out strange, wrong somehow. A lie and a truth twisted together.

"I know," Kyle replied. He pulled her close, his mouth finding hers in a kiss that was full of need. "I love the monster I helped create."

They stayed like that for a moment, two broken people clinging to each other in the wreckage of their choices. Then Kyle pulled away, his expression hardening back into that careful handler's mask.

"Get some rest," he said. "We've got a few more hours before we reach town."

Grace nodded, watching him walk away. The emptiness yawned wider, but tomorrow's execution would help. Would give her that high she craved. But she was starting to suspect it might not be enough either. That maybe nothing would ever be enough again.

You'll need bigger doses, Landry said, appearing beside her. *The returns keep diminishing. That's how addiction works.*

"I'm not addicted," Grace said automatically. But even she didn't believe it anymore.

The convoy rested for thirty minutes, then pressed forward. Frank stumbled behind the truck, his feet leaving bloody trails. Cornish appeared in the distance, storm-damaged buildings rising against the afternoon sky.

Grace filmed their approach, narrating about liberation and revolution and finale content. But underneath the performance, the craving gnawed at her.

Kill more, the ghosts suggested. *Bigger executions. Multiple victims. Make it a festival.*

Grace's hands tightened on her phone. They were right. She'd already figured out the pattern. Each death gave less satisfaction than the last. So the solution was simple. More deaths. More suffering. Keep escalating until she found the dose that worked.

Elena brought a brief high, but she was just as insane as Grace but more of a Primadonna. Grace glanced to where Rebecca was readying Elena for her camera moment. She brought fresh intelligence and would prove that Frank was wrong. She was going to hang someone tomorrow, and she didn't care who it was.

Cornish's outskirts loomed closer. Grace saw the perfect spot. The town hall with its front steps. Wide and dramatic and visible to everyone. Perfect staging for tomorrow's performance.

"We'll camp here tonight," Grace announced. "Set up perimeter security. I want everyone rested for tomorrow's content creation."

Frank collapsed behind the truck, unconscious or simply unable to go further. Grace filmed him lying in his own blood, careful to get the best angle on his destroyed feet and broken expression.

"Behind the scenes content," she narrated softly. "Showing authentic consequences for negative energy. Tomorrow's finale is going to be revolutionary, everyone. The kind of content that breaks engagement metrics and redefines what platform success looks like."

Grace turned her phone toward him, capturing his kneeling form against the backdrop of ruined buildings. "Let's check in with our special guest! Frank, tell our amazing followers what you've learned about community engagement and positive energy!"

Frank raised his head, and Grace acted like she was zooming in on his face. The defeat in his eyes would translate beautifully to her audience. She felt it was authentic, emotional content that you simply couldn't fake.

But then he opened his mouth and ruined everything.

"Grace," he croaked, "there's nobody watching. There's no audience. You're talking to a dead phone."

"Frank, what the hell are you doing? You're completely destroying the narrative flow! Can't you see we're creating premium content here?

"The reviews are coming in," Grace whispered, reading feedback that scrolled across her vision like ghostly subtitles. "Oh, no. Oh, no… no, no, no…the engagement numbers are terrible. Someone's been sabotaging my platform."

She turned back to Frank with sudden clarity, seeing him clearly for the first time. Not a community member struggling with personal growth, but a saboteur deliberately tanking her metrics. The pieces fell into place with horrible precision.

"It's you." Grace's voice dropped to something more dangerous than screaming. "You're the one posting negative reviews. You're working for my competitors, trying to destroy everything I've built."

"Grace, please—" Frank began, but Grace cut him off with a dismissive gesture of her hand.

"No more negative content!" Her voice rose to levels that made several followers step backward. "I am so tired of people trying to destroy my platform! This is premium subscriber content, and you're killing my engagement rates with your toxic energy!"

She lowered her phone slowly, the emptiness already building again despite filming Frank's suffering.

"This is going to be absolutely incredible footage!" Grace announced, walking backward while filming Frank's journey toward the building and up the steps. "Natural lighting, authentic setting, real consequences for negative energy! Our platform analytics are going to go through the roof!"

Her community managers worked with professional efficiency, positioning Frank on the front steps while Grace provided running commentary about camera angles and audience engagement. The rope flew out of the upper story window, the noose end landing on the stoop behind him. She stood smiling, they'd done this before, and understood the technical requirements for quality content creation.

"Any last words for our followers, Frank?" Grace held her phone close to his face, capturing his expression in beautiful high definition. "Want to apologize for trying to sabotage our amazing community building efforts?"

Frank's head lifted slightly. His eyes found Grace's face, and she felt a small hit of satisfaction from the hatred burning there. He tried to speak but his throat was too raw from screaming.

"Save your voice," Grace advised, moving closer with her phone. "You're going to need it for today's performance. Very important that the audio is clear for my followers."

Frank's voice came out as a barely audible whisper, "You're bat shit crazy." Then he looked up at the group standing around watching as they prepared to hang him. "Can't you all see? Can't you see what is happening here?" He pleaded, but each of them just looked at the ground. He looked into her eyes with a venom that was incredible, and Grace smiled, lifting the phone to capture it. Then Frank hissed. "Your mother abandoned you because she's ashamed of what you've become."

Kyle grabbed her arm, pulling her away from Frank's earshot. "Grace. We need to talk about what happens after."

"After the hanging? We plan the farm assault with Elena's intelligence. I already outlined the content strategy last night."

"No." Kyle's grip tightened. "After everything. After Cornish. After you get your revenge on Hannah and Maddie. What happens then?"

Grace blinked at him, confused by the question. "Then the platform continues growing. We expand operations. Create more revolutionary content. Build the empire."

"With what followers?" Kyle's voice dropped lower. "Grace, look around. We're down to maybe thirty people. Half of them are terrified of you. The other half are planning to run the first chance they get. This isn't sustainable."

The words tried to penetrate Grace's defenses, tried to force her to see reality. But the ghosts were already there, building walls against Kyle's truth.

He's trying to sabotage you, Dice said. *Right before your biggest content drop.*

He's scared, Landry added. *Scared of how powerful you've become.*

"You're just nervous about today's execution," Grace said, patting Kyle's cheek. "Pre-performance jitters. Very normal. But don't worry, baby. Today's content is going to be so incredible that everyone will remember why they follow the Queen." Grace's entire world tilted sideways. Gripping something deep and raw in the place where her parents' voices used to provide constant encouragement and validation. She looked around desperately, searching for their familiar faces in the crowd of followers.

The static behind her eyes exploded into white noise. For a moment that lasted forever, Grace saw everything with perfect clarity. The terrified faces of her prisoners. The broken phone in her hands. Frank's naked, beaten figure standing on his tip toes with the rope tightening. The blood under her fingernails. The smell of death that followed her everywhere.

The truth crashed over her like ice water and she gasped, stumbling backward as reality tried to reassert itself.

Nothing. Just empty air and the growing certainty that something was very, very wrong with her platform.

But the camera was still rolling. It had to be. The alternative was unthinkable.

Grace's mind worked frantically to patch the cracks in her delusion, layering new fantasies over the crumbling foundation of her sanity. The effort left her dizzy and nauseous, but content creators had to maintain professionalism even during technical difficulties.

Now for the main event, Travis said. *Frank's waiting.*

Grace turned toward the town hall, seeing the sun had climbed high enough for perfect lighting. Frank still hung suspended, barely conscious from pain and exhaustion. The crowd had gathered without being told, drawn by morbid fascination or survival instinct that demanded they witness what came next.

Time for the finale," Grace announced. "Everyone gather around! This is going to be revolutionary content that redefines what platform success looks like!"

She moved toward Frank, feeling that emptiness in her chest finally starting to ease. This was it. Frank's execution combined with Elena's arrival. Double content drop. Maybe this would finally be enough.

Pete and Nate positioned themselves near the rope. Rebecca stood in the crowd, face carefully neutral. The Burke brothers watched from the edge, both boys pale and tense. Kyle leaned against a wall, arms crossed, expression unreadable.

Grace raised her phone, framing the perfect shot. Frank hanging from the town hall. The crowd assembled below. Storm-damaged buildings provided authentic apocalypse aesthetic.

"Before we begin," Grace said loudly, "I want everyone to understand what today represents. This isn't just an execution. It's a demonstration. A teaching moment. An example of what happens when someone consistently brings negative energy to our community."

She moved closer to Frank, tilting his chin up with her pistol barrel. His eyes opened, filled with pain and rage and something that might have been resignation.

"Frank questioned the platform," Grace continued. "He contradicted our strategic planning. He tried to convince me that my parents weren't watching, that my followers didn't exist. He brought toxic energy that threatened everything we've built."

Tell them about the consequences, Dice urged.

"And now," Grace's smile widened, "he experiences authentic consequences for his choices. This is advanced community management, everyone. Pay attention. Learn from Frank's mistakes."

Frank found his voice, rasping and broken. "Grace. Please. I have information. About the farm. About routes and defenses. I'm valuable alive."

"You were valuable," Grace corrected. "Past tense. You became a liability when you couldn't appreciate what we were building."

She stepped back, gesturing to Pete and Nate. "Gentlemen, if you please. Let's give our followers some revolutionary content."

Frank's eyes went wide. "Grace, wait. Listen to me. Your mother would be ashamed of what you've become. Your parents would look at you and see a monster."

The words detonated like a bomb in Grace's chest. Her vision flickered. For one horrible moment, she saw everything clearly. Her parents' faces. Not proud and encouraging. Horrified. Ashamed. Looking at their daughter and seeing something unrecognizable.

No, Travis said sharply. *Don't let him break you. Not now.*

He's trying to sabotage the content, Landry added. *Right at the climax.*

Finish it, Dice demanded. *Show everyone what happens to people who try to destroy your platform.*

Grace blinked hard, forcing the moment of clarity away. Frank was lying. Trying to hurt her with the last weapon he had left. Her parents weren't ashamed. They were watching. They were proud. They had to be.

"Pull the rope," Grace said softly.

Frank's feet left the ground completely. The rope went taut. His body jerked once, twice, legs kicking reflexively. His face turned purple. Eyes bulging. Mouth working soundlessly.

Grace filmed every second, phone raised high. "Notice the authentic physical responses," she narrated, "The way the body reacts to oxygen deprivation. Very educational content. Very valuable for our followers studying survival techniques."

But the high she'd expected, the rush that was supposed to fill the emptiness, didn't come. Grace watched Frank's death with growing desperation, waiting for that incredible feeling to flood through her system.

Nothing.

Frank's movements slowed. His face darkened further. His body went through its final convulsions. And Grace felt nothing but that terrible gnawing emptiness growing worse instead of better.

Why isn't this working? Grace thought desperately. *This should be enough. This should fill it.*

Diminishing returns, Travis said quietly. *You need bigger doses now. Frank's just one person. You need more.*

Frank's body went still. Grace lowered her phone slowly, staring at his corpse with something approaching panic. She'd been so sure this would work. So certain that Frank's execution would give her the high she needed.

But all she felt was empty. Used up. Like an addict realizing their usual dose no longer worked.

"Beautiful content," Grace said mechanically, her voice lacking its usual enthusiasm. "Revolutionary execution. Authentic consequences. Very engaging for our followers."

The crowd stood in shocked silence. Nobody moved. Nobody spoke. They just stared at Frank's body swaying gently in the morning breeze, understanding that Grace had crossed a line that couldn't be uncrossed.

Kyle stared at her, and Grace saw something break behind his eyes. Not surprise. Not shock. Just sad, tired acceptance. He'd finally realized she was completely gone. That whatever girl had existed before Portsmouth was never coming back. He turned to walk away and she called out to him, "Kyle? Are you leaving?"

"I'm staying with you," he said quietly. "Until the end. Whatever that looks like."

Grace kissed him, although the exchange was filled with fear and reservation, it carried the weight of their twisted love. "That's what I like to hear. Loyalty. Commitment. Platform dedication."

Nobody cheered. A few people nodded with hollow eyes. Most just stared at Frank hanging from the town hall, understanding that if they showed the wrong emotion, they might be next.

Grace felt the emptiness yawn wider. This should excite them. Should fill them with enthusiasm for the incredible content they were about to create. But their fear read as disappointment, as failure to appreciate her vision.

They don't understand yet, Travis assured her. *But they will. After today's performance, everyone will see what you've built.*

Grace understood. Frank's hanging wasn't enough by itself. She needed escalation. Needed something that would push this from good content to revolutionary.

Elena arrived mid-morning.

Grace heard the commotion first. Shouts from the perimeter guards. Then a figure stumbling into camp, mud-caked and exhausted. A young woman, late twenties maybe, with that desperate refugee energy that made for compelling content.

Grace raised her phone immediately, filming the woman's approach. "Spontaneous arrival content! This is incredible! Everyone, we're getting organic dramatic development!"

The woman collapsed near the center of camp, gasping with exhaustion. Her clothes were torn and filthy, her face marked by genuine trauma. Or very good acting. Grace couldn't quite tell which.

"Please," the woman gasped. "I need help. I escaped. They threw me out, and I've been walking for days."

Grace moved closer, phone capturing every detail. "Tell me everything. Our followers need to hear your story. This is exactly the kind of authentic human drama that drives serious engagement."

The woman looked up, and Grace saw calculation behind the performance of helplessness. This refugee understood how to play an audience. Knew how to craft a narrative. Grace liked her immediately.

"My name is Elena," the woman said, her voice breaking with what sounded like real grief. "I lost everything. My baby died and the man I loved chose someone else. The community that was supposed to support me turned on me instead. Protected the people who destroyed my life."

Grace's excitement spiked. Personal betrayal. Romantic conflict. Community corruption. This was premium content material.

"Which community?" Grace asked, though she already suspected the answer.

"The Thompson farm." Elena's voice turned bitter. "Just north of here. They act like they're building something good, but they're just another power structure that protects their favorites and discards anyone who becomes inconvenient."

Perfect, Travis breathed. *She's giving you everything you need.*

Grace felt the anticipation building. Elena wasn't just a refugee. She was an insider with intelligence about the target. Someone who understood betrayal and wanted revenge. A kindred spirit who'd feed Grace's delusions instead of challenging them.

"Tell me everything," Grace said, kneeling beside Elena. "Every detail about the farm. About the people who hurt you. About the toxic dynamics we're going to help you overcome."

Elena's story poured out in carefully crafted fragments. The Thompson farm. James Thompson and his military background. His son-in-law who'd served overseas. The families living there. The defenses they'd built. And most importantly, the people Elena blamed for her suffering.

"There's a woman named Maddie," Elena said, her voice dripping poison. "She thinks she's so special with her engineering projects and her perfect relationship. But she destroyed mine. Took the man I loved and made the whole community choose her over me."

Grace's breath caught. "Maddie? Maddie Foster?"

Elena's eyes sharpened. "You know her?"

"She destroyed my life too," Grace said, feeling something slot into place. "Her and Hannah Mitchell. They sabotaged my big opportunity. They tried to ruin everything I'd built."

This is it, the ghosts chorused. *This is what you needed.*

Grace helped Elena to her feet, supporting her like a sister. "You found exactly the right place. We're planning to liberate the Thompson farm. To show them what happens when communities betray their most vulnerable members. And you're going to help us create the most revolutionary content anyone has ever filmed."

Elena's smile was sharp and hungry. "I want to watch their faces when they realize what's coming. I want them to understand that discarding people has consequences."

"Exactly!" Grace clapped her hands together. "Consequence content! Authentic accountability! This collaboration is going to break every engagement metric!"

She turned to address the camp, phone raised high. "Everyone! Meet Elena, our new intelligence consultant! She's going to help us plan tomorrow's liberation operation! This is exactly the kind of strategic partnership that defines successful platforms!"

Kyle appeared at Grace's side, studying Elena with narrow eyes. "Convenient timing. Show up right before we assault the place, offering insider intelligence."

"Because she escaped," Grace said impatiently. "She's a refugee seeking justice. Can't you see how perfect this is?"

Kyle and Elena locked eyes for a moment. Some silent communication passed between them that Grace couldn't quite read. Then Kyle nodded once, sharp and final.

"Your platform," he said to Grace. "Your call."

Grace felt a rush of validation. Kyle was trusting her judgment. Recognizing her leadership. Understanding that Elena was exactly what the operation needed.

"*Frank?* Grace thought. *Are you there?*

A moment of silence. Then Frank appeared beside his own corpse, looking down at it with detached curiosity. His ghost was more solid than the others, more present somehow.

"That was quite a show," Frank said conversationally. "Real crowd-pleaser. Though I notice your engagement metrics aren't climbing the way you expected."

Grace's hands started shaking. "Why didn't it work? Why don't I feel anything?"

"Because you're chasing something that doesn't exist," Frank replied. "The high isn't from the killing. It's from the delusion that killing means something. That it fills some void. But Grace, honey, that void isn't real. It's just untreated mental illness."

"Shut up," Grace whispered. "You're supposed to be my advisor now. You're supposed to help with the platform."

"Oh, I'll help," Frank said with a cold smile. "I'll help you understand exactly what you've become. What you're going to keep becoming until someone finally stops you."

Grace turned away from the ghost, focusing on Elena instead. The woman watched Frank's body with satisfaction and fascination, clearly pleased by the demonstration.

"That was perfect," Elena said. "Exactly the kind of strong leadership people need to see. No wonder you've built such a successful operation."

The validation helped slightly. Not enough to fill the void, but enough to ease the worst of the panic. Elena understood. Elena appreciated what Grace was building.

"Thank you," Grace said, feeling tears prick her eyes. "Most people don't get it. Don't understand what it takes to create revolutionary content."

"I understand completely," Elena replied. "And I'm going to help you create the most incredible finale content anyone has ever seen. The Thompson farm liberation is going to be legendary."

Grace grabbed Elena's hand, holding tight. "Tell me everything. Every detail. We need to plan this perfectly."

They moved away from Frank's corpse, settling near the supply trucks. Elena launched into a detailed description of the farm's layout, defensive positions, and key personnel. Grace filmed everything, capturing Elena's intelligence for her followers.

"The main house here," Elena explained. "James Thompson and his family. That's where Maddie lives now. Where she plays house with the man she stole from me."

"Hannah's probably there too," Grace said. "Her and Maddie; both of them thinking they escaped consequences. Thinking they destroyed my platform and got away with it."

"They're going to learn," Elena promised. "Tomorrow, we show them what betrayal costs."

This is good, Frank's ghost said, appearing beside them. *Planning content. Strategic collaboration. But you know it won't be enough, right? Tomorrow's assault? Even if you kill everyone at that farm, it still won't fill what you're looking for.*

Grace ignored him, focusing on Elena's intelligence. The woman knew everything. Guard rotations. Weak points in the defenses. Where supplies were stored. Most importantly, where Maddie and Hannah would be.

"We could hit them at dawn," Elena suggested.

"Maximum content," Grace agreed. "I'll film everything. Every moment of liberation. Every face when they realize the Queen has arrived."

Kyle watched from a distance, his expression unreadable. He'd given up trying to stop her, Grace realized. He was just following now. Staying with her until the inevitable end.

Rebecca moved through camp quietly, distributing supplies, checking on people. Playing her role perfectly. Grace barely noticed her anymore. Just another loyal follower doing her assigned tasks.

The Burke brothers stayed near their vehicle, both boys looking sick. Tommy kept glancing at Frank's body, still hanging from the town hall. Grace wondered if he was reconsidering his commitment to the platform. If he understood the consequences of wavering loyalty.

Evening came. Grace had Frank's body left hanging, wanting everyone to see it. Wanting the message to be clear. This is what happened to negative influences. This is the price of questioning the Queen.

She sat with Elena near a cooking fire, both women discussing the farm assault with manic enthusiasm. Elena fed every delusion, validated every plan, encouraged every violent fantasy. It felt good. Felt like finding someone who finally understood.

Two unstable women, Frank's ghost observed, *feeding each other's madness. This is going to end spectacularly badly.*

"Tomorrow," Grace said to Elena, "we film the most revolutionary content anyone has ever created. Liberation content that redefines what platforms can accomplish."

"Tomorrow," Elena agreed, her smile sharp with anticipated revenge, "they finally understand what they took from us."

Kyle appeared as darkness fell. "Grace. We need to talk about tomorrow. About what happens if things go wrong."

"Things won't go wrong," Grace said firmly. "We have insider intelligence. Superior numbers. The element of surprise. It's going to be perfect."

"Grace." Kyle crouched beside her, his voice dropping low. "What if Hannah and Maddie aren't the villains you remember? What if Portsmouth didn't happen the way you think?"

The question tried to penetrate Grace's defenses. Tried to make her examine the memory she'd built her entire revenge fantasy around. But the ghosts were there immediately, shouting down Kyle's doubt.

Don't listen to him, Travis said. *He's trying to sabotage tomorrow's content.*

They betrayed you, Dice added. *You remember it perfectly.*

The reality TV scouts, Landry insisted. *Hannah and Maddie destroyed your opportunity.*

"I remember exactly what happened," Grace said coldly. "They sabotaged me. They tried to ruin everything. And tomorrow, they pay for it."

Kyle stared at her for a long moment. Then he nodded slowly. "Okay. We do it your way. All the way to the end."

He walked away, leaving Grace with Elena and the ghosts. Her phone buzzed with imaginary notifications. Comments flooding in about tomorrow's assault. Followers anticipating the finale content. Hearts and likes and engagement metrics promising that this time, finally, would be enough.

Grace scrolled through blank screens, reading validation that didn't exist, planning violence that would never fill the void. Frank's corpse swayed in the darkness behind her. The ghosts whispered their encouragement. Elena smiled her hungry smile.

And the emptiness just kept growing, demanding more and more and more.

She didn't want to face the possibility that she'd keep chasing this high until she destroyed everything, including herself.

Spoiler, Frank's ghost said softly. *You're already destroying yourself. Have been since it all began. Tomorrow just makes it official.*

Grace closed her eyes, holding her phone tight, and pretended she didn't hear him.

Grace woke to Elena's laugh.

Sharp and brittle, cutting through the pre-dawn darkness like broken glass. Grace sat up in her tent, disoriented, listening to Elena's voice outside.

"Oh, they're going to suffer so beautifully," Elena was saying to someone. "Maddie especially. I want her to watch everything she loves burn before I let her die."

Grace pushed out of the tent, finding Elena sitting with two of the followers near a dying fire. The woman's face was animated, alive with vindictive pleasure as she described in detail what she wanted to do to the people at the Thompson farm.

"The children, too?" one of the followers asked nervously.

"Especially the children," Elena replied. "Maddie loves those little bastards. Thinks she's some kind of savior taking them in. I want her to hear them scream."

Grace felt something cold slide down her spine. She raised her phone automatically, filming Elena's performance, but something about it felt wrong. Off. Like watching herself from outside her body.

She sounds just like you, Frank's ghost said, appearing beside Grace. *Isn't that interesting?*

"That's not true," Grace whispered. "I don't talk about hurting children."

You ordered two of them drowned yesterday, Frank replied. *Mike and Jenny. What were they, early twenties? Still kids really. What about that girl you shot? Don't you remember?*

Grace shook her head, trying to clear it. Elena wasn't like her. Elena was damaged, vengeful, unstable. Grace was creating content. Building a platform. Completely different motivations.

But watching Elena describe torture with that manic smile, Grace felt her stomach turn. Because Frank was right. Elena sounded exactly like Grace did when she talked about Hannah and Maddie. That same vindictive pleasure. That same need to make them suffer.

"Morning content check," Grace said loudly, moving toward the fire. "Elena, maybe we should focus on strategic planning instead of... specific revenge fantasies."

Elena's eyes snapped to Grace, and, for just a moment, something ugly flickered across her face. Resentment maybe. Or competition. Then her smile returned, bright and artificial.

"Of course! Sorry, I got carried away. It's just so exciting knowing we're finally going to make them pay."

Pay for what? Grace's mother's voice whispered. Faint, distant, like a radio signal barely reaching through static. *What did they actually do to her?*

Grace spun around, searching for her mother's face in the darkness. "Mom? Where are you? I can barely hear you."

"Grace?" Elena stood, concern painted on her features. "Who are you talking to?"

"My parents. They're here. They're always here watching the content." Grace's voice climbed with desperation. "Mom? Dad? Don't leave me. Not now. Not when we're so close."

But the spaces where her parents usually stood remained empty. Their voices had been fading since Frank pointed out they weren't real, and now Grace could barely feel their presence at all.

They were never really here, Frank said. *Just your psychosis manifesting validation you desperately needed.*

"Shut up," Grace hissed at the ghost. "You don't know anything."

Elena watched this exchange with calculating eyes. "The stress is getting to you. That's normal. Big day coming up. Lots of pressure."

But Grace caught something in Elena's tone. Not concern. Something closer to satisfaction. Like Elena enjoyed watching Grace fracture further.

The convoy began preparations as dawn broke. Grace moved through the camp filming, but her usual enthusiasm felt forced. Empty. Everything felt wrong this morning. Frank's corpse still hung from the town hall, bloated and stinking in the heat. The smell made Grace's stomach turn.

That's what all your content creation amounts to, Travis said, appearing beside the body. *Rotting meat and trauma.*

Grace ignored him, focusing on Elena instead. The woman was helping organize the assault teams, talking to the Burke brothers about something. But Grace noticed how Elena's eyes gleamed when she described violence. How her smile widened when planning suffering.

"We hit the kids first," Elena was telling Sean Burke. "Make the adults choose between defending them and defending the main compound. Create chaos and trauma that breaks their organization."

"That's..." Sean's face went pale. "That's pretty ruthless."

"That's strategy," Elena corrected. "You want to win or not?"

Grace raised her phone, filming the exchange. Elena's tactics made sense from a pure strategy perspective. But something about the way she described it, the pleasure she took in planning children's terror, made Grace feel sick.

She's you, Dice whispered. *Without the influencer filter. Just raw psychosis and revenge.*

"I'm not like that," Grace said quietly.

You forced two people to drown yesterday and laughed, Landry reminded her. *You maimed Amy for suggesting different makeup. You're exactly like that.*

Grace's hands shook. She scrolled through her phone desperately, searching for validation from her followers. But the comments felt distant today. Muted. Like they were coming from very far away.

Kyle appeared, his face drawn with exhaustion. "Convoy's ready. We can move out whenever you give the word."

"Good." Grace tried to inject enthusiasm into her voice. "Today's the day we've been building toward. Revolutionary content that redefines platform success."

Kyle studied her face. "You okay? You seem... off."

"I'm perfect," Grace lied. "Just pre-performance nerves. Very normal before major content drops."

But she wasn't perfect. Something had shifted overnight. Watching Elena, listening to her describe violence with that manic pleasure, Grace was starting to see herself reflected back. And the reflection was ugly.

Finally, her mother's voice whispered, so faint Grace almost missed it. *Finally you're seeing clearly.*

"Mom?" Grace spun around, tears stinging her eyes. "Please don't go. Please stay. I need you."

But her mother's voice faded completely. Her father's, too. The warm, encouraging presences that had validated every choice since Earl's cabin were gone. Leaving Grace with nothing but ghosts of her victims and the growing suspicion that maybe, possibly, she'd become something monstrous.

You think? Frank asked sarcastically.

The convoy moved out as the sun climbed higher. Grace rode in the lead truck beside Kyle, phone pressed against the window. Behind them, maybe twenty-five people now. Half the force she'd started with. The rest had deserted or died or simply given up.

Elena rode in the truck bed, still talking excitedly about the assault. Grace could hear her voice through the rear window, describing in detail what she wanted to do to Maddie.

"I want her to see her man's face when he realizes I destroyed everything they built," Elena said. "I want her to feel exactly what she made me feel when she stole him."

Stole him, Grace's mind echoed. *Like Hannah stole my opportunity. Like Maddie sabotaged my platform.*

But the memory felt slippery today. Less clear. Grace tried to hold onto it, tried to remember exactly what Hannah and Maddie had done in Portsmouth. The reality TV scouts. The sabotage. The betrayal.

The details wouldn't come into focus.

That's because it didn't happen that way, her mother's ghost whispered, one final message before vanishing completely. *They tried to save you, baby. Tried to stop those men from hurting you. But you can't see it anymore. The psychosis ate the truth.*

"No," Grace whispered. "That's not right. They destroyed my platform. I remember."

Do you? Frank asked. *Or do you just remember what the illness told you to remember?*

Grace squeezed her eyes shut, trying to block out the doubt. She'd built everything on that memory. The betrayal in Portsmouth. Hannah and Maddie's sabotage. That's what justified all of this. The platform. The followers. The executions.

If that memory was false, if her mother's ghost was right, then what did that make Grace?

A serial killer, the ghosts answered in unison. *A murderer chasing a high that doesn't exist.*

The road that would lead them to the Thompson farm appeared in the distance around noon, and they pulled up to the intersection and stopped

"There," Elena breathed, her voice thick with anticipated revenge. "Right up there. That's where they think they're safe. Where Maddie plays house with my life."

Grace studied Elena's face. The woman's expression was twisted with hate and hunger. Her whole body trembled with the need to hurt people who'd wronged her.

Grace recognized that expression. Had seen it in mirrors. In reflections. In Kyle's eyes when he looked at her with that mix of fear and fascination.

She's your doppelganger, Travis said. *Your shadow self. Everything you are without the delusion that it's justified.*

"We're not the same," Grace said, but the words felt hollow.

"What?" Elena turned to her, confusion crossing her features.

"Nothing. Just... talking to my followers." Grace raised her phone, filming the farm. "Final approach content. Revolutionary assault preparation."

But her hands shook. The emptiness in her chest had grown so large it felt like it was consuming her from the inside. Yesterday's execution hadn't helped. They'd set up camp to plan the assault but it hadn't helped, either. Grace was starting to understand that nothing would ever fill this void.

Because the void isn't real, Frank explained patiently. *It's just untreated schizophrenia and trauma manifesting as addiction. You're chasing a high that was never sustainable.*

She'd heard those words before and pushed the thoughts away. The convoy now taking cover in a tree line, Grace called a planning session, gathering everyone around Elena's hand drawn map. But Grace found herself watching Elena more than listening to the tactical briefing.

The way Elena's smile widened when describing violence. The pleasure she took in planning suffering. The complete lack of remorse for what she was about to help facilitate.

Grace saw herself. Truly saw herself for the first time since Portsmouth. And it was horrifying.

"Grace?" Kyle's hand on her shoulder. "You with us?"

Grace blinked, refocusing. Everyone was staring at her, waiting for direction. Elena looked irritated at the interruption.

"Sorry. Just checking engagement metrics." Grace forced enthusiasm into her voice. "Elena, continue with the briefing."

Elena launched back into her plans. Explaining where they'd find Maddie and make her suffer. But Grace barely heard the details. She was too focused on that mirror Elena represented.

This is what you look like, Dice said quietly. *From the outside. This is how everyone sees you.*

Grace thought about Frank hanging from the town hall. Mike and Jenny drowning while she laughed. Amy's shattered knee. Sherman's decomposing body displayed on the truck hood. Travis shot for mocking her. All the bodies stretching back to Earl's cabin.

And she'd enjoyed it. Gotten high from it. Chased that rush like an addict until it stopped working.

Just like Elena was doing now. Using old trauma to justify new atrocities. Feeding delusions about righteousness and justice when really it was just... hurt people hurting people. Broken women breaking others.

"Grace!" Elena's sharp voice cut through her thoughts. "Are you listening? This is important."

"I'm listening," Grace lied.

But she wasn't. She was watching Elena's face, seeing her own madness reflected back, and finally, finally understanding what she'd become.

The planning session stretched into late afternoon. Grace went through the motions, approving strategies, assigning roles. But her heart wasn't in it anymore. The emptiness had grown so large it crowded out everything else.

You're crashing, Travis observed. *Coming down hard from yesterday's execution. You need another fix soon, or you're going to break completely.*

Grace knew he was right. The addiction demanded more. Needed escalation. Required bigger doses. But watching Elena plan torture and murder, Grace couldn't shake the growing horror at what that meant.

She'd become an addict. Not to drugs or alcohol, but to violence. To power. To the rush that came from complete control over life and death. And like any addiction, it was destroying her. Had already destroyed who she used to be.

Rebecca moved through the camp, distributing supplies, checking equipment. When she passed Grace, their eyes met briefly. Rebecca's expression was carefully neutral, but Grace saw something underneath. Not fear or compliance.

Calculation.

She's waiting, Frank's ghost said. *Waiting for you to fracture completely. Then she'll strike.*

But Grace couldn't muster the energy to care. Let Rebecca plot. Let everyone plot. None of it mattered. Tomorrow's assault would happen whether Grace was present or not. The addiction had momentum now. It would carry through to its inevitable conclusion.

Evening came. Grace sat apart from the camp, phone in hand, scrolling through blank screens. Elena found her there, settling beside her with false camaraderie.

"Big day tomorrow," Elena said. "Nervous?"

"No." Grace's voice came out flat. "Just thinking."

"About what?"

Grace turned to look at Elena fully. Really look at her. Saw the hunger in her eyes. The need to hurt people who'd wronged her. The complete conviction that her revenge was justified.

"About how you and I aren't that different," Grace said quietly.

Elena's smile sharpened. "I know. That's why I came to find you. We're both survivors. Both women who refuse to let betrayal go unanswered. Both willing to do what needs to be done."

Both completely insane, Landry added. *Both using trauma to justify murder.*

"What if..." Grace paused, the words difficult. "What if they didn't actually betray us? What if we're just... broken? Sick? Using old hurts as excuses to hurt others?"

Elena's expression went cold. "Don't you dare. Don't you fucking dare try to rewrite what they did to us. Maddie destroyed my life. She chose that man over me. She made the whole community reject me after I lost my baby."

"Or maybe they just... moved on," Grace whispered. "Maybe they built something good, and we can't stand it because we're stuck in our own pain."

Elena stood abruptly, her face twisted with rage. "You're weak. You're backing down right when we're so close. This is exactly what they want. They want us to doubt ourselves, to think we're the problem."

But we are the problem, Grace thought. *That's the horrible truth Elena can't face, and I'm only just starting to see.*

"I'm not backing down," Grace said, the lie automatic. "Just... thinking out loud. Pre-assault nerves."

Elena studied her with suspicious eyes. "You better not fuck this up, Grace. I didn't come all this way to watch you have a crisis of conscience."

She stalked away, and Grace watched her go straight to Kyle. Watched Elena laugh at something he said, her hand touching his arm. Watched Kyle's expression stay neutral but not dismissive. Not pulling away from her touch.

Grace felt something hot and acidic flood her chest. Not the emptiness. Something worse. Jealousy mixed with recognition.

Elena was younger than Grace by a few years. More conventionally attractive when she wasn't mud-caked and traumatized. And she had that same manic energy that had drawn Kyle to Grace in the first place. That dangerous edge that made her fascinating instead of just crazy.

She could replace you, Dice whispered. *Kyle's already seen how broken you are. Maybe he's looking for a newer model.*

Grace raised her phone, filming Elena and Kyle's interaction. Elena leaned close, whispering something that made Kyle's jaw tighten. His hand moved to his rifle, not threatening but present. The body language of someone being circled by a predator.

But he didn't walk away. Didn't shut down the conversation. Just stood there, letting Elena orbit him with her hungry smile and vindictive energy.

She's doing it on purpose, Travis said. *Showing you she could take him. Showing you she's just as broken and dangerous as you are. Maybe more.*

"No," Grace whispered. But the fear was there now, burrowing deep. Elena wasn't just her mirror. She was her competition. Another psychotic woman who understood the addiction to violence. Who could give Kyle that same dark thrill.

And Kyle had already admitted he was addicted to watching monsters. What if Elena proved to be a more interesting monster?

Grace watched Elena's hand linger on Kyle's arm. Watched her lean in close enough that Kyle could smell her perfume, whatever stolen scent she'd found in the ruins. Watched her smile up at him with calculation disguised as camaraderie.

This is how she operates, Frank's ghost said. *She finds people's weaknesses and exploits them. She knows Kyle is your anchor. So she's showing you she could cut that rope any time she wants.*

Kyle finally stepped back, putting distance between himself and Elena. But the damage was done. Grace had seen the way Elena looked at him. Like prey or a possession. Like another thing to take from someone who'd wronged her.

Except Grace hadn't wronged Elena. They were supposed to be allies and fellow survivors of betrayal.

But maybe that's not how Elena saw it. Maybe Elena saw Grace as competition. Another broken woman in her territory. Someone who needed to be replaced.

Or maybe, Landry suggested, *Elena is just as paranoid and possessive as you are. Maybe she sees threats everywhere because that's what psychosis does.*

Grace stood abruptly, moving toward them before she could think better of it. Elena saw her coming and smiled that sharp, knowing smile.

"Grace! We were just talking about you. About how tomorrow's assault is going to be legendary. Right, Kyle?"

Kyle's eyes met Grace's, and she saw exhaustion there. Resignation. But also something else. A warning maybe. Or a plea for Grace to not make this into another drama.

"What were you really talking about?" Grace asked, phone raised between them like a shield.

"Strategy," Elena said smoothly. "Kyle was telling me about some of your past operations. Very impressive tactical choices. Very... ruthless."

The word hung in the air like smoke. Ruthless. Not strategic. Not effective but ruthless. Elena was categorizing Grace's violence, comparing notes, measuring herself against the competition.

"Kyle's my partner," Grace said, hearing how childish it sounded. How possessive and desperate. "He understands my platform. He's been with me since the beginning."

"Of course he has," Elena agreed, her smile widening. "I'm sure your bond is very special. I was just saying how lucky you are to have someone who gets it. Who understands what it takes to create real change."

But Grace heard what Elena was really saying: *I could understand, too. I could give him the same thing. Maybe better.*

Kyle shifted uncomfortably, clearly recognizing the dynamic playing out. "Grace, we should review tomorrow's plans and make sure everyone knows their assignments."

"Yes," Grace said, not looking away from Elena. "We should."

Elena's eyes glittered with something Grace recognized from her own mirror. Competition. Hunger. The need to prove she was more dangerous, more committed, more worthy of attention.

She's going to be a problem, Travis said. *Not tomorrow. But soon. She's showing you what you are, and you can't stand it. And she's circling Kyle because she knows it destabilizes you.*

Grace turned away first, hating herself for it. Hating how Elena's presence made her feel threatened and exposed. Hating how watching Elena touch Kyle sent jealous rage through her system that felt almost as good as the violence high.

"Come on," Kyle said quietly, his hand finding Grace's lower back. The touch was possessive, reassuring. *Mine*, it said. *Still mine.*

But for how long? Grace wondered. How long before Kyle saw Elena as the fresher, more interesting monster? The one who hadn't completely shattered yet? Who still had some spark of unpredictability instead of just empty, desperate addiction?

Who was she now? What had she become? The girl who was going to Harvard felt like someone else entirely. Someone who existed in another lifetime. Before Portsmouth. Before Earl. Before she discovered the addictive rush of power over life and death.

You're Grace Reynolds, Frank's ghost said gently. *Trauma victim. Untreated and spiraling. You were always going to end up here. The only question was how many people you'd take down with you.*

"I can still stop," Grace whispered. "Can't I? I can still choose differently."

Can you? Frank gestured toward Elena. *Or have you gone too far? Done too much? Become too addicted to the high to ever quit?*

Grace didn't have an answer. She just sat there in the gathering dark, holding her dead phone, watching Elena rally the troops with manic enthusiasm. Seeing herself reflected in every gesture. Every smile. Every promise of righteous revenge.

And understanding, finally, that tomorrow's assault wasn't about justice or platforms or revolutionary content.

It was just two broken women feeding each other's delusions until they both destroyed themselves and everyone around them.

Kyle found Grace after midnight. She was still sitting alone, phone clutched against her chest like a shield.

"You're not okay," he said. Not a question.

"No," Grace admitted. "I'm really not."

Kyle settled beside her, close but not touching. "Elena's a mistake. She's going to push this into something even you can't control."

"I know." Grace's voice broke slightly. "She's me, Kyle. She's what I look like from the outside. And it's horrible."

"I know." Kyle's arm wrapped around her shoulders. "I've been watching you become her since her arrival. Watching both of you spiral together."

"Why didn't you stop me?"

"Because I'm as addicted as you are." Kyle pulled her closer. "To the danger. To watching how far you'll go. To the sick thrill of loving a monster."

She sat with Kyle in the darkness, holding her dead phone, and waited for dawn to come.

It was almost dawn when Grace made her decision. Elena had to die. Not for strategic reasons. Not for platform content. But because Grace couldn't stand looking at that mirror anymore. Couldn't face what Elena represented about her own descent.

20

Grace woke and again heard Elena's laugh threading through the pre-dawn darkness, but today it was more like fingernails on a chalkboard. It made her cringe at the very sound of it.

It wasn't the manic enthusiasm from yesterday. Today it was different. Lower, even intimate. Grace abruptly sat up in her tent, Kyle's side of the bedding already cold, and listened to Elena's voice outside mixing with Kyle's deeper rumble.

Grace pushed through the tent flap, her phone already raised. The dying campfire cast orange light across Elena and Kyle standing close together. Too close. Elena's hand rested on Kyle's arm, her fingers curved around his bicep like she owned him. Her head tilted up toward his face, hair catching firelight.

"I'm just saying," Elena was telling him, her voice pitched low and conspiratorial, "someone with your tactical experience could lead this operation better than—" She trailed off, noticing Grace approaching. Her smile sharpened. "Morning, Grace! We were just discussing assault strategy."

Grace's phone captured Elena's hand on Kyle's arm. Captured the way Elena leaned into him. Captured Kyle's neutral expression that didn't quite push her away.

She's circling him, Frank's ghost said, appearing beside Grace. *Showing you she could take him. Showing you she's better for him than you are. Maybe more of the monster he needs.*

"Strategy," Grace repeated, her voice bright and artificial. "In the wee hours of the morning. How professional." Elena's hand slid down Kyle's arm before dropping away. The touch lingered too long. Deliberate. A message. "The early bird gets the content, right? Isn't that what you always say?"

Kyle stepped back, putting distance between himself and Elena. But the damage was done. Grace had seen it. The way Elena touched him. The way she looked at him like prey. Like a possession. Like another thing to take.

She sees you as competition, Frank said quietly. *Another broken woman in her territory. Someone who needs to be replaced.*

Grace filmed Elena's face, capturing the calculation behind her smile.

She could replace you, Frank continued. *Kyle's already seen how broken you are. Maybe he's looking for a newer model. One that hasn't completely shattered yet.*

"We should get everyone up," Grace said, lowering her phone. "Big day ahead. Revolutionary content that will redefine platform success, right, Elena?"

"Exactly what I was telling Kyle," Elena agreed, her smile widening. "This assault is going to be legendary. Right, Kyle?"

Kyle's eyes met Grace's, and she saw exhaustion there. Warning. Or maybe just resignation. "I'll wake the crew," he said, moving away from both women.

Grace watched him go, then turned back to Elena. The woman stood by the fire, backlit by flames, looking satisfied. Triumphant. Like she'd just won something.

She's showing you she could take him anytime she wants, Frank whispered. *And you can't stand it. Can you?*

No. Grace couldn't stand it. The jealousy burned hotter than the violence high. Hotter than the need for revenge against Hannah. Elena was circling Kyle, threatening the one real thing Grace had left.

The convoy stirred as dawn broke. People emerging from tents, checking weapons, preparing for the assault. Grace moved through the camp filming, but her focus kept returning to Elena. To the way Elena laughed with some of the followers. To how her hand found Kyle's arm again when he passed, casual and possessive.

She's doing it on purpose, Frank said. *Making sure you see. Destabilizing you right before the assault.*

Grace's jaw clenched. The emptiness in her chest yawned wider despite yesterday's execution. Frank's death hadn't filled it. Elena's presence just made it worse. Made Grace feel threatened and exposed and replaceable.

They began packing up as morning light painted the sky orange and red. Grace climbed into the lead truck beside Kyle. Elena settled into the back with several followers, her voice carrying through the rear window.

"Today they understand what happens when you discard people! Today Maddie learns that betrayal has consequences!"

Grace's hands tightened on her phone. Elena kept talking about Maddie. About the Thompson farm. About revenge. But Grace saw what Elena was really doing. Positioning herself. Making herself essential. Showing Kyle she could be just as useful. Just as dangerous.

Just as interesting, Frank added.

Grace looked through the window as they waited for their teams to ready their gear, noting the storm's aftermath stretched in every direction. And through it all, Elena's voice kept threading from the truck bed. Loud and enthusiastic. Just like Grace, she was performing.

Water covered the pavement, ankle deep, muddy and brown from storm runoff. The convoy sat, engines idling.

"Maybe we should just stage here," Kyle said, killing the engine. "Review our approach and make a few final preparations."

Grace nodded and climbed out, her combat boots splashing in the muddy water. The sun beat down mercilessly. Heat waves shimmered across the flooded road. Behind them, followers emerged from vehicles, weapons ready, faces showing exhaustion and doubt.

Elena jumped down from the truck bed, landing in the water with a splash. She moved immediately to Kyle, pulling out maps, pointing at routes. Her body language open. Engaged. Flirtatious beneath the tactical discussion.

Watch her, Frank said. *Watch how she operates.*

Grace filmed them from a distance. Elena's hand on Kyle's arm again. The way she leaned close, invading his space. The way she smiled up at him like they shared secrets Grace wasn't part of.

The jealousy mixed with that familiar craving. The need for control. For validation. For the high that would prove she was still the Queen. Still the most dangerous woman here. Still Kyle's monster.

She's threatening everything, Frank whispered. *Your connection to Kyle. Your position. Your platform.*

"She needs to go," Grace said quietly.

Then make it happen, Frank replied. *Before she takes him from you.*

But Grace couldn't just kill her. Not without reason. Not without justification. The followers were already doubting.

Already questioning. Grace needed the execution to look justified. Needed Elena to be the problem.

So make her the problem, Frank suggested. *You're good at that.*

Grace watched Elena with Kyle for another moment. Watched the easy way Elena touched him. The comfortable way she occupied his space. Then Grace moved toward Rebecca's old cage mounted on the flatbed truck and took a moment to film the lonely space.

It's her turn to be in the cage, Frank said. *Her turn to pay the price for treachery.*

Grace lowered her phone slightly when Rebecca drew near and dropped her voice so only Rebecca could hear. "Elena's been giving me intelligence about Cornish. About the Thompson farm. About defenses and personnel."

Rebecca's expression didn't change. But something flickered behind her eyes.

"She says Maddie's there," Grace continued. "Says the farm is vulnerable. Easy target." Grace paused. "But what if she's lying? What if her intelligence is bad? What if she's been feeding me false information this whole time?"

Rebecca's lips curved slightly. Not quite a smile. Just acknowledgement.

"If Elena's intelligence is wrong," Grace said slowly, "if she's been sabotaging this operation from the inside, that would make her a traitor. Wouldn't it?"

Rebecca held Grace's gaze for a long moment. Then she raised her eyebrows tilting her head. It was sharp but deliberate. Giving Grace exactly what she needed.

There, Frank said. *Your justification. Elena's a saboteur. A spy. Feeding you bad intelligence to undermine the assault.*

Grace straightened, raising her phone again. The pieces falling into place. She didn't need Elena to actually be a traitor. She just needed the appearance of it. The justification. The reason that would make the execution look necessary instead of jealous.

Grace commanded that Elena be the next one to occupy the cage, and her orders were carried out. Elena was bound and smacked around by the men, some even ripping her clothes before tying her up and shoving her into the hot metal cage.

Elena called out for Kyle to help her, but he just ignored it. For hours she begged anyone that passed by to help her but none dared defy Grace. The hot sun beat down on Elena who's dirty face showed the streaks from sweat and tears.

Occasionally, Grace would stop what she was doing to briefly film but only with quiet commentary about her treachery and betrayal. She'd worked herself right up into a murderous fury by the time she made a decision.

"Kyle!" Grace's voice cut across the staging area. "Get everyone gathered! I need witnesses for this content!"

Kyle's head turned. Even from a distance, Grace saw his expression shift. Confusion turning to concern turning to resignation. He'd seen this before and knew what was coming.

The followers assembled slowly, reluctantly. Forming a rough semicircle in the ankle-deep water. The Burke brothers exchanged glances. Pete and Nate flanked Kyle, hands on their weapons. Everyone understood something was about to happen.

Grace moved to the truck where they'd secured Elena in the makeshift cage. The metal was already scorching from the morning sun. Elena's expensive clothes were torn and soaked with sweat and filth.

"Grace?" Elena's voice came out uncertain. "What's going on?"

Grace raised her phone, filming through the chain link. "Morning content session. Accountability documentation. Very important for platform transparency."

Elena's eyes darted to Kyle. Looking for reassurance. For intervention. But Kyle's face stayed carefully neutral, he was not helping her and not stopping Grace.

He's choosing, Frank said. *Watch.*

"I've been reviewing your intelligence," Grace said, her voice carrying across the staging area. "About the Thompson farm and about Maddie."

"It's good intelligence," Elena said quickly. "I lived there. I know the layout and their defenses."

"Do you?" Grace's smile sharpened. "Because Rebecca says otherwise. Says your information is wrong. Says you've been feeding me bad intel this whole time."

Elena's face went pale. "That's not true! Rebecca's lying! She's the one trying to sabotage you!"

Perfect, Frank breathed. *She's panicking. Making it worse.*

"Please, Grace, please!" Elena shrieked, her hands gripping the scorching metal despite the pain. "I supported you! Maddie's the real saboteur! She wants your audience and your power. She's poisoning everyone against you. I've seen it! I swear!"

Grace was well aware that Rebecca hadn't said anything, but used it as she approached the cage like a prowling wolf. Each step measured. Calculated for maximum dramatic effect. The stench around the cage was overwhelming. Elena's terror-sweat mixed with the smell of human waste and rotting flood debris.

"Oh, sweetheart," Grace purred, tilting Elena's chin up with the barrel of her pistol. The metal was burning hot from being in the sun, and Elena's eyes went wide as it touched her skin. "Your personal arc is collapsing. Negative engagement, disloyalty…" She tapped the gun playfully against Elena's cheek. "…irrelevance."

Elena sobbed, her makeup streaking down her face in grotesque rivers. "You don't understand," she gasped. "It must have been a bad moment of info, I got things mixed up, but I'm a loyal follower! I'll do anything. I'll stream, I'll hype you, I'll attack whoever you say. Just… please, I can turn this around! I can help you go viral again."

But you're not doing this because of bad intel, Frank whispered. *You're doing this because she touched Kyle. Because she threatened what's yours.*

Grace knew Frank was right. The intelligence didn't matter, it wasn't even true. Whether Elena was lying or telling the truth didn't matter. What mattered was that Elena had circled Kyle and tried to show Grace how easily she could be replaced. She made the fatal mistake of threatening the one real connection Grace had left.

But the followers couldn't know that. They needed to see justified execution. Accountability and not simply a jealous rage.

"Viral," Grace mused, rolling the word around her tongue like fine wine. "Such a beautiful concept. Spreading, infecting, taking over everything it touches." She crouched, lowering herself until their eyes met. "You hear that, Frankie? She wants to be useful."

Frank materialized beside the cage, his rotted form dripping. *Desperation doesn't sell,* he drawled. *Loyalty's cheap when it's bought at the gallows. She's dead weight, and you're trending.*

"Open the door," Grace barked the order out without acknowledging Frank.

Grace tilted her head, feigning consideration. Her hair fell across her face. She pushed it back with theatrical slowness. "Do you know what happens to leeches who feed without giving back, Elena? They get burned off."

She leaned in to look at her more clearly. "Push her closer so the camera can see every line on her face."

One of the men shoved her forward with a stick between her shoulder blades, and Elena winced. Grace zoomed in on the expression and raised an eyebrow.

"No, Grace! Please," Elena sobbed, her bound hands struggling against the momentum shoving her forward.. "I'll change. I'll do anything. I'll get you more followers, I'll fight, I'll—"

Grace silenced her with a slap. The sound echoed across the water. Elena's head snapped to the side, blood trickling from her split lip.

"My dearest revolutionaries," Grace announced, turning to her gathered audience. Her arms spread wide. "You know the rules. Loyalty is rewarded. Betrayal?"

Frank appeared again, pressing close. *Punished, darling. Publicly.*

Grace gestured to Pete and Nate. "Get her out. Let's make this properly cinematic."

They dragged Elena from the cage. She collapsed in the muddy water, her bound hands splashing desperately.

"I'll change. I'll do anything. I'll get you more followers, I'll fight, I'll—"

Grace waved her cracked phone like she was broadcasting to millions. "The time for chances passed when you chose betrayal. It was obvious from the beginning what you were doing," Grace purred. "But don't worry, sweetheart, you still have a part to play. Every tragedy needs a proper climax."

Elena sobbed out denials. Calling herself loyal. Blaming Maddie. Blaming Rebecca. Her body shuddered with every broken word, the heat making her delirium worse, until her strength gave out and she collapsed face-first in the water.

"Up," Grace barked.

Pete and Nate hauled Elena up by her hair. Strands came away in their fists. Elena's scalp bled where they'd torn free. Her face was raw and burned from the relentless sun all day.

Grace stalked forward, pistol drawn. Pressed it to Elena's thigh.

"This is what happens to traitors," Grace said, her voice rich with imagined fanfare. She could hear the crowd's roar. Feel their bloodlust feeding her own.

This is what happens to women who threaten what's mine, Grace thought.

She squeezed the trigger.

Elena's scream pierced the air as the bullet tore through muscle. She crumpled to the ground, clutching her leg, blood mingling with the muck. Her screams became hoarse sobs as she writhed, convulsing.

"I can be better," Elena wailed, her desperation raw. "Please, Grace, please, it wasn't supposed to be like this. I just wanted to belong. I just wanted to be someone."

Just like you, Frank said. *Desperate for validation. For belonging. For someone to see her. Someone like Kyle, perhaps?*

"Oh, you'll be someone," Grace murmured sweetly, circling Elena like a predator. Water lapped at her boots. "You'll be a warning."

Grace shot again, this time into Elena's side. The bullet punched through flesh with a wet sound. Elena's back arched in agony. The convulsions returned, her body jerking violently. Blood spread across the muddy puddle, dark red arterial blood rolling into the shallow water.

The high started building. Not as strong as Grace needed. Not filling the void. But something. Proof she was still the Queen. Still the most dangerous. Still Kyle's.

Grace leaned down, whispering close to Elena''s ear. "You thought you could take him, didn't you?" Her eyes flashed to Kyle before looking deep into Elena's. "You thought wrong, and this is your final scene, Elena. Don't ruin it by whining."

Elena's eyes went wide and she sobbed, snot and tears mixing on her filthy face. "I'm sorry. I was stupid, Grace, please don't."

But it is about you, Grace thought. *About you touching Kyle. About you threatening to replace me.*

"Spies and traitors suffer their fate," Grace said aloud, gesturing to the invisible cameras. "Millions of them. You're more famous now than you've ever been… Or ever will be."

Grace smiled, raised her voice to the gathered followers. "Now, my dears, for the grand finale. No loose ends or failed arcs. Just victory."

She pressed the barrel to Elena's forehead, savoring the shivering terror in her victim's eyes. The metal was scorching hot from the shots she'd already fired. Elena's skin turned instantly red where it touched.

Elena's eyes found Kyle's face in the crowd. Desperate. Pleading. But Kyle's expression stayed blank. Carefully neutral and not intervening.

He's choosing you, Frank said. *Over her. He's staying with you.*

"Smile for the audience," Grace whispered.

She pulled the trigger.

The crack echoed across the sweltering landscape. Elena's head snapped back before collapsing lifeless onto the burning ground. Blood and brain matter painted the earth behind her in abstract patterns.

Grace stood over the corpse, phone raised high, filming from multiple angles. The high built stronger. Not enough. Never enough. But something. Validation that she was still the Queen and still Kyle's.

"This," Grace declared, "is how you build an empire."

She turned, arms raised in triumph. "See that, my loves? Traitors don't get redemption arcs—they get finales."

But when Grace looked at her followers, she saw only horror. Tommy Burke had his hand over his mouth. Sean's face was pale. Rebecca stood at the edge, her expression carefully blank but her eyes calculating.

Kyle stood frozen. His face showed something Grace couldn't quite read. Not fear or fascination. Something worse.

Pity.

Engagement is up, Frank's ghost said quietly. *But is it enough?*

Grace lowered her phone slowly. Stared at Elena's corpse. Felt the high already fading. Already leaving her empty again.

It wasn't enough.

It would never be enough.

"Load up!" Grace's voice came out too bright. Manic. "We have a farm to assault! Revolutionary content to create! My followers are waiting!"

Nobody moved. They just stared at her. At the monster standing in ankle-deep water with blood on her hands and a dead woman at her feet.

"I said LOAD UP!" Grace screamed.

The followers scattered. Running back to the vehicles. Some crying. Others just numb.

Kyle approached slowly. Stopped beside Elena's body, looking down at it with that unreadable expression.

"That was about me," he said quietly. Not a question.

"She was competition," Grace replied. Her hand moved to his chest. Possessive. Desperate. "You're mine, Kyle. Not hers. Mine."

Kyle looked at her for a long moment. Then he nodded slowly, with resignation in his eyes. "Yeah. I'm yours. Until the end."

He walked away, leaving Grace standing over Elena's corpse. The sun beat down mercilessly. Heat waves shimmered. The emptiness yawned wider despite Elena's death.

You killed her because she made you see yourself clearly, Frank said. *And you couldn't stand the reflection.*

The convoy loaded up. Grace climbed into the lead truck, her sequined top spattered with Elena's blood. Kyle took the driver's seat without speaking. Behind them, the followers prepared for assault with hollow eyes and defeated expressions.

They rolled forward. Past Elena's body. Toward the Thompson farm access road. Toward Hannah and Maddie and the revenge fantasy that consumed Grace's existence.

Grace raised her phone, filming their approach. "Final assault content. Revolutionary platform documentation."

But her hands shook. The manic enthusiasm felt forced. Empty. Elena's execution hadn't filled the void. Had just proved that Grace was exactly what Frank said.

A monster. Chasing an addiction that would never satisfy.

The farm access road appeared ahead, leading uphill through trees. Grace could see defensive positions in the treeline. Vehicles blocking the approach. People moving with military precision.

"They're ready for us," Kyle said flatly.

"Good." Grace's smile felt wrong on her face. "Authentic resistance makes better content."

The convoy stopped at the bottom of the access road. Everyone climbed out, checking weapons. The Burke brothers took positions. Pete and Nate established a perimeter.

Grace stood in the middle of it all, phone raised, filming everything. But she felt distant. Disconnected. Like watching someone else play the role of the Queen of Likes.

This is it, Frank said. *The finale. Everything you've been building toward.*

The first gunshot cracked across the morning air.

Someone screamed. One of the followers went down, blood spreading across gravel. Grace spun, filming the chaos erupting around her.

Bullets sparked off vehicles. People scrambled for cover. The Burke brothers returned fire toward the treeline above. Defenders used elevation and cover to rain hell down on Grace's exposed position.

Grace laughed. The sound bubbled up from somewhere broken and wrong. She stood in the middle of the killing field, phone raised high, filming the carnage.

"Beautiful!" she shouted over the gunfire. "This is revolutionary content! Authentic conflict with real stakes!"

Kyle tackled her behind a vehicle as a bullet sparked where she'd been standing. "What the fuck are you doing?"

"Creating content!" Grace twisted free, raising her phone again. "My followers need to see this!"

"Your followers don't exist!" Kyle grabbed her shoulders, forcing her to look at him. "Grace, we're dying here! We need to retreat!"

"We're not retreating!" Grace shoved him away. Her eyes scanned the treeline frantically. "Hannah's up there! I can see her! She's actually here!"

"Where?" Kyle scanned the trees. "I don't see anyone!"

But Grace had seen something. Or thought she had. A glimpse of movement. Blonde hair through the trees. It had to be Hannah. Everything led to this moment.

More of Grace's followers went down. The Burke brothers weren't firing anymore. Just crouching behind cover, weapons lowered. Pete and Nate backing toward vehicles, preparing to flee.

The assault was collapsing; Grace's empire crumbling. But all she could see was that glimpse through the trees. All she could feel was the desperate need to reach Hannah. To make it all mean something.

Kyle's hands framed her face. Tears cut tracks through the dirt on his cheeks.

"Grace. Baby. Look at me."

Grace's eyes focused on his face. Saw absolute desperation.

"Come with me," Kyle said, his voice breaking. "Right now. We leave. We run. Just you and me. We disappear into the woods. Start over somewhere. Anywhere. I love you. I love you so fucking much. Please. Please, baby, let me save you."

Grace stared at him. At the man who'd enabled her madness. Who'd stayed through executions and torture. Who'd loved the monster she became. Who was now begging her to choose him over the revenge that consumed her.

For one perfect, crystalline moment, Grace wanted to say yes. Wanted to drop her phone and run. Wanted to let Kyle save her from herself.

His forehead pressed to hers. "I don't want to lose you. Please don't make me lose you. Choose me. Right now. Choose me."

The words tried to penetrate. Tried to reach whatever was left of Grace Reynolds beneath the madness. Kyle was offering her a way out. An escape. A chance to stop before it was too late.

Then Grace heard it again. It was faint and distant. Maybe real. Maybe imagined.

"Mom!"

Grace's head turned toward the sound. Through the chaos and gunfire, she saw movement in the treeline. A figure that could be Hannah. Could be anyone. Could be another hallucination.

But Grace's fractured mind latched onto it. Hannah was there. Hannah was real. This was the moment everything had been building toward.

"She's here," Grace breathed. "Kyle, she's actually here."

Kyle's face crumpled. "No. Grace, please—"

But Grace was already pulling away. Already raising her phone. Already chasing that final confrontation. That ultimate validation.

"I can't," Grace whispered. "I can't stop. Not when she's right there."

Kyle's hands dropped. His whole body sagged. "Then I can't help you anymore."

Another explosion. Another scream. Grace's followers breaking completely now. The handlers slipping away into the woods.

Grace stood in the middle of it all, phone raised, laughing that broken laugh. Bullets kicked up gravel around her boots. People died around her.

Kyle stood beside her. Not running or fleeing with the rest. Just watching Grace destroy herself. His face showed such profound sadness. Such longing. Like he wanted nothing more than to grab her and run but knew she'd already made her choice.

"I love you," he said quietly, barely audible over the gunfire. "I'll always love the monster I helped create. But I can't watch this anymore."

21

Bullets tore through the air like angry hornets. Grace stood on the hood of the lead truck, phone raised high, spinning in a slow circle to capture every angle of the chaos.

"This is AMAZING content!" she screamed over the gunfire. "Look at these authentic battle aesthetics! Bullet holes in the trucks are going to make INCREDIBLE merch opportunities! Apocalypse fashion with real combat damage!"

Someone grabbed her ankle. Kyle hauled her down as a round sparked off the metal where her head had been. Grace giggled, stumbling in the gravel, her sequined top catching sunlight.

"Did you see that near-miss?" Grace raised her phone toward Kyle's face. "That's the kind of authentic danger my followers LIVE for! Real stakes! Actual mortality content!"

Kyle's expression was unreadable. Blood streaked his face from a cut above his eyebrow. His hands shook slightly as he checked his rifle. "Grace, we need to fall back. Now."

"Fall back?" Grace's laugh came out shrill. "We just got here! The engagement metrics are EXPLODING!"

More of Grace's followers were down. Bodies sprawled in the gravel at the bottom of the access road. The Thompson farm defenders held the high ground, pouring fire down on Grace's exposed position. Tommy Burke crouched behind a vehicle, his weapon lowered, his face showing he was done fighting.

Grace filmed it all. The blood spreading across gravel like abstract art. The way bodies twitched when rounds found them. The smoke rising from burning vehicles creating perfect dramatic backlighting.

"Blood spatter patterns are very on-trend," Grace narrated breathlessly. "Very gritty realism. My followers appreciate authentic survival aesthetics. This is revolutionary platform content!"

"Grace!" Pete's voice cracked across the killing field. "We're pulling out! Now!"

But Grace wasn't listening. She was too busy filming the Burke brothers as they threw down their weapons. Too focused on capturing Sean's face as he raised his hands in surrender. Too invested in documenting her empire's collapse to understand what it meant.

Kyle grabbed her arm. Hard. Painful. "Grace, LOOK AT ME."

Grace's eyes focused on his face. Saw something there she'd never seen before.

Finality.

"We're done," Kyle said quietly. "This is over. Come with me right now, or I'm leaving without you."

"Leaving?" Grace's voice climbed toward hysteria. "We can't leave! Hannah's up there! I SAW her! This is the moment everything's been building toward!"

"There is no Hannah!" Kyle shook her. "There's just you chasing ghosts and getting people killed for content that doesn't exist!"

Grace tried to pull away but Kyle's grip tightened. His face was inches from hers. She could see tears cutting tracks through the dirt on his cheeks.

"I love you," Kyle said, his voice breaking. "I love you so much it's destroying me. But I can't watch you do this anymore. I can't be part of this. Come with me. Right now. We run. We disappear. We start over."

For one crystalline moment, Grace felt something crack inside her chest. Kyle loved her. Kyle was begging her to choose him. Kyle was offering her a way out.

"Kyle, I—"

An explosion cut her off. One of the rear vehicles erupted in flames. Grace's head turned automatically toward the sound, her phone rising to capture it. The fireball. The smoke. The perfect dramatic content.

When she looked back, Kyle's expression had changed. The desperate hope was gone. Replaced by grief.

"That's what I thought," he said softly.

He released her arm. Stepped back. Once. Twice. His weapon lowering. His whole body radiating exhaustion and defeat and a longing so profound it made Grace's breath catch.

Kyle's eyes stayed locked on her face. Drinking her in. Memorizing her. His expression showed he wanted nothing more than to stay. To grab her. To drag her away from this.

But knowing he couldn't.

"I'm sorry," Kyle whispered. "I'm so sorry I helped make you into this."

Then he turned and walked away. Moving toward the woods. Away from Grace and away from the madness.

His shoulders slumped. His head down. Every line of his body showing the cost of the choice. But he kept walking.

Grace's hand reached out. Extended into empty air. Her mouth opened but no sound came out. The one person who stayed. The one person who understood. The one person who loved the monster.

Gone.

"Kyle?" Grace's voice came out small. Broken. "Kyle, please."

But he didn't turn around. Didn't look back. Just disappeared into the trees. The longing in his final look burning into Grace's mind like a brand.

She'd lost him.

After everything. After building an empire on delusions and blood. After believing she was creating revolutionary content. After killing and torturing and destroying everything in her path.

She'd lost the one real thing she had.

Grace's legs buckled. She collapsed beside the truck, her phone slipping from her fingers. The screen cracked as it hit the gravel. As dead and useless as it had always been.

Around her, the battle was ending with surrender. Grace's followers throwing down weapons. The handlers who'd enabled everything slipping away into the woods like smoke.

Grace pulled her knees to her chest. Wrapped her arms around them. And started to laugh.

The sound came out broken and wrong. Bubbling up from somewhere deep and shattering into pure madness, crystallizing into audio. Grace laughed and laughed, rocking back and forth, while blood soaked into gravel and smoke drifted across the access road.

She'd created the ultimate content drop.

And no one was watching.

No one had ever been watching.

Boots crunched on gravel nearby. Grace looked up through swimming vision. Rebecca stood there. No longer playing compliance. Flanked by Tommy Burke and others who'd turned.

Rebecca's face showed no triumph. No vindication. Just profound exhaustion and something that might have been pity.

"It's over, Grace," Rebecca said quietly.

Grace stared at her.

"Where's Kyle?" Grace asked, her voice distant. "Did you see where Kyle went?"

Rebecca glanced toward the woods. "He's gone. They're all gone. All of them. Everyone who used your sickness for their own purposes."

"He loved me." Grace's hands moved through the gravel, searching. Her fingers found something cold. Metal. A knife on a fallen fighter's belt. She pulled it free. "He said he loved me."

"I know," Rebecca said, her weapon staying pointed at the ground. "I believe he did. In his own broken way."

Grace studied the knife in her hand. The blade catching morning light. Real. More real than anything had felt in months. More real than the validation she'd chased. More real than the content she'd created. More real than the platform she'd built from delusions and blood.

The fighting had stopped completely now. People moved slowly. Sorting wounded. Surrendering. The Queen of Likes' empire collapsing in real time.

Grace looked up at Rebecca. Really looked at her. "Mrs. Mitchell?" Her voice came out small. Confused. "What's happening? Where are my parents? They were just here, they were watching the stream..."

Rebecca's expression crumbled. "They're gone, honey. They've been gone for a long time."

Grace's face twisted. For a moment she looked like the lost child she'd always been. "They're gone," she whispered. "Why aren't they watching? Where did they go?"

"The phone doesn't work, Grace," Rebecca said gently, stepping closer. "It hasn't worked for months. There's no audience. There never was."

Grace stared at the cracked device in the gravel beside her. Understanding flickered across her features. "No," she whispered. "No, that's not right. Frank told me the numbers were good. The engagement was—"

"Frank is dead," Rebecca said softly. "You killed him, remember? You hanged him in town."

Grace's eyes went wide with horror. "No, he's right here. He's been helping me plan the content. He said—" She stopped, her gaze darting around frantically. "Frank? Frank, where are you?"

But the ghosts were gone. All of them. Travis and Sherman and Derek and Elena and Frank. The voices that had validated every choice. That praised her commitment and demanded she continue.

Silent.

Grace's breath came in ragged gasps. "They left me. Everyone left me."

Rebecca forced her voice steady. "It's over, Grace. Please. Let me help you."

At the edges of the chaos, Grace caught glimpses of the handlers melting away. Disappearing. Abandoning their puppet now that she was no longer useful.

Grace swayed on her feet, shoulders shaking. Her hand trembled around the knife. "Mrs. Mitchell," she choked. "I didn't mean to. I didn't—"

"I know," Rebecca said, stepping forward slowly, hands open. "I know you didn't mean it. You were sick. You needed help, and nobody gave it to you."

Grace's breathing was ragged now, her chest hitching with suppressed sobs. "I remember," she whispered. "I remember Hannah laughing. I remember when we used to dance in your backyard. I remember when I was..." She paused, her voice breaking. "When I was at Harvard. Oh God! Am I even human?"

"You're still human," Rebecca said desperately. "You're still that girl who loved her friends, who wanted to make people happy. That's still in there, Grace. We can find her again."

But even as she spoke, Rebecca's expression mirrored the shift in Grace. The clarity fighting with the madness. Reality trying to reassert itself while the delusions screamed their denial.

"The algorithm doesn't like redemption arcs," Grace said suddenly standing, her voice taking on that manic quality again. "Frank says it's too predictable. The audience wants—"

"There is no audience!" Rebecca screamed, her composure finally cracking. "There is no Frank! There are no likes, no followers, no engagement! It's just you, Grace! Just you and these people!" Rebecca's arms went wide to each side showcasing the hollow faces staring at them.

The words hit Grace like physical blows. She stumbled backward, her face cycling through confusion, recognition, and desperate denial. "No," she whispered. "No, you're wrong. They're watching. They have to be watching. Otherwise, what was it all for?"

Grace's mind fractured in real time, trapped between two realities. The one where she was a beloved influencer creating content for millions, and the one where she was a murderer standing in the ruins of her own making.

"Come with me," Rebecca pleaded, reaching out her hand. "We can fix this. We can get you help. Hannah would want that. She'd want us to save you."

Grace stared at Rebecca's outstretched hand. For a moment, hope flickered in her eyes. She took a step forward, then another, her movements hesitant but deliberate. "Hannah," she whispered. "Is she—is she really alive?"

"Yes," Rebecca said, tears streaming down her face. "She's alive, and she's safe, and she still loves you. She never stopped loving you."

Grace's face crumpled completely. "I tried to kill her," she sobbed. "I tried to kill my best friend. For fucking content that doesn't even exist?"

"But you didn't," Rebecca said urgently. "You didn't kill her. That means something. That means you can still choose differently."

For a moment, the clearing went quiet except for the sound of Grace's ragged breathing. The war raging inside her between the broken girl fighting against the monster she'd become and reality battling delusion. Love struggled against the madness that had consumed her.

Then Grace's expression changed. The lucidity settled. Hardened. Her eyes cleared with terrible understanding.

"You're trying to tank my ratings," Grace said, her voice flat. Then she stopped. Blinked. "No. That's not..." She looked around at the hollow faces. At the bodies. At the blood. "There are no ratings. Are there?"

The shift was small but devastating. A flicker of true recognition cutting through everything. Grace saw it all clearly for the first time since Portsmouth. Since Earl. Since the drowning.

She saw what she'd become.

"Stay back Mrs. Mitchell," Grace whispered, the knife rising to her own throat.

Rebecca screamed, "No!"

Grace's chest hitched. Her fingers shook as she pressed the blade against her skin. The metal caught the sunlight like liquid fire shimmering into her eyes. Her body trembled.

"May God forgive me," Grace whispered.

"Grace, please," Rebecca sobbed, reaching out desperately. "Please don't do this. Hannah needs you. I need you. We can fix this together."

But Grace was already gone. Lost in the space between realities. Between the girl she'd been and the monster she'd become. "Tell them," she whispered, her voice barely audible. "Tell them I was trying to make something beautiful."

The blade flashed in the merciless sun.

The slash was brutal, sudden, efficient.

Blood sprayed in an arc, bright red against the bleached landscape. Grace gasped, her mouth opening in a silent apology. The knife clattered to the ground. She stumbled, knees buckling.

Pain registered. Sharp and immediate. But underneath it, something else. The warmth of blood gushing down her chest felt like release. Like demons pouring out of the wound. Like the ghosts and the madness and the desperate need for validation all flowing away with her life.

She felt free of them.

For the first time since it all began, Grace felt clean.

Her body folded inward like a broken doll. She hit the baked earth with a sick, final sound. The world lurched. Tilted. The sky wheeled overhead in shades of orange and pink.

Grace's vision narrowed. Darkness circling in from the edges. She tried to move but her body wouldn't respond. Could only lie there in the gravel, feeling the warmth spreading beneath her.

A voice called her name. Distant. Familiar. "Grace! Grace, honey, stay with me!"

Her mother's voice?

Except Grace knew, deep down in the last rational corner of her mind, that it wasn't her mother. It was Rebecca. It had always been Rebecca. Her parents were gone. Had been gone.

But it sounded so much like her mother.

Grace tried to turn her head toward the sound. Managed to roll slightly. Looking up at the sky. So blue. So clear. So beautiful.

Around her, the world was going still. Weapons dropping. People falling to their knees. Shoulders shaking with sobs. The Queen of Likes' followers finally understanding what they'd been part of.

Grace wanted to tell them she was sorry. Wanted to explain that she'd been sick. That she'd needed help and was still in there somewhere, drowning.

But when she tried to speak, only blood bubbled from her lips.

Kyle.

She tried to whisper his name. To call him back and tell him she chose wrong. That she should have run with him. That she loved the man who loved a monster.

But no sound came. Her throat wouldn't work. The blood flowed too fast.

Kyle.

The darkness circled tighter. Grace's vision narrowed to a pinpoint. She lay on the ground looking up at the blue sky as it faded. The voices grew distant, and the warmth of her blood pooling beneath her turned cold. Her thoughts cycled through the moments since that day, skipping between the historic brick buildings at Harvard and Maddie's laugh at her spinning in the bright sunshine. All the moments since showed the monster she truly was and the friends she'd lost along the way. As the last rays penetrated her vision, she tried to speak one last time.

"I'm sorry."

Thank you for reading. Please consider leaving a positive review.

"It's not the end of the world at all," he said. "It's only the end for us. The world will go on just the same, only we shan't be in it. I dare say it will get along all right without us."

- Nevil Shute

Also by DJ Cooper

Dystopia Series

Beginning of the End

Long Road

Revelations

Dark Days

Apocalypse Fire Series

Endure the Chaos

Survive the Chaos

Beyond the Chaos

Cincinnati Fall Series

Cincinnati Fall 1

Cincinnati Fall 2

Cincinnati Fall 3

Nine Meals From Anarchy Series

Sun's Fury

Terminus State

Insurrection Series

Deception

Evasion

Abolition

WordPeddler Magazines

COMING SOON

https://fire-n-ash.com

Acknowledgements

Queen of Likes is a story of not just survival but of human desire to persevere. In book one *Wasted World*, the separate journeys through areas mired with challenges around every corner. Followed by *Decayed World* where the stunning revelation of a new threat, The Queen of Likes Emerges and a subsequent war for their very survival in *Altered World*. The queen is on a mission to take down Hannah and Maddie, while she broadcasts to her dead phone every detail. This maddening dive into the world of psychosis has been a journey like no other.

If you would like to stay updated on this and emerging stories in my new Fire & Ash World, visit my website at https://authoroftheapocalypse.com

I am incredibly grateful to all who read this and my other stories. A passion I never knew existed until I sat down one day to write and now, I try harder with each book, chapter, paragraph and sentence to make it better than the one before. If it were not for the amazing readers who give up their time to walk these tales along with me, I would not be able to do so. It is for you I try to make each one more than the last. I love hearing from readers even if you don't like it. Without feedback I can't do better next time.

I am thankful that through the terrible things not just in this book but also in life I have friends and family to see it through.

-DJ